Knight's Keep

The street was dark and deserted. It seemed that as my footsteps increased so did those behind me. They were heavy, determined and unmistakably male.

I glanced over my shoulder and saw the figure of a man reflected in the dim light of a sputtering gas lamp. It looked solid, bulky, and menacing. Alarm clutched me. I suppressed it firmly and hurried on – but the man hurried too. I felt fear lick my heart and forced myself to break into a run. Suddenly, mercifully, I was home and hurrying up the front steps, fumbling for my door key as the man came ever nearer . . .

Available in Fontana by the same author

Glenrannoch
The Watchman's Stone
Dragonmede

RONA RANDALL

Knight's Keep

Collins
FONTANA BOOKS

First published in 1967 by William Collins Sons & Co Ltd
First issued in Fontana Books 1977

© Rona Randall 1967

Made and Printed in Great Britain by
William Collins Sons & Co Ltd Glasgow

CHAPTER ONE

I never dreamed that I would live at Knight's Keep. I never dreamed that the rambling Elizabethan mansion would become as familiar to me as the countryside surrounding it, nor that I would know happiness, passion, and finally terror there before its bonds set me free. But that is what happened, and it happened at a time when I was most vulnerable.

Perhaps that is why I went there in the first place, grateful for a refuge. I no longer fitted into my own background. The teeming London streets where I had been born and had grown up no longer had a place for me. Fate had suddenly set me apart.

With stiff-necked pride, my warm-hearted neighbors avoided me. I knew why. They didn't want to "impose." Perhaps they were even a little awed because the orphaned daughter of the clergyman they had loved was suddenly elevated above them. The elevation was in their minds, not mine. Whatever their reasons, they withdrew. I felt shut out and alone, for the first time in my life.

"You'll be leaving us, of course," they said. "Good luck, miss," and went back into their overcrowded homes and shut their doors, not merely emphasizing the gap between us, but widening it once and for all.

I felt more bereft than I had felt at Uncle Silas's death, for my sorrow then had been tinged with a sense of relief. No longer would I worry about him, or fear for him when he wandered about the sprawling London streets, invariably getting lost; no longer would I wonder how to cope with his moods and idiosyncrasies, praying that they wouldn't grow worse as he grew older, fearing the day when he would have to be taken away. "To be taken care of, my dear." That was how Dr. Harlow would put it when the time came, but I knew what it would really mean—locking him up, restricting him, certifying him as insane when he was really a dear, harmless old man who wouldn't hurt a fly.

Uncle Silas had always been eccentric. That was part of his charm. The day he wandered into the church crypt which my father always left open for tramps and the homeless, he was noticeable not only because of the clothes he wore, but the way he wore them. A shabby beaver hat at a rakish angle; a monocle on a black velvet ribbon; a frock coat that had seen better days; a malacca cane twirling negligently in a gloved hand.

Gloves! None of the tramps who came to the crypt for the bowl of soup and the hunk of bread that my parents scraped their pockets to provide—for the church was a poor one, always low on funds—ever wore gloves, let alone frock coats and monocles.

Everything about him was shabby but elegant, his Vandycke beard neatly clipped, his threadbare shoes polished. I discovered later that he rubbed them up with the lining of his jacket, not having the money to pay a shoe-shine boy or even for a penny tin of polish, and anyway the lining didn't show. . . . And his gloves, once dove gray and now badly faded, had been of the finest doeskin.

He was an aging dandy, like one of those down-on-their-luck music hall artistes who sometimes came to see my father, hearing he was good for a touch.

But Uncle Silas didn't come for that reason. He came because it was cold outside. He refused the bowl of soup I offered, waving it away negligently. "Give it to the poor johnny over there, my dear!" But I could tell that he was hungry, all the same.

My father was in his study preparing his Sunday sermon. My mother was busy in the house. Only Mrs. Burchell, the Verger's wife, and I, were on duty in the crypt. It was my job to ladle out the soup and hand it over with a hunk of bread, and hers to question the long line of forgotten men and women to find out if they had anywhere to sleep and, if not, to give them a blanket and a corner to lie down in. The crypt of St. Saviour's had become well known in this part of London, tucked away between Long Acre and Covent Garden. The line increased daily, and included all sorts, all ages, all colors, and all creeds, but it had never before included a monocled gentleman, even a shabby one.

I was fourteeen then, and I remember feeling very grown up that day because instead of wearing my hair loose and straight over my shoulders, I had tied it back with a large blue bow, to match my dress. The dress was one my mother had cut down for me, but anyone would have thought it was new. She had trimmed it with lace, the remains of an Early Victorian gown, and the frills about my wrists delighted me.

"Don't let it trail in the soup, my dear," the monocled gentleman said. "That is very beautiful lace. Very good lace."

I'm sure I would have been concerned for this man even if he hadn't recognized how good the lace was, but this indicated that he was accustomed to the best and the thought distressed me. *I* only knew the lace was good because my mother told me so. The gown had belonged to a former employer, for my mother's family had been in service for three generations and she herself had been a lady's maid at Knight's Keep before my father, a theological student, had gone there to tutor the young Lord Elam, the Earl of Ashford's heir, during the summer vacation, and scandalized everyone by falling in love with the coachman's daughter.

His own father, a high-ranking member of the church, had disowned him on their marriage. The son of a *Bishop*, marrying a servant! He was doomed, of course. Doomed and possibly damned. The snobbish Bewleigh family never even met my mother or bothered about me, and since my father had disgraced such an eminent name it wasn't surprising that he never rose to be more than a struggling parson in a poor London parish, conveniently far from the family home in Gloucestershire and therefore unlikely to embarrass them.

I suddenly became aware that the monocled dandy was studying me intently.

"Forgive me, my dear—but what is your name?"

"Jane Bewleigh, sir."

"And your father—is he Vincent Bewleigh?"

"He is," I said in surprise. "Do you know him?"

"I—saw his name on the board outside the church."

He was still staring at me and, feeling uncomfortable, I said at random, "Are you sure you won't have some soup?"

His hesitation was barely perceptible. He needed that soup badly and could no longer wave it away with an indifferent hand.

I don't know what made me go in search of my father, but leaving poor Mrs. Burchell to cope single-handed I flung my cloak over my shoulders, ran up the stairs from the crypt and across the churchyard to the Parsonage. It was a gaunt barracks of a house, impossible to keep warm, and I knew that my father would be huddled over his desk in a greatcoat with a double-tiered shoulder-cape, for his stipend didn't run to extra fires.

I stood for a moment in the doorway, waiting to be noticed.

He concentrated so intently on his sermons that it wasn't always wise to disturb him. In the light from the oil lamp on his desk I saw that his mittened fingers were blue, and on an impulse I ran across to him and flung my arm about his neck.

I adored my father. He was the gayest, kindest person in the world, with the exception of my mother. Each sparked off in the other all that was warm and fine. They had given me the good things of life—the really good things. Love and security and kindness. We had never had money, but if they ever missed it or needed it, they never passed their anxiety on to me. Our home was rich in happiness. What more did we need?

"And to what do I owe this unexpected demonstration of affection?" he asked indulgently, smiling the wonderful smile that drew everyone to him. Lame dogs, skeptics, tough costermongers who had never set foot inside a church, and even the prostitutes with which this quarter abounded, all liked and respected the Vicar of St. Saviour's.

"I love you," I told him now, giving him a final hug. "I love you very much and I'm glad to have you as my father."

"And you left Mrs. Burchell to carry on alone so that you could come to tell me that?" he asked skeptically.

"No—there's a man down there. I wish you'd see him. He isn't like the rest. He's a—gentleman," I finished, for that really was the only word.

"So is old Hopkins who sells jellied eels on the corner— as honest and decent a gentleman as ever was born, my dear."

"I know, but this one is different. He is educated, cultured —and pathetic somehow."

"An actor down on his luck, perhaps."

"I don't think so. Come and see him, Father, before he goes away. He may never come back!"

He patted my cheek affectionately. "My dear Jane, you are just like your mother—always falling for some hard-luck story."

"And what about you? Anyway, he hasn't told a hard-luck story. He simply asked my name."

My father didn't like that. He was always quick to sense any unwanted overtures to his wife and daughter. Age made no difference in this quarter. Girls of fourteen were considered women, and often looked it. Some were prostitutes long before that. You couldn't grow up as a parson's daughter in a seamy London district and not know the facts of life.

My father pushed his chair aside. "I'll take a look at this man," he said gruffly.

"Father—he isn't that kind at all!"

But despite my protests he was now anxious to inspect the stranger. Many were the times my father had thrown men out physically for trying to lay hands on me, or for making unwelcome suggestions to my mother or Mrs. Burchell. I knew he didn't really like the idea of my helping in the crypt, but I was well able to take care of myself. If my mother could help down there, so could I.

I remember running beside my father across the church yard, trying to keep up with his immense stride, and I remember pulling up when he reached the crypt, simply because he halted so abruptly, staring across at the man.

He was sitting against the wall, his beaver hat on his knee, his legs elegantly crossed, his eyes closed. His face was white and Mrs. Burchell was watching him anxiously.

"Oh, Reverend, I'm glad you've come! I think this man is ill—"

My father said nothing. He was staring at the stranger in a puzzled sort of way, then in one stride he was beside him, his hand upon his shoulder, his face concerned.

"Silas! It *is* Silas, isn't it?"

The man opened his eyes. For a moment they didn't seem to focus properly, then recognition dawned and he said weakly, "Vincent—"

He tried to get up, but the pressure of my father's hand on his shoulder forced him to be still.

"Jane—fetch your mother."

The man protested. "No! I don't want her to see me like this—"

"Fetch her, Jane. Tell her that someone is here. Someone she knows."

"Who shall I say?" I asked stupidly.

"Silas Be—"

"Silas Davenport," the old man put in quickly. "She will have forgotten the name, and it doesn't matter if she has."

It wasn't until after his death that I discovered that his surname wasn't Davenport. Nor was he my uncle, but I always knew that. He was just a dear friend from the past who my parents took into their home, a friend who became Uncle Silas to me, a forgetful old man who had to be looked after because he was incapable of looking after himself. So it was natural to continue caring for him when my parents died two years later. He was all the family I had left.

That was one of the winters when the Thames was frozen over and London made sport on the ice. It was so solid that roundabouts and swings were set up in the middle of the river, and military bands played on their brass instruments far into the night, and oxen were roasted on huge revolving spits, and chestnuts and pigs' trotters were sold piping hot, and not even the heat of the braziers melted the frozen river.

At least, not for a long time.

The disaster came suddenly. The sound of cracking ice echoed like pistol shots in the night air and the hissing of braziers sinking beneath the ice floes was like the savage spitting of serpents, but worst of all were the human screams as bodies catapulted into the icy waters, struggled, and were silent.

And among them were my parents, skating hand in hand. One moment I saw them waltzing and laughing together; the next, they were gone, and I was screaming wildly on the river bank, with Uncle Silas gathering me close against him so that the picture was blotted out.

That day was my mother's birthday. We had gone to the frozen Thames to celebrate it because the entertainment was free and the whole of London was enjoying the festivities, besides which my parents loved skating and had few opportunities for it.

Characteristically, they had included many parishioners in the party—old Nell, who ran the laundry around the corner, and Miss Dobson, who ran the Church School, and Hopkins, the jellied-eel vendor, and the Burchells and their children, and Tom Kelly who sold newspapers, and widowed Dora Smee the dressmaker, and many more. I remember how gay we all were as we bowled along to Westminster Bridge, my parents and Uncle Silas and I piled into Ned Baxter's hansom cab, with Ned's wife up beside him on the box, and all the neighborhood following in coster-carts and pony-traps or on foot.

And I remember going home eventually with my hand in Uncle Silas's, too stunned to speak, and how he looked down at me and said over and over again, "I'll look after you, my dear. I'll look after you always, I promise. . . ."

But really, of course, it was I who had to look after him,

and I knew it. It was what my parents would have wanted me to do.

I don't know why I never asked questions about Uncle Silas. Perhaps I instinctively sensed that they wouldn't be answered. He always side-stepped the inquisitive approaches of neighbors, and so did my parents. To me, he was a lame dog who had to be helped, an old friend down on his luck, a man who had obviously been reared as a gentleman and no longer had a place in society. A gambler, perhaps, who had lost his money through his own foolhardiness or extravagance. Whatever the reasons, they belonged to his past, and by my parents' choice he belonged to our present. It was a situation I just naturally accepted.

I quickly learned to love him. He was kind and endearing, and when the gauntness due to hunger and neglect disappeared, he was handsome too. He held my parents, and particularly my mother, in great affection. I don't know when it was that I suspected he loved her and that once upon a time he had probably loved her very, very deeply, as a man loves a woman, with desire. It seemed to me that he was very much older than she, and perhaps this was the reason why he had failed to win her, although I knew that she could never have loved any man as she loved my father.

Silas used to say that I was like her, and as I grew older, and particularly after they were gone—for he seemed to break up rapidly after that—he sometimes used to confuse me with her, calling me by her name and actually believing that I was she. That was when I began to get worried about him, fearing that his memory was going.

He did strange things, too. Like hoarding. Anything, everything. Pieces of candy that old Mrs. Tucker gave him when he wandered into her shop; cigar bands of gold paper, although where he got the cigars from I never really knew, for he had no money to buy them. I assumed people gave them to him, although no one in the vicinity could afford cigars. He also hoarded copies of *The Times*, which was rather tiresome because they cluttered up the small rooms we rented from Dora Smee after we moved out of the Parsonage.

We lived in Dora Smee's house until Uncle Silas died. I was twenty then, and worked with Dora, earning enough to buy our food and making clothes for myself, and even shirts for Uncle Silas, out of pieces of material left over from customers' orders. Dora and I built up quite a thriving little dressmaking concern between us, but it was hard work and sometimes involved sewing long into the night. It was then that Silas took to wandering out more and more, and because I couldn't keep an eye on him I had no idea where he went.

"Don't worry about 'im, ducks. 'E'll come 'ome, dragging 'is tail be'ind 'im," Dora would say in her cheerful cockney voice. But very often I had to go in search of him, or a Peeler would find him wandering and bring him home.

I can't remember when he first began talking about the carriage. A green carriage. It didn't mean anything, of course, because London was full of carriages, green and maroon and brown and cream being fashionable colors. I supposed he used to dream of driving around in one, like a gentleman. Anyway, I took no notice of these ramblings, but I was worried about his increasingly irresponsible behavior.

"You know, dearie, you oughta put 'im away, reely you oughta," Dora said one day. "It's not fair on a young thing like you, looking after a doddering old man."

"He isn't doddering! He's a little vague at times, that's all."

"Nutty, dearie. That's wot. All this talk about a green carriage following 'im around!"

"I've never heard him say that it was following him."

"Well, I 'ave. Told me about it t'other day, 'e did. 'I'll watch out for it tonight, Dora,' 'e sez. 'I'll watch out for it, and then I'll stop it and arsk the driver why 'e's always following me.' That's wot 'e said, dear, trooly."

"But it doesn't make sense! Why should a carriage—any carriage—be following him?"

"Exackly!" Dora said triumphantly. "It's all nonsense— *but not to 'im.* It's like I said, dearie—" She tapped her forehead significantly. "You reely oughta put 'im away."

My needle flew furiously, but my hands were suddenly shaking—my voice, too, as I declared, "Never! I'll look after him, just as my parents would have done."

Dora sighed. "Well, be it on your own 'ead, ducks. Don't say I didn't warn you. But think about it, all the same. T'ain't fair on a little slip like you, 'aving to worry about an old man who thinks 'e's being chased by green carriages! What sort of life do you 'ave, divided between this sewing room and your Uncle Silas? What chance will you ever get to meet a nice fella and get married?"

I smiled a little wryly at that, for even without being tied to my uncle, I would have no opportunity to get married. I had nothing in common with the young men in this neighborhood and since I wasn't likely to meet any others I had long since resigned myself to spinsterhood. It was foolish to dream about marrying a man as fine and gentlemanly as my father, for such an opportunity would never come my way.

Which shows how impossible it is to predict the future.

We finished work early that day, and I was glad to hurry upstairs to our sitting room and light the fire. For economy's sake I never lit it during the day if Uncle Silas had gone off for one of his walks. I hoped he would be home early, for a sudden fog had descended. Even the sound of the muffin man's bell was deadened, like a drum at a State funeral.

I flung a shawl about my shoulders and ran down to the street to buy a pennyworth for tea. At a farthing each it meant two muffins for each of us. I would toast them before the fire, and draw the curtains, and light the lamp, and maybe Uncle Silas would like a game of chess afterwards.

If I hadn't gone out to get those muffins I wouldn't have seen it happen. Even now, I'm not sure exactly how it did. All I remember is the sudden sound of carriage wheels as I turned to go back into the house. I heard the muffin man's bell begin to clang again as he went on his way, then clatter abruptly into silence. I spun around just in time to see Uncle Silas come shuffling out of the fog, stumbling across the road in his haste to reach the footpath. Beneath the flickering gaslight from a street lamp I saw his face contorted with terror.

He mouthed incoherently, but his words were drowned by galloping hooves and the jingle of harness and the rattle of wheels, and suddenly a vehicle came looming out of the fog, driven by a demon driver who lashed the horses unmercifully in direct pursuit of the old man. Or so it seemed. For a fraction of a moment my mind was frozen in horror, and then I rushed to pull my uncle to safety.

I was too late. He lay sprawled on the ground like a broken puppet. He had made a pitiful attempt to cover his head and even as I reached him I felt a rush of air as the carriage narrowly missed me then continued on its mad gallop into the night. In the spluttering jet of a street lamp I caught a flash of green as it sped by, then vanished into the fog.

The muffin man was shouting and cursing and shaking his

fist. "*Bastards!*" he yelled. "*Murdering bastards! Murdering, bloody toffs! To hell with all bloody toffs!*"

Out of the fog people came running. In a matter of minutes a group had gathered, but in far less time than that there was no longer any sound of retreating carriage wheels. They were gone forever.

I heard myself babbling incoherently, "Someone fetch Doctor Harlow—quickly, *quickly!*" and Dora put her arm about me, murmuring, "Yes, lovey, yes—'e'll be 'ere soon. Young Tommy Wilson's gorn to fetch 'im—" And through the haze of shock and the whirl of voices I could hear Tommy scampering off down the street. Doctor Harlow's surgery was five blocks away. What if he came too late? I clung to Dora and sobbed, "He may be out! He may have gone to see a patient, and there's no other doctor around here!"

"There, there, ducky, don't take on. Tommy'll fetch 'im as quick as 'e can, don't you worry."

The muffin man and old Hopkins from the corner were picking Uncle Silas up to carry him indoors, and Dora was propelling me back into the house. My knees seemed to cave under me as I climbed the steps. We were halfway up when an authoritative voice said from below, "Don't move him! Let me take a look."

Dora and I turned. A man had emerged from the fog—a stranger. He was taking command just as if he had every right to and the two men were obediently replacing Uncle Silas on the pavement. Something cracked in me then. I couldn't bear the sight of my uncle lying there on the stones, like a worn-out vagrant. I flew down the steps and turned on the man like a tigress. "Who are *you* to give orders? Bring my uncle indoors, Hopkins—I won't have him lying there!"

The man put me aside and stooped over Silas. "Leave him alone!" I cried, and flung myself on the stranger. "What right have *you* to touch him?"

"Every right." The man put me aside again and rapped, "Someone take this girl indoors. She's a nuisance. And stand back, all of you—I'm a doctor."

The fight went out of me. I leaned against Dora, limp as a rag. A doctor. Thank God for a doctor! I was so relieved that it didn't occur to me to wonder who he was, or where he came from, or how he happened to be in a district that had only one doctor anyway. This part of London was too poor to to support two. But none of that came into my mind until later.

The man's fingers were on Silas's pulse. He stooped and listened for his heart-beats, then lifted his eyelids and gently closed them again. I knew without being told that Uncle Silas was dead.

The man straightened up.

"All right," he said quietly. "You can take him indoors. Moving him can't do any harm now."

I just stood there, staring at the man. He said quietly, "I'm sorry. He was killed almost instantly. The wheels went right over him."

"I know," I whispered. "I know."

Dora said gently, "Come on in, dear, come on in," and somehow I climbed those steps again, forgetting the man and the crowd and the bitter cold that ran through me—forgetting everything but the fact that Uncle Silas was dead. Killed. Trampled to death by galloping hooves and flying wheels.

Inside the house I sank weakly onto the stairs, and to my surprise the man was stooping over me, feeling my pulse. Then he opened his Gladstone bag. "Put her to bed at once," he said to Dora, "and give her this draught. Sleep is what she needs."

Then he was gone, striding along the dark passage and disappearing into the foggy night as mysteriously as he came.

Twice, I thought as I drank the sedative the unknown doctor had left for me. Twice I had seen death strike suddenly and violently, the first by accident, the second by—could it *really* have been design, or had that demon driver merely been trying to control a team of runaway horses?

No one would ever know, for no one would be able to find out. Accidents were commonplace in foggy London in the late eighteen-hundreds. The Peelers couldn't be everywhere— there just weren't enough to patrol all the streets. People shouldn't wander around alone in pea-soupers, especially old people, they would say.

Besides, what difference would it make? Finding Uncle Silas's executioner wouldn't bring the old man back, and now, at any rate, he was at peace.

That was the first time I openly acknowledged to myself that he had been a tormented man, and it was my last thought before I sank into a sleep so deep that it lasted well into the next day. As I struggled back to consciousness a loose end was troubling the back of my mind, as if it had lain there waiting to be dealt with when I emerged from stupor. *"The wheels went right over him,"* the stranger had said, just as if he had seen the accident happen. But that was impossible. No one had been around at the time. No one but myself and the muffin man—and, of course, the demon driver.

Could it have been the man himself, returning to see what damage he had done and, on finding he had killed a man, pretending to know nothing about it? Or was that the carriage that Silas declared had been pursuing him for weeks, until it finally claimed its victim? If both conjectures were correct, then I had been face to face with my uncle's murderer.

CHAPTER TWO

"Lord-luvva-ducks," said Dora, "I thought you'd never come 'round! Gawd knows wot that doctor-chap gave you, but it certainly knocked you out. Getting scared, I was, wondering if 'e'd put an end to you!"

She bit her tongue sharply and I said, "It's all right, Dora—you needn't be afraid of reminding me that Uncle Silas is dead."

"Well, so long as *you're* not dead too!" she said thankfully.

My head felt like a turnip stuffed with cotton wool. I had never been drugged before and if the after-effects were like this, I would take good care never to be again.

But apart from that I felt better. Shock had receded and gratefully I drank the tea Dora put before me. With the first cup the heavy, doped feeling began to subside.

"I wonder who he was," I mused, "and where he came from."

"*That's* wot Doctor 'Arlow wanted to know! By the time young Tommy fetched 'im, the man 'ad gorn and you'd passed out. ' 'Ow should I know who 'e was?' I said. 'Lucky for us 'e 'appened to be passing.' "

She was right, of course. All the same, I couldn't help wondering about the stranger whose arrival had been so opportune. "Perhaps he was visiting friends in the neighborhood," I said aloud, although what educated person would be likely to have friends in the immediate vicinity I couldn't imagine.

"Taking a short cut through Covent Garden, I shouldn't wonder," said Dora, which seemed a more logical explanation. On a night like that no cabs would be available in the Strand and to cut up Drury Lane and across Covent Garden Market to Long Acre, possibly on his way to Leicester Square, would be a step anyone would take providing he knew the way.

It wasn't until after the funeral that I went through Uncle Silas's things. He was buried beneath the dusty plane trees of my father's former church, and his coffin was wheeled there on a coster's barrow because these people had loved him and wanted to take him on his last walk through the London streets, and perhaps they knew that I couldn't afford a grand hearse, for such things cost money.

The whole neighborhood turned out, falling in behind Dora and me as we walked the short distance to the graveyard, and afterwards they went out of their way to show their sympathy, anxious that I shouldn't feel alone.

They were rough, illiterate, and poor, but their hearts were warm. Always there had been a sense of division between myself and my neighbors—I, the daughter of their clergyman, and they, the cockneys of his parish, but the few well-to-do parishioners from not-far-distant Bloomsbury, who had sat in their grand front pews to listen to his sermons, never showed the kindness and friendship to me after his death that these poor people did.

"*I'll* do this job for you, dear," Dora said when she came upstairs and found me wrapping up Uncle Silas's clothes. "What d'you want done with 'em?"

"I thought I'd take them along to Mrs. Burchell—her husband is still Verger and will know the most needy families. It's a pity the new vicar closed the crypt. Mrs. Burchell told me he couldn't afford to run it."

Dora sniffed. "Well, your dear pa managed to. If you arsks me the present Reverend 'asn't much time for anyone without money. Never does the rounds like your pa useter—only goes calling on the people in the posh Squares over Bloomsbury way. No wonder the church is 'alf empty now. Not like it was in your father's time. Dearie me, are these the only things your uncle owned?"

"That's all," I said, as I folded the last garment.

I found some wrapping paper and tied the bundle, looking for the last time at Uncle Silas's frock coat. It was the one he had been wearing the day he first came into our lives, and he had kept it all these years, brushing it and pressing it but, for all his care, being unable to preserve the nap. There were shiny patches where it had rubbed clean off.

" 'Ave you been through 'is drawers, dearie?"

"He only has one—the top one, over there."

Dora opened it. "Blimey! Look at all this junk!"

The drawer might have belonged to a small boy, it was so cluttered, mostly with rubbish. There were a few stale candies, all neatly laid in a row along one side—the side near his bed. Did he reach out in the night and help himself to one, lying there in the darkness, nibbling like a child? Tears pricked my eyes. The only thing to do was throw everything away.

I lifted the drawer out and tipped the contents onto his bed. Pieces of string, cigar bands, paltry little knick-knacks, a piece of lace . . .

I recognized the lace at once. It was a collar my mother had once worn. I put it to my cheek, sniffing the fragrance which still lingered about it, a fragrance that brought her back more poignantly than anything else could have done. And Uncle Silas had kept it all this time, a last relic of the woman he had loved. . . .

Suddenly Dora picked something up and held it out to me. I could scarcely see it through my tears.

"It's addressed to you, lovey. You'd better open it."

It was a sealed envelope, with my name written in a flowing hand—a hand quite unlike my uncle's in later years, so it would seem to have been written some time ago. Beneath my name was the added line, *"To be opened in the event of my death."*

The note wasn't long. It was dated the day after I lost my parents.

My dear little Jane,

I promised to look after you always, and so I shall. When the time comes for you to read this, I want you to go at once to Mr. Mortimer Claythorne, of Claythorne, Draycott and Claythorne, No. 19, Lincoln's Inn Fields. Had your parents lived, the little I possess would have gone to them—now it comes to you because, with them, I hold you most dear in all the world.

May the Lord bless, preserve and keep you in happiness

all the days of your life, for your sweetness, so like your dear mother's, and your unselfishness, inherited from both your parents, does well deserve it.

Silas Davenport Carlton Bedell, Bt.

And then, quite inexplicably, he had carefully penned another line.

Repelle, Domine, virtutem diaboli.

Dora was peering over my shoulder, reading laboriously. Long before she reached the end I was staring in stunned disbelief at the signature.

"Lord love us, what does it mean?" she breathed.

"It means that what little he possessed, he has left to me."

"Well, bless my soul, I'd never've thought 'e possessed anything!"

"Nor I," I managed to say.

"There, there, love—don't take on! Mop your eyes and I'll put the kettle on for a nice cuppa tea." But before bustling from the room she cast another glance at the note, which I still held between nerveless fingers.

Her brow puckered. "Strange, isn't it, dearie? We all thought 'e was skint. Oh, we knew 'e was a gent, orlright, but 'e never seemed to 'ave tuppence to rub together!"

"I doubt if he had. That was why my parents took him in. He came to them when he had nowhere else to go and no means of support. I remember my mother telling me that he had once been well-to-do, but times had changed for him."

"Then wot's 'e got to leave you?"

"He says 'what little he has'—a few personal belongings, I expect, no more. But I shall be glad to keep them in memory of him."

"Then this little lot isn't all 'e 'ad in the world?"

"Apparently not."

"Funny 'e didn't keep everything with 'im."

"I expect he lodged them with his solicitors and simply left them there when he made his home with us."

"Wonder wot they'll turn out to be!" Dora said excitedly.

I hazarded a guess. "A few pictures, perhaps. Books. Maybe a few portraits of his family. Things like that."

"I wonder who 'is folks were and wot became of 'em? Dead, I suppose."

I didn't answer. I couldn't, because now I knew where my parents had met him, and what part of their lives he

19

had been associated with. And that, perhaps, was their reason for never referring to it. Apart from telling me of their swift love affair, they rarely recalled the days when my mother had been daughter of the coachman at Knight's Keep and my father a holiday-tutor to the son of the Ashford family, who owned it. And the Lady Ashford of those days had been a Bedell before her marriage. Silas's sister?

Once or twice, to satisfy my eager questions, my mother had described the old Elizabethan mansion, and the vast grounds, and the snobbishness that then prevailed in England of the Shires, but it was plain that it meant nothing to them. My mother wasn't ashamed of having been a coachman's daughter, nor, later, a lady's maid like her mother and grandmother before her, nor was my father ashamed of marrying into a sphere considered by his snobbish family as being socially beneath him. My parents had rejected the past and rejected it gladly for a far happier life together.

But they hadn't forgotten Silas. I could now understand their shock when he wandered into the crypt that day, as hungry as the line of beggars, but wearing his pride as elegantly as his shabby tail-coat and beaver hat and faded gloves. Perhaps he had been their only friend at a time when everyone else turned their backs, and for this reason they remembered him with affection and gratitude and took him into their home. Or perhaps the gesture was one of typical kindness, because he was now a lame dog as much in need as any, but I knew that in their hearts they had always had a deep affection for him, and that there must have been a reason.

Dora's voice recalled me with a jerk. "What are all those names at the bottom, dearie?"

"Silas Davenport Carlton Bedell," I said slowly. "And to think that I never knew him as anything but Silas Davenport."

"And that bit at the end—Bt. Wot's that s'posed to mean?"

"It's short for Baronet."

Dora gave a faint shriek. "You don't mean your old uncle was a reel live *Baronet!*"

"It seems so."

"And never let on! Not even to you?"

"My parents must have known. He was their friend long before I was born."

Dora's eyes were agog. "And wot's all that—there at the

bottom—all those funny-looking words? Like some foreign language!"

"It's Latin," I told her. "A dead language now. That means it isn't spoken any more, but only used by scholars, like my father. He used to teach it, in his spare time."

"Blimey! I wonder what it means?"

I pretended not to know, because suddenly I didn't want to talk any more. I said perhaps it was a family motto, and added, "I'd love that cup of tea."

She bustled away at once, concerned and excited and, I guessed, eager to spread the news around the neighborhood. I could tell that she was awed because she had been sheltering a baronet beneath her roof. It would be something to boast about for the rest of her life. If I hadn't been feeling so stunned, I would have been amused.

Alone, I reread the letter, puzzled and vaguely troubled by the carefully penned Latin at the end. Of all things, why did he have to add those words? I knew very well what they meant, for my father had taught me Latin as well as French, to supplement the three R's which was about all the local free school catered for.

"*Repelle, Domine, virtutem diaboli.*" Drive back, O Lord, the power of the devil. . . .

A shiver ran down my spine.

CHAPTER THREE

The next day I decided to call on Mr. Mortimer Claythorne to claim the few possessions Uncle Silas had left me. I knew they would be pitifully few, but was touched by his thought, and even a little amused by his reference to "Looking after me." All these years his wandering mind must have believed that fortune had not completely abandoned him.

I took pains with my appearance, carefully brushing and pressing the dark serge coat I had made for myself, trimmed with velvet left over from a customer's order. I had made a velvet toque to match, and although my gloves were cheap in quality I made sure they were spotless. Dora produced an elegant muff due to be delivered to a lady in Grosvenor Square. "Won't do no 'arm to borrow it for an hour or two," she insisted, and although I felt guilty I was glad of its distinction, for I didn't want to arrive at the solicitor's office looking like a poor relation.

"And take a cab," Dora insisted, opening her worn purse and counting out some change. "Might as well do the thing in style and I 'ope this Claythorne chap sees you arrive!"

I hoped so, too. I had always been fearful of patronage and knew very well that a legatee calling to collect a few pathetic possessions couldn't hope to be received with much deference, so at least I could try to create a good impression. But I put Dora's much-needed money aside. I had a few shillings of my own which would cover the cost of a cab to Lincoln's Inn Fields. The return journey didn't matter—I could do that on foot.

A hansom was clip-clopping by as I left the house, and I must say I felt very grand as I stepped inside. The cabby opened the trap-door in the roof and said, "Where to, Lidy?" and with great aplomb, as if riding around London by cab was an every-day thing to me, I gave him the address, then sat back elegantly in the corner, enjoying the drive eastwards. The day was clear and sunny; I felt relaxed and at ease.

Perhaps that was why I was caught unawares, pitching forward and striking my head violently on the floor when another cab stupidly tried to pass in an area too narrow to do so. We were driving through an alley into Drury Lane when it happened—so quickly that I was only aware of the sudden sound of wheels rattling alongside. My driver swerved to avoid a crash, but was too late. The overtaking vehicle ripped off our rear wheel and we pitched over drunkenly. It was then that I crashed onto the floor, felt the violent blow, and plunged into darkness.

When I came around the cabby was dragging me out, and the air was blue with oaths. Both drivers were cursing each other and even through the mists of shock I could see that the second one was an ugly customer, an ex-jailbird if ever there was one. "D'yer want the 'ole perishing street to yerself?" he was shouting, and as my driver propped me against a wall he yelled back, "I'll 'ave the Peelers onto you, you ruddy fool! What the 'ell d'you think you're doing, trying to push by in a bleedin' alley? Look at me cab—'oo's goin' ter pay for *that*? As for the passenger, she might've been killed!"

Their voices sounded doubly loud to my stunned senses. I leaned against the wall and took deep breaths to steady myself. I was shaking like a leaf, my head hurt violently, but I knew instinctively that no bones were broken. As the driver said, I'd had a lucky escape.

I became aware that people were hanging out of tenement windows and others diverging onto us along the narrow street. I hated being the center of attention and took a firm hold on myself. A kindly woman said, "Are you all right, ducks?" and began to brush me down. "Never saw the likes of it!" she flung at the reckless driver. "A man like you shouldn't be allowed at the reins. This pore young lidy might never've got to where she was going!"

My senses were clearing. I saw the second cabby advancing on the woman belligerently. He was certainly a very ugly customer and I knew that at any moment there would be a free-for-all. I had to get away.

"My bag—" I gasped. "I've lost my bag—"

The driver of my cab was fishing my reticule out of the overturned vehicle, cursing because the other man's cab had escaped with mere scratches *and* no passenger to worry about. He found my toque, sadly squashed, and the elegant muff which, I was thankful to see, was quite unharmed. With shaking fingers I rummaged for coins and thrust them into his hands. By now he was yelling blue murder at the second driver and the whole neighborhood seemed to be joining in. My cabby left me to the woman's care and enlisted a couple of men to help him right his cab. The broken wheel lay in the gutter and I stepped over it gingerly as I forced myself to walk.

The woman hurried after me. "Sure you're all right, Miss?" she asked anxiously. "Maybe you oughter come in 'n sit down."

I thanked her, but insisted that all I needed was fresh air. My step grew steadier as I turned the corner of the alley and emerged into Drury Lane. I knew I looked a sorry sight and with shaking hands tried to restore some shape to my battered toque. I would certainly make an impression when I did eventually arrive at the lawyer's office, but not the impression I had planned!

Using a shop window as a mirror I tidied myself, then sought an apothecary and asked for a draught of *sal volatile.* He made me sit down for a while and gradually I began to feel much better. All I would suffer would be a few bruises and a headache.

"You had a narrow escape," the man said when I told him the story. "The second driver must have been insane, trying to overtake in that narrow alley. And if he had no passenger, why was he in such a hurry, or even going that way? He could hardly expect to pick up a fare in that quarter."

I couldn't answer those questions. The incident was over as far as I was concerned, although I felt sorry for the driver of the wrecked cab.

So after all I didn't arrive at the offices of Claythorne, Draycott and Claythorne in grand style. Even so, I was received with a courtesy which surprised me, for it was tinged with an unexpected deference. I was shown into the office of Mr. Mortimer Claythorne without delay and offered the most comfortable chair in the room.

"May I offer you some refreshment, Miss Bewleigh?"

I hesitated, then accepted. "A cup of tea would be most welcome," I said, and told him why. He was a courtly old gentleman and deeply concerned.

"Good gracious me!" he exclaimed. "How appalling if you had been prevented from getting here!"

I couldn't see why. After all, I had only come to collect a few minor articles, and said so. At that, his bushy eyebrows raised.

"Am I to understand, my dear young lady, that you have no idea of the nature of your inheritance?"

"Naturally not, sir, but since my uncle was a poor man I presume that the 'little' to which he referred in his letter to me can only consist of a few personal items. Of course, if there are such things as pictures or books, I must ask you to be so kind as to arrange for their delivery."

He held up a tapering white hand. "I see I must make things quite clear to you. Sir Silas had no material possessions. He sold them all when he sold his home many years ago."

"Where was his home?"

"The family place in Kent—a manor called Beechwood Close, a few miles from Lympne."

"Near Knight's Keep, where my mother worked?"

"Quite near. Both the Ashford family and the Bedells were old-established Kentish people, linked by the marriage of Silas's sister, Ruth. Silas also had a brother, Joseph, who emigrated to New Zealand and eventually died there childless, so Silas was left with the family home."

"And he never married?"

"Never—surprisingly, for he was a handsome man and very eligible. He was my senior at Oxford, and even as an undergraduate he was very attractive to women. I always suspected that there was one particular woman in his life, a woman he wanted but never won, but I was never taken into his confidence about it. Nor was anyone, I imagine."

The tea arrived, and as I drank it I asked, "But why did he sell his house? And after he sold it, where did he go?"

Mr. Claythorne looked down at his hands and said painfully, "He was—sick. Not physically, but perhaps one might say mentally. He was not insane, I do assure you—"

"I know that. He lived with us during the final years of his life."

"Yes—of course. Then you will know that he was merely harmless and eccentric."

"Yes."

"But housekeepers would never stay with him for long. They found him tiresome. He would go for long, solitary walks and forget to come back for meals, and behavior like that is annoying to conscientious housekeepers. He was moody, too, and given to long spells of introspection. And so eventually he lived quite alone, becoming more and more neglected. One day he was found in a state of collapse, due entirely to malnutrition. With no one to prepare his meals, he just didn't trouble to eat."

"Who found him?"

"His nephew, Lord Ashford—or Lord Elam as he was then. You may have heard of him."

"I have. My father tutored him for a while."

"So I recall. During a summer vacation, I believe—when he met and married your mother."

"You knew my parents?" I asked eagerly.

"Alas, no. Only of them. It was good of them to befriend Silas in his time of need."

"What I don't understand is how he came to such a pass. Surely he was financially well provided for?"

"He most certainly was, and the sale of his manor house added to his fortune."

"Then what happened to the money?" I asked, surprised.

"Precisely nothing. For a while Silas went as a voluntary patient into a hospital where people in failing health could be cared for. During that time—and forever after—he drew nothing but a very small proportion of the interest, so the principal increased steadily and is now worth a great deal."

"But didn't he know?" I cried. "Poor darling, didn't he *know*?"

"Of course," the solicitor answered calmly. "I kept him informed."

"But when we found him he was destitute!"

The solicitor cleared his throat in some embarrassment.

"My dear young lady, you didn't find him—*he* found *you*. Or, rather, he found your parents. He appealed to me to help in tracing them. I gather he held them both, and particularly your mother, in high regard."

"How long did he stay in the hospital?"

"Not long enough. He walked out one day, and never went back."

I could imagine him doing that, just wandering away in his vague fashion.

"This hospital. Was it—was it a—"

I couldn't utter the word "asylum," but Mortimer Claythorne knew what I meant.

"Not exactly, Miss Bewleigh. Your uncle—I know you think of him as that and I know he liked you to—was somewhat irresponsible, but far from insane, as the doctors informed his brother-in-law."

"But surely he knew that? Surely it was evident to everyone that poor Silas was simply lonely and needed looking after—and perhaps a little childish in some ways?"

"The doctors made that quite clear."

"Then why didn't he take care of Silas later?"

"For one thing, no one knew where he had gone. It was I who found him eventually, living in a most distressing and impoverished fashion in a room in Camden Town. He was so convinced that he was poor that it was the hardest job in the world to dissuade him. I brought him back here and showed him the state of his investments, but even then he didn't really grasp their full value, merely that he had, after all, what he called 'a fairly decent estate' to bequeath to whomever he chose. It was then that he asked me to trace your parents—and back he went to those wretched lodgings while I did so. I could never persuade him to change his mode of living. 'I have enough,' he insisted. 'I don't need money. It is foolishness to spend, although I have never been able to convince my sister's husband on that point.' " The solicitor gave a dry little laugh. "Matthew was always rich enough not to worry about spending. He inherited not only Knight's Keep but the whole of the Ashford fortune. He was always a little out of patience with Silas, and I suppose it was understandable."

I felt a lump in my throat so big that I could scarcely speak.

"When he came to us he was shabby and hungry. It was heartbreaking. . . ."

The solicitor said gently, "Believe me, the shabbiness was quite unnecessary. So was the hunger. But he had developed the fanaticism of many aging people—the conviction that to spend money on himself was a dire mistake. Even to spend at all! No matter how hard I tried to persuade him otherwise, the conviction remained. Because certain investments had deteriorated he was constantly afraid that the rest would follow suit. He was quite unable to grasp that depleted investments had been more than counterbalanced by the increase of others. Facts and figures were beyond him. 'I mustn't touch any of it,' he insisted, 'or I shall have nothing to leave them.' By 'them' he meant your parents. He thought of no one else. And eventually there actually was no one else but his nephew Justin, who became the Earl of Ashford and inherited Knight's Keep when his father, who was much addicted to foreign travel, died following one of his expeditions—Africa, I believe."

"Then surely, as Silas's one remaining relative, Lord Ashford should inherit now?"

"That was not Silas's wish. "They need it, Justin doesn't,' he said when he made his will, and frankly I agreed. As soon as I traced your parents, the matter was settled. Silas placed everything in my hands, and the will is legal and indisputable. He bequeathed everything to Vincent and Lucy Bewleigh, and, in the event of their predeceasing him, to such descendants as they might have. In other words you, my child. 'It will be a comfortable little nest-egg for them,' he said." The solicitor smiled as he spoke the words. "All Silas would allow me to pay out to him was a trifling sum each month, barely enough to keep him in cigars, so that the 'little' he possessed should remain intact. It did more than that—it increased and flourished, with the result that you are now a rich young woman. A very rich young woman indeed."

CHAPTER FOUR

"I don't believe it," I stammered incoherently. "I don't believe it. . . ."

"Then let me show you."

And there it was, proof positive. Facts and figures revealing that I was richer than I could have been in my wildest dreams, had I ever indulged in them. The wealth seemed to me almost unlimited, and I had no one to spend it on but myself.

Quite illogically, I was frightened. Playing make-believe, as Dora and I sometimes did, about what we would do if we ever came into a fortune was one thing, but to suddenly possess one was another. It assumed the proportions of a terrifying burden that I had no idea how to handle. Besides, the "fortune" of which Dora and I had day-dreamed, as we sewed fine seams for fine ladies, had consisted of what had seemed to us wealth indeed—a few hundred pounds, perhaps even a thousand—but my inheritance was beyond all that. It was enough to keep me in more than comfort for the rest of my life.

"I won't know how to handle it," I said helplessly, suddenly aware that I was shaking.

Mortimer Claythorne said kindly, "You need have no worry on that account. We will handle it for you. You can draw on the capital at any time, and we will arrange for a good income to be paid to you each month. You need suffer none of poor Silas's fears—your estate will not diminish. It is safely tied up."

At Silas's name, the tears began to run unheeded down my cheeks. "Poor Silas—poor dear Silas, depriving himself for us. . . ."

The solicitor said briskly, "You mustn't look at it like that, Miss Bewleigh. Silas may have deprived himself materially, but not in the way that was important to him. More than anything in life he wanted to be near your mother. I believe he loved her. Without her, life had proved empty and worthless, so riches meant nothing to him. He got the thing he most wanted in the end—a home beneath the same roof, the daily sight of her, the reassurance that she was happy and well loved, the sharing of her life in a small way—a big way, to him. He belonged, at last, to Lucy and her family. The final years of his life were among the happiest he ever knew and after her death the one thing, the one person, who made it worth while was yourself—her daughter. He once told me that you were the reincarnation of your mother, when young. Few people are lucky enough even partially to recapture their dreams in old age, but Silas did. So take your inheritance, my dear, and be happy with it, as he wished. Your nest-egg, as he called it, will give you security for the rest of your life, and that is what he wanted."

But still I wasn't completely happy.

"Has the present Lord Ashford any family?" I asked.

"He married, I understand."

"Then I would like them to have it. They are the rightful heirs, not I."

At that, Mr. Claythorne became quite irritated.

"My dear young lady, I have had enough of dealing with stubbornness! Silas tried my patience many times. I beg you not to do the same. This will is legal and indisputable, as I have already told you."

"But Lord Ashford might not think so."

"He cannot gainsay it!"

"Has he been notified of his uncle's death?"

"Besides writing to him, I inserted the usual announcements in the obituary columns."

"Have you heard from him?"

"Not yet."

"Then please write to him again. Tell him I don't wish to accept this inheritance. What will I do with so much money? It will bewilder me!"

"Only at first. It is amazing how quickly one becomes accustomed to wealth," the solicitor said dryly. Then he added earnestly, "My dear young lady, if I am to act for you I must obey your wishes, but pray give this matter some thought. I will delay any such letter until you have done so."

"Oh, I won't refuse it all," I said sensibly. "I will accept enough for my needs, enough to make life comfortable and secure, so that when I am old I shall want for nothing."

The solicitor actually laughed.

"A child like you should not be worrying about old age!"

"But you haven't seen the things I have seen, nor grown

up in a neighborhood like mine. You haven't seen the effect of poverty on young and old. My father's parish was full of such things—starvation, and tragedy, and squalor. I shall take enough money to help certain people I know who need it, and enough for my own needs, but for the rest—no. Too much money could set me apart. How would I live? In splendid isolation, friendless and alone?"

Mortimer Claythorne gave a snort of impatience.

"A girl like you will never be alone. You are much too pretty. You will marry—and marry well. In fact," his dry voice finished, "you are now such a good catch that you will have to be very careful not to fall into the hands of a fortune hunter. At any rate, not until the Married Women's Property Act comes into force on the first of January next," he joked, "then by law it will remain your own."

So now, I thought wryly, the only eligible husband for me had switched from a rough youth of my district to the other extreme—a man wealthy enough not to need my additional money. All the more reason for depleting my fortune, I decided. A young woman with a modest but comfortable income would be in a far safer position. She needn't look askance at any possible suitor, wondering whether it was herself or her money that he wanted.

"Please, Mr. Claythorne, will you do as I ask? Write to Uncle Silas's nephew."

"Very well," he agreed unwillingly. "I will tell him that you wish to share the legacy, but I shall make it absolutely clear that such a decision is not obligatory, but entirely voluntary on your part. I hope the man will have the decency to refuse."

I walked home from Lincoln's Inn in a daze. I scarcely remember passing the stage door of the Drury Lane Theater and entering Covent Garden Market. I was quite unaware of my surroundings, of the market porters cocking admiring eyebrows at the sight of a young woman walking across the basket-laden cobblestones, or of the flower sellers taking up their stands beside the pillared entrance of the opera house, waiting for the toffs to arrive for the evening performance.

It was late afternoon and dusk was drawing in. The market was a litter of refuse and abandoned carts. It was far too early for the glittering opera audience to arrive in their carriages and landaus and hansoms, but the flower girls liked to claim their pitches well in advance. Their raucous voices screeched about my ears as they bandied coarse jokes or abuse at each other, or shrieked across the cobbled market to the porters who invited them into the gin bars. It was a fantastic world, this corner deep in the heart of London, where squalor ruled by day, and with darkness, changed into glitter and opulence.

Some premonition told me that soon I would leave all this. Where I should go, I had no idea, but already I felt a different person. I had a substantial sum of money in my reticule, and a bank account book that Mr. Claythorne had already arranged for me. He had insisted upon the advance and I had never carried so much cash on my person in my life, nor ever dreamed I would.

On an impulse I stopped and bought an armful of nosegays from an astonished flower-seller. There were buttonholes for the gentlemen and posies for the ladies, and I gathered up a whole handful intermixed, and gave her a sovereign for the lot.

Of course that was a mistake. I was besieged at once by the others and before a fight could break out I thrust sovereigns at them all and hurried away, slowing down as I neared Long Acre. In five minutes I would be home.

It was then that I heard the footsteps. Not that I heeded them, except to quicken my own because the street was dark and deserted. Perhaps the accident on the way to Lincoln's Inn had unnerved me a little because it seemed that as my footsteps increased so did those behind me. They were heavy, determined, and unmistakably male.

Turning a corner, I tried to run, but could not. It was then I realized that although I had forgotten the accident in the excitement of Mr. Claythorne's news, I had not completely recovered from it. I was still somewhat shaken, and my heart thumped ridiculously.

The footsteps turned the corner. I glanced over my shoulder and saw the figure of a man reflected in the dim light of a spluttering gas lamp. It looked solid, bulky, and menacing, recalling the jailbird of a cab driver who had nearly killed me. Alarm clutched me. I suppressed it firmly and hurried on—but now, without a doubt, the man hurried too. I felt fear lick my heart and forced myself to break into a run. The flowers scattered from my hands but I dared not pause to pick them up. I was convinced that the thug following me, if not the dangerous cab driver, had seen me distributing sovereigns outside the opera house and was bent on robbery.

Suddenly, mercifully, Long Acre opened before me and soon I was home and hurrying up the front steps, fumbling for my door key as the man came ever nearer. He was within a few yards of the area railings when at last I shot the key into the lock and turned it. As I did so I cast a fleeting glance over my shoulder and saw him hurrying in my wake, his face obscured by the upturned collar of his greatcoat. No—it wasn't the sinister cab-driver, nor even a thug. He was well dressed but that didn't lessen my fear—nor did the thought which came to me later, that there had been something familiar about him.

I slammed the front door shut and leaned against it, my heart palpitating with relief. Outside, the man's footsteps halted, then walked on. I could hear them disappearing down the street, heavy and frightening, vanishing like a bad dream.

Dora was waiting, with the kettle on the hob and a pile of sewing on her lap.

"My, but you've been a long time, dear. Never mind—show me the prizes!"

I managed to laugh. "There weren't any prizes, Dora."

She looked crestfallen. She had been anticipating some nice pictures for the walls and maybe a vase or two.

"Not a *thing*?" she gasped.

"Only money," I told her, as negligently as possible.

She stared, then with characteristic skepticism asked: "'Ow much?"

"I can't name it in round figures."

She sniffed. "That I'll warrant! Your pore old uncle was skint. Didn't I tell you?"

"My poor old uncle was far from skint. He was rich, Dora. And so am I now."

Her jaw dropped so wide I thought it would never close again. The pile of sewing scattered as her hands flew to her face. After staring for one incredulous moment, she gasped, "Come orf it—you're pulling me leg!"

It took some time to convince her. I showed her the bank account book as evidence, but she had never seen one in her life so that didn't impress her much. Money, to her, was good hard cash. But in the end she managed to take it in, and when she did, it was my turn to be shocked. Before my eyes she changed from a warm and friendly figure into a distant stranger.

She stood up and smoothed her skirts self-consciously. "I—I'll make you some tea—" she said, as if anxious to get away.

"You're always making tea!" I joked, but my voice seemed hollow in the shabby room, and it was the voice of an intruder, someone who didn't belong any more.

That was the first indication that a gulf had suddenly come between me and my warm-hearted neighbors and that what had previously been affection for their late parson's daughter could change abruptly to awe.

As the news spread, so the gulf widened. They didn't begrudge me my good fortune, but it alienated them. It placed me beyond them. "You always were a lady," said Ned Baxter's wife. "Now you'll be able to live like one. That's right'n proper, miss." But instead of friendliness there was deference in her voice.

I made a desperate attempt to placate them, particularly Dora. I had plans for her—good ones. A dress shop in one of the exclusive West End streets. "You'll like that, won't you?" I pleaded. "It will be much better than eking out a living as a dressmaker."

To my astonishment, the idea didn't appeal at all.

"Now what would the likes of me do in one of them posh places? I don't even talk right. It needs someone genteel—like you. Someone wot speaks proper. Oh no, miss, I'd be all at sea, thanks very much. I've lived in this 'ouse ever since I wed Joe Smee and I get by fine. Of course, I'll miss you—you're a rare 'and with the needle, if I may say so."

"What's all this?" I cried, exasperated. "'If you may say so,' indeed! Next you'll be saying 'By your leave!'"

"We-ell," she admitted uncomfortably, "you can't say as 'ow things ain't different now. You'll forget about the likes of us—the likes of me—when you're living like a grand lady."

"Stop it, Dora! I won't listen to such talk!"

"You'll 'ave to listen," she said quietly, "because you can't pretend that things ain't different now. You'll leave us, and a good thing, too. This district ain't right for the likes of you, and never was. Gawd bless your mum and dad, they stuck it 'cos they 'ad to, but don't tell me they wouldn't be glad to know you were getting out of it."

I knew this to be true, and could say nothing. The one

thing that had troubled my parents was bringing up their daughter in such an area. Dora was right—they hadn't done it from choice, but from necessity, because my father's incumbency had been here.

"So you want me to go," I said helplessly.

"You didn't imagine you'd stay on 'ere, did you?"

"I mean, you want me to go immediately—"

It was a week after my visit to the lawyer's office, a week after the accident which might have cheated me out of my inheritance. I had never bothered to tell Dora about that, or about the man who had followed me home through the darkened streets. Both were unimportant now.

I was sitting in the workroom with Dora for the simple reason that I refused to be shut out of it. I was hand-sewing a hem and glad to have an occupation, but it was plain that Dora didn't like the idea at all.

"You've got to go," she repeated stubbornly, "so the sooner the better. What did this lawyer chap say you were to do?"

"A lawyer doesn't tell you what to do—he does what *you* tell *him*."

"Blimey!"

Her expression of astonishment was a joy to me. I laughed for the first time.

"He makes suggestions, of course," I added.

"Proper ones, I 'ope!"

"Oh, very proper, I assure you," I said solemnly. "In other words, he advises his client."

"Is that wot you are—a client?"

"Yes. He will handle my affairs, such as arranging for Lord Ashford—that's Uncle Silas's nephew and only living relative—to share this inheritance. I don't want it all and feel he is more entitled to it than I. When that is settled I shall do as Mr. Claythorne suggested."

"And wot was that?"

"Buy a small house in Kensington or Belgravia and engage a companion. Dora, if you won't accept the dress shop, will you come and live with me?"

"As your maid, you mean? I couldn't be one of them there companions, now could I? I'd be more comfy-like as a maid, anyway. Well, miss, I might consider it, but wot's all this about sharing the legacy with this wot's-'is-name? Your Uncle Silas wanted *you* to 'ave it, else why should 'e leave it to you? Come to your senses and take wot's rightly yours. And don't go slinging it about, neither. *I* know you've been giving money to all the scroungers in the neighborhood already, and don't try to deny it."

"Well, if my friends won't take it, my real friends like you—"

"Real friends don't want to make a touch, miss, and if this Lord Ashford feller does, I'll wring 'is neck, that's wot."

But there was no necessity for that, for Lord Ashford refused my offer. His uncle was entitled to bequeath his estate wherever he willed, he wrote, and furthermore he himself had no need for it. He was delighted to hear that the daughter of his former tutor had been provided for and was deeply grateful to her for taking care of his uncle in the final years of his life.

His letter to Mr. Claythorne was cordial. So too was his invitation to me. "Please convey to Miss Bewleigh my wish that she should accept the hospitality of Knight's Keep for a prolonged visit. Both Lady Ashford and myself would extend to her a very sincere welcome."

What was it someone had once said? That when one door closed, another opened? But never had I imagined that the doors of Knight's Keep would be opened to me, offering me hospitality and refuge just at a time when I was wondering where I could go, and hating the idea of establishing myself in my own household without friends or family to keep me company—venturing alone into an alien world where I knew no one.

But at Knight's Keep a welcome awaited me. It offered me sanctuary at the precise moment that I needed it. I could go soon, make new friends, and take my time over deciding where and how I should live. These were the reasons that I seized upon for accepting the invitation, but in my heart was a deeper one. I wanted to visit the place where my parents had met. I wanted to tread the paths where they had walked together, and see for myself the scene of their love affair.

I had imagined it so often—the stately Elizabethan mansion set in sweeping parkland; the mews quarters tucked away in the stable block where my grandparents had lived and my mother had been born; the rooms where she had worked as a lady's maid, and the dark corridors in which she had met my father. He had told me once how he had first seen her, coming towards him along one of those corridors, carrying a silver candlestick in her hand, her skirts rustling about her ankles, "And the flame of the candle casting a light on her face, like the reflection of a halo." And after that, their secret meetings, their whirlwind love. . . .

How could I resist such an invitation? And how, being human, could I not feel a certain triumph in the thought of visiting Knight's Keep as a guest and social equal? It would be a vindication of the couple who had dared to defy everyone. Tongues had wagged in the village of Lympne at the time; the whole of Kent had echoed with the story of the bishop's son who had disgraced the family name by running away with a maid from the Keep. And now their daughter was going there, invited, welcomed, socially acceptable—and rich. So she would be able to hold her head up proudly and confidently.

The prospect was enticing. I was about to embark on a life of elegance and grace, where people lived in harmony, where there could be neither ugliness, fear, nor treachery.

For how could it be otherwise in a house which was famous as one of the loveliest in all England?

CHAPTER FIVE

I departed for Knight's Keep exactly a month later. It took every minute of that time to prepare for the visit, for I was determined to do the thing in style. A Bond Street salon, famous as the shrine of a dapper French hairdresser, created an elegant coiffure for me, sweeping my blonde hair back from my brow and cascading it down the back in a cluster of curls. I was shown how to ring the change with a chignon if I wished, and how to adorn it by night with jewels, or feathers of osprey. I bought hats and gowns and gloves and mantles, cloaks and furs and shoes and parasols, and all from leading fashion houses.

My taste both pleased and surprised the high priestesses of these establishments, for I had walked in looking like some insignificant girl in inferior clothes—and was received as such until it became obvious that here was a customer who wanted nothing but the best and could pay for it. After that the picture changed. Bales of silks and satins and velvets and brocades were unrolled for my inspection; designs were produced, and fitters, and tape-measures, and sighs of ecstatic approval over my figure and deportment. It now seemed that I was a delight to dress. I repressed the cynical thought that perhaps all this gush and enthusiasm might have been less had the bills not been so high.

But the result was gratifying, and because I insisted on being supplied quickly, my wardrobe was complete in record time. As I tried on the finished garments I grew more poised and confident with each one. Oh yes, I could go to Knight's Keep with my head high! I could step into the midst of the landed gentry without any feeling of inferiority, for when a woman knows that her looks and her clothes cannot be faulted, she can win most battles.

Finally, my entire wardrobe was carefully packed into a big satin-lined trunk and dispatched to the Charing Cross depot of the South Eastern Railway, to be put in the guard's van of the train which was to take me to Sandling, the nearest station to Knight's Keep. There I would be met by one of the Ashford carriages, Mr. Claythorne informed me.

"And may you have a very happy visit, my dear. If I may say so, Silas's relatives are about to receive a very charming guest."

We were standing on the platform and I reached up impulsively and kissed his cheek. His pleasure and embarrassment amused me, but I was so grateful for his fatherly interest that I could think of no better way of expressing it.

If he was surprised by the delegation from the Long Acre district who, like himself, had come to see me off, he hid it well, and was amiable and courteous to them. Dora was there, tearful and awed and excited by the occasion. She had never ridden in a steam train—nor, indeed, had I—and actually to watch me step into a first class carriage, dressed in a gown and coat of dark blue velvet to reveal the swirled drapery across the hips and the straight sweep of skirt beneath it, and the elegant fall of both coat and gown over the bustle frame at the back, thrilled her as much as watching an actress make her entrance on to the Dury Lane stage, only this time she was not viewing from the gallery, but from a front seat in the stalls.

At first she refused to come, but I had begged her to. I wanted to see familiar faces as I departed from the great city that had been my home from birth. The Burchells were there too, with their family of children, and I had driven to Charing Cross in Ned Baxter's hansom, newly polished for the occasion. His wife wept openly and pretty soon they were all sniffing rather copiously and calling goodbye in choked voices.

Perhaps they made a rather incongruous picture, gathered around the open door of my compartment and straining to see what it was like inside. I caught a glimpse of the dapper solicitor standing on the brink, regarding them all with a mixture of amusement and embarrassment and yet, I felt, oddly touched by them. Nevertheless, as he pushed his way towards me and stepped into the train to place on the seat a copy of the *Lady's Companion*, I knew that he deemed it a very good thing that I was leaving such companions behind.

The compartment was empty, for the solicitor had reserved it to insure privacy. I was sorry in a way, for fellow travelers might have been interesting, but on the other hand, I would be able to relax and savor to the full every moment of this first journey of my life. I was tremendously excited, and had the hardest job in the world to appear calm and collected.

Dora thrust her way towards me and piped, "Now don't go talking to no strangers, miss—'specially men!"

"I shall have no opportunity to," I assured her, laughing. I was still laughing when Mr. Claythorne shook my hand and said, "I must confess that I endorse the good woman's warning, my dear Miss Bewleigh, although I have taken the precaution of ensuring that you will be unmolested."

Pompous and wordy to the end, I thought with some amusement, and begged him to have no concern for me. "I am well able to look after myself," I said quietly, "and life has taught me a certain astuteness. That is why I know you are glad to see me leave these people behind, and a little ashamed because you feel that way. I understand why you do, but in turn you must understand why I wanted them here. They were my friends. They have been good to me. They loved my parents, and so I love them, and always shall."

He said gruffly, "Bless you, my dear—bless you—" Then he lifted my gloved hand, brushed it lightly with his lips, stepped down onto the platform and shut the door. A "Reserved" label was stuck on to the glass window which formed the top half, and as I released the leather strap the heavy plate glass slid down within the door. I leaned out and called a final goodbye as the guard's whistle blew the departure signal, and the green flag waved.

There was a united chorus, a waving of hands, a sudden

shunting of the engine, and slowly the train began to move.

It was then that the unexpected happened. I was still waving goodbye when suddenly the door was flung open from the platform and I was thrust aside so abruptly that I collapsed into the corner seat. Into the compartment a man leaped, a big and heavy man who then slammed the door behind him, flung a Gladstone bag into the luggage rack, and exclaimed, "Made it, b'Gad! I thought that damned cab driver would never get here."

I recognized him at once. It was the stranger—the doctor who had appeared so mysteriously on the night of Silas's death, and his arrival now was equally unexpected.

I caught a fleeting glimpse of Dora's astonished face before the train gathered speed and carried me away, and her astonishment was only equalled by my own. The man studied me intently for a moment, then said, "Good God, it's you—the girl from Long Acre."

"I recognized you, too," I said. "This gives me the opportunity to thank you for what you did."

"I did nothing. Alas, there was nothing I could do for your uncle."

"How did you know he was my uncle?" I asked swiftly, wondering just why this man appeared at unpredictable moments and why he made me feel so uneasy.

"You called him your uncle." His voice was bland, but his eyes were not. They were shrewd, observant, taking in every detail of my appearance. I knew he was mentally comparing my new aura of prosperity with the girl he had first seen with a shawl about her shoulders. He was a man who missed nothing.

I asked suddenly, "How did you know the wheels had gone over him?"

"My dear young lady, I am a doctor. I can tell when a man's ribs have been crushed, and the difference between marks left by the hooves of horses and those made by wheels. Besides, a carriage had charged past me around the corner. It was a very simple deduction," he finished, leaving me feeling completely foolish.

"And yourself?" he asked. "You slept well that night?"

"Too well. I don't know what you prescribed, sir, but I was unconscious for hours."

"A dose of laudanum. Not enough to harm you. You were suffering from severe shock and needed prolonged sleep."

"I suppose I must thank you for that, too." Because I found this man disconcerting I was unwilling to be under an obligation to him for anything.

"You need thank me for nothing," he answered abruptly. "I am a doctor. I was doing my job."

"For which I paid no fee."

"For which I wanted no fee."

"It was strange that you should have been in the vicinity at the time, sir. There is only one doctor in that neighborhood."

"It was not in the least strange. I often cut through Covent Garden from the Strand to my lodgings at the top of St. Martin's Lane."

He had a logical explanation for everything.

The train gave a loud shriek, making me jump. The man promptly leaned forward and pulled up the window. "A tunnel," he explained as he fastened the leather strap. "We must close the window or we will be covered in smoke."

And then he saw the notice, carefully fixed to the pane of glass.

"And now I suppose I must apologize. I had no idea this compartment was reserved."

"Of course you didn't. The window was down."

"Of all the damned silly places to stick a notice! It should have been on a side window, where it could be seen."

The train gave another shriek and dived into the tunnel, drowning conversation and plunging us into darkness. The sudden transition made me tense. I felt as if I were cooped up in a pitch-black cage from which there was no escape, alone with a man who looked strong enough to break me with one arm, and if he moved I wouldn't even hear him.

I told myself not to be ridiculous and that we would be out of the tunnel in a minute, but the minutes stretched on in an eternity of darkness.

The roar of sound was deafening, but beneath it the thudding of my heart beat against my ear drums. I sat rigid, trying to think of anything and everything but the nearness of this man.

Suddenly his foot touched mine.

I jerked away, my heart leaping to my throat, and even as I did so the train rushed from darkness into light and I saw to my consternation that he had merely uncrossed his legs and settled back into his corner. My alarm had been ridiculous and I could only hope it didn't show, for I had the sudden conviction that if he so much as suspected my fears his strong, rather ruthless face would break into a broad grin of amusement.

"As I was saying, ma'am," he continued, as if the conversation had never been interrupted, "I must apologize for the intrusion. It didn't occur to me that a whole compartment would be reserved for one person—except for Royalty, perhaps."

"Doesn't Royalty travel by the Royal train?" I answered lightly.

"Ah yes, to be sure."

I was perfectly composed now, but surely those shrewd gray eyes held amusement?

"I'm afraid you must be burdened with my presence until we reach Tunbridge Wells, ma'am, when I promise to move to another compartment. Until then you are forced to tolerate my company—unless you prefer me to jump out on the line?"

I laughed. "I don't think that will be necessary, sir."

"Nor am *I* prepared to do it, so I'm afraid you must offer me the hospitality of your private compartment until we reach the first stop—after which," he finished with a hint of derision, "I should advise you to keep that window well up, to ward off intruders."

He ended the conversation by taking a heavy volume from his Gladstone bag and settling down to read without sparing me another word or glance.

I found myself smarting under this abrupt rejection, like a hostess being dismissed in her own drawing room, so I picked up the *Lady's Companion* and pretended to be equally absorbed. But concentration proved difficult. I was disturbingly aware of the man, and cast furtive little glances over the pages of the journal. He was lost to the world and to me, so I was able to study him unobserved. His jaw was one of the strongest I had ever seen, and his mouth was equally resolute. I felt he was the sort of man who, having once made up his mind on a point, would never yield. Surrender was a word he had probably never heard of, and from the depth of his concentration I knew that he was capable of shutting out all extraneous thought or disturbance.

I wouldn't like to make an enemy of him, I decided. I wouldn't like to have to beg for mercy from him. I wouldn't like to oppose him, or pit my will against his, for he was a man who would pursue his own ends quite relentlessly, and God help anyone who got in his way.

I decided that he wasn't a likeable character despite his surface courtesy. Had he been born into the harsh world I had known, he would have been a very tough customer indeed. Not necessarily a crooked one, but a merciless one. A fighter. A man who never gave up.

Why I gave so much attention to an analysis of his character I failed to understand, for he was nothing but a stranger who had stumbled into my life and, I hoped, would very soon leave it. His appearances were too unexpected to be mere coincidence. It almost seemed as if he were dogging my steps.

The thought gave me a sickening little jolt and I heard again the heavy tread of a man following me through the darkened streets of Covent Garden.

I was thankful when the train steamed into Tunbridge Wells and the man closed his heavy book with a slam, donned his coat, picked up his hat, pulled on his gloves, flung the volume back into his Gladstone bag, bowed politely, and walked out of my life.

But before he disappeared something caught my attention. He walked down the platform with the collar of his greatcoat turned up, his face concealed—just like that menacing figure in the dark.

CHAPTER SIX

The train stood in Tunbridge Wells station for quite a time, waiting for a connection from Maidstone, and from the windows I tried to catch a glimpse of the beautiful spa which had been so fashionable in Regency days. My mother had once told me of visiting there as a girl, when the present Lord Ashford's mother was attending a grand ball at the Assembly Rooms, where the famous Beau Nash had once been Master of Ceremonies. She had told me of the grandeur, and the fine Regency terraces, and the elegant area called The Pantiles, and the lords and ladies who still went in those days to take the waters.

The rest of the journey was uneventful and I gave myself up to viewing the gentle countryside of Kent as it unfolded in an endless panorama outside my windows. In blossom time the famous orchards would be a sea of color. It was a little sad to think that when spring came I should have left this lovely corner of England, but of course I couldn't stay at Knight's Keep indefinitely and by that time I should have rearranged my life completely—in London, of course, because that was my background. Country life was unfamiliar to me and I had no idea how I should react to it.

But as a change, a holiday, a respite, I welcomed it, and as the train crawled into sleepy Sandling and I stepped down onto the narrow platform I realized that never had I smelled air so sweet. There was a tang about it, too. The distant tang of the sea.

I stood irresolutely, looking around for a porter. The station was so tiny that it boasted only one, and I lifted my hand, in its elegant glove of blue French suède, to summon him. As I did so, a masculine arm reached down and picked up my valise. "Allow me," an already familiar voice said, and I looked up into the eyes of the stranger again. This man certainly seemed to haunt me and I liked him less and less.

The guard was hauling my trunk onto the platform and very soon it was being trundled over the narrow bridge that spanned the railway line, linking the platform with the main entrance of the station. Holding up my velvet skirts I walked behind the porter, the stranger beside me.

"You are being met, I presume?" he said.

I told him that a carriage was being sent for me, at which he gave a curt nod and said no more. He seemed to be uninterested in where I was going, or who I was, for which I was thankful, but as we descended the wooden steps at the end of the footbridge he took hold of my elbow. I wanted to jerk away but refrained, reminding myself that he was only showing normal courtesy to a lady.

Outside the tiny station two carriages stood. One bore a crest on the door, and was an elegant affair in maroon edged with gold. The coachman, in his cockaded hat and smart maroon livery, stood holding the horses' bridles, and it seemed to me that at the sight of that carriage my companion halted briefly, but the next moment he was saying, "The unpretentious carriage with the unpretentious driver belongs to me, ma'am, so I can only presume that the Ashford affair has come to meet you."

I admitted that it had.

"You're not going to Knight's Keep, I hope?"

"I am indeed, sir, and I hardly think—"

"—that it is any business of mine," he finished calmly. "That makes no difference. I urge you not to go there."

"You *what*, sir?"

"I urge you not to go there, ma'am. You would do well to wait for the next train back to London. It is due in only fifteen minutes."

"You are either impertinent, or out of your mind!"

"I have been told that before, but it troubles me not in the least. What does trouble me is the fact that you should—"

He broke off as the door of the carriage opened and a man stepped down. He was a man of some distinction and he stood looking at us for a brief moment, then he removed his hat, smiled, and bowed. His smile was the kindest I had ever seen.

"Miss Bewleigh? I am Lord Ashford. I prefer to introduce myself rather than wait for the good doctor to do so."

The stranger put down my valise, nodded curtly, and was about to walk away when Lord Ashford put out his hand and caught his arm.

"My dear Daniel, permit me to thank you. I see you've been taking care of my guest. I had no idea you knew each other."

The doctor rudely shook away Lord Ashford's hand.

"We didn't," he said curtly, "but we do now. Good day, ma'am." He began to walk away, then turned suddenly. "Bewleigh, did he call you?"

"But, of course," my host said. "She is Miss Jane Bewleigh. The name is probably familiar to you because when we were boys her father tutored us for a while. Remember? You used to come over to the Keep to share those tedious Latin lessons with me. Your pardon, Miss Bewleigh—it is unforgivable of me to keep you standing here. Permit me—"

He handed me into the carriage, tipped the porter while the coachman attended to my luggage, stepped in beside me, and covered my knees with a thick fur rug. A minute later we were driving away from the tiny country station—and from the strange and unpredictable doctor.

"I trust you found the journey not too tedious, Miss Bewleigh?"

"Indeed, no. It was rather exciting. The first long journey I have ever made."

"How refreshing to meet someone so honest!"

"Honest, Lord Ashford? Why shouldn't I be?"

"Not many young women would admit to being inexperienced. I find it charming."

"But what use would it be to pretend? Until your uncle died, I was poor."

"I am sorry to hear that. I'm sure you deserved better from life. Your parents, too."

"They were content. Their lives were full and happy, and so was mine."

"But not so full and happy as it is going to be, I'm sure." His eyes were as kind as his smile. "I remember your parents well, despite the fact that I was only fifteen at the time. Or perhaps that's why I do remember them. I was at an impressionable age." His smile broadened. "Moreover, I hated Latin and when Bewleigh departed I was delighted to be released from it. It all happened towards the end of the summer holidays, so until my school reopened it wasn't worth employing another tutor to replace the runaway one. It was all very exciting. Romantic, too."

"Do you remember my mother?"

"Of course. She was my first love."

He laughed at my astonishment. It was a good-natured laugh which I was to become very familiar with, and which was to delight me as it did then.

"A man never forgets his first love, Miss Bewleigh, and at fifteen the experience is acute. Oh, she was never aware of me! I was a schoolboy, no more, but to me she was a goddess. She looked like a dream, she walked like a dream. She was also as remote as a dream, because she rarely talked to me."

"It was hardly—"

He held up an immaculately gloved hand.

"Please, do not say it was hardly her place. I shall never remember your mother as a servant, because to me she was never that. She was a young woman of charm and grace, gentle and well-mannered. Too well-mannered—I longed for her to talk to me, but she rarely did. She was conscious of being my mother's personal maid, I suppose. When she fell in love with Bewleigh, I was both heart-broken and elated— heart-broken because I knew I could never win her (oh yes, at fifteen a boy weaves all sorts of dreams about a goddess!), and elated because she proved to be both courageous and passionate. It was wonderfully romantic, too—even the scandal. A runaway romance! What could be more thrilling than that? You see what a sentimentalist I am."

"You were also a realist," I reminded him, "glad to escape from your Latin lessons."

"Oh yes, that entered into it. I though my heart was broken because the object of my adoration had gone beyond my reach forever, and yet, as you say, I was realistic enough to enjoy my release from tedium. And the excitement! The fun of it all! The glorious, poetic justice—"

"What poetic justice?" I asked, a little puzzled.

"To that detestable man the Bishop, his father. Such a snob the man was, and damned patronizing to a schoolboy of fifteen. He actually had the audacity to pat me on the head, as if I were a child. That was after it all happened, when he came rushing to Knight's Keep to chastise his son, and found it was too late. I listened outside my father's study, quite without shame, relishing every moment of the Bishop's discomfiture. 'I shall never be able to hold my head up again!' he wailed. I remember thinking, 'Serves you right, you old—' I won't repeat the word, Miss Bewleigh. A schoolboy's vocabulary can be disgusting."

"I'm sure I would have echoed it, Lord Ashford."

He laughed, and continued reminiscently, "It was a rare time, and it *did* serve the old Bishop right. He was a mean devil. Sent his son to Cambridge but kept him so tight for money that he had to work in the vacation to earn some cash."

"My father often blessed him for that—otherwise he would never have met my mother."

"Or stolen my love. Or broken my heart."

"I'm sure it was very resilient," I answered solemnly.

He laughed. "Hearts are, at fifteen." The gay note suddenly disappeared. "It is only later that they can be broken."

We were descending a hill, and in the distance lay the sea. I could see a small town nestling beside the water, and a wide sweep of bay. He followed my glance.

"That is Hythe—one of the Cinque Ports. We turn at the bottom of this hill. The village down there to the right is Saltwood, and if you look over here, a little closer—" He put out his arm and drew me nearer, so that I leaned across in front of him and looked down into a valley. "Do you see it?" he said. "That is Saltwood Castle."

His face was very close to mine, his voice almost against my ear. I experienced a sudden, sharp awareness of him, so intense that I jerked away. For a moment he was still, not looking at me, giving no indication that he was aware of my sudden withdrawal or wondered as to the cause of it. But my heart was thumping in a ridiculous fashion.

He continued easily, "It is a very famous castle. Quite small, but it played a big part in history. Do you know why?"

I shook my head.

"It was there that Thomas à Becket's murder was plotted. Your scholarly father must have taught you history, so I am sure the murder of Archbishop Becket must be familiar to you.

"Of course. It took place in Canterbury Cathedral on December 29th, 1170—the very day after four impetuous knights hurried home across the Channel from France, because Henry the Second's fiery Plantagenet temper had blazed in the council-room, 'Not one who will deliver me from this low-born priest!'"

"Well done! What an accurate memory you have. Your father must have been proud of his pupil."

"You are laughing at me," I said, blushing a little for I had indeed been carried away. "History was a favorite subject of mine," I explained.

"Then you have come to the right part of England." He halted the coachman. We were halfway down the hill and to the right the lovely castle could be seen across the meadows. So this was where William de Tracy, Reginald Fitzurse, Richard le Breton and Hugh de Morville had taken shelter for the night and plotted their world-shaking crime, and next morning had gone riding down the long Roman road to Canterbury.

"It doesn't seem possible that men's thoughts could have been bent on murder in such a gentle spot," I said.

"Murder is no respecter of surroundings. If it were, the precincts of the country's greatest cathedral wouldn't have been chosen for it." He signaled to the coachman, and we moved on. "I must take you to see the martyrdom. You'll find it interesting."

"Interesting, yes—but terrible."

"You are sensitive," he said quietly, "so on second thoughts I won't take you to see the martyrdom."

"But I want to. I've always wanted to see Canterbury and its great cathedral."

"Then you shall," he said, smiling again. "You shall see whatever you want to see—and Kent has plenty to offer in the way of history. Plenty of castles, too—some small, like Saltwood and Lympne and Chilham, and larger ones standing high above the sea, like Walmer and Dover."

"Knight's Keep has its history too, I understand."

He shrugged. "Nothing exceptional. No priests' holes or secret passages; no crimes to darken its past. In fact, the Ashford family has always been singularly respectable—and dull." His charming smile flashed again, and I thought how fortunate Lady Ashford was to have such a husband.

We climbed another hill, the sea behind us, then turned down a lane between wild fields. I saw a milestone announcing that Lympne was three miles distant, and my excitement quickened. Soon we would be at Knight's Keep.

I was aware that Lord Ashford was studying me with interest, and when I turned and looked at him he said, "Forgive me—I was trying to recall your mother's pretty face. Time had obscured it in my mind, but now I see you, it seems to me that you resemble her."

"So my father always said. Uncle Silas, too. *Your* Uncle Silas," I corrected hurriedly, "although he always liked me to call him that."

"I'm glad you did. Poor Silas never had a family of his own; never anyone to love." He put out his hand and touched mine. "I want you to know how grateful I am to you for all you did for him."

I wanted to ask why he himself had done nothing, but refrained.

"I know what you're thinking, Miss Bewleigh. You are wondering why I didn't look after my uncle. The truth is that he quarreled with my father and the breach was never healed. These rifts happen between families, I'm afraid, and it doesn't occur to a young man to go in search of relatives with whom his parents have split. If that seems selfish, I'm afraid it's true. I was so busy living my own life that I never gave my long-lost relative a thought."

"Please—you don't have to explain. Not to me."

"I don't have to, but I want to. When your solicitor told me of your generous impulse to share the legacy, he stated that you felt it your duty to do so. I want you to know that because of the rift between my parents' families I felt no such duty was involved. So in case you still feel any embarrassment over accepting Silas's fortune, you can dismiss it once and for all. I am glad for you, believe me. It was right that you should be rewarded."

"You're very kind."

"Nonsense. I inherited from my father all that was rightfully mine. I need no more. He was a rich man, and even his lust for travel didn't deplete his wealth. He had great wanderlust, had my father."

"And you, sir?"

"Indeed no. I'm a home-loving fellow. Knight's Keep means more to me than any place on earth. I could not contemplate living anywhere else, and rarely leave it—not even for trips to London. I hope you won't find our life dull down here."

Our life, he had said, reminding me that he shared it with a wife, a fact I had been in danger of forgetting. I felt a little guilty, for the invitation had been a joint one and I should have remembered that.

I don't know why I felt a vague disappointment, unless it was because the first attractive man I had ever met, the kind of man I had secretly dreamed about as young and silly girls do dream, was married and therefore beyond my reach.

We were entering a village and soon the carriage turned down a side road. I caught a glimpse of another castle—the Castle of Lympne, Lord Ashford told me—and then we turned again and went bowling along a lane that wound endlessly between thick hedges and overhanging trees. The village was left behind, and I recalled that my mother had once told me how secluded Knight's Keep was, standing well back from the cliffs, surrounded by endless parkland, with the Romney Marshes spreading out far below.

I had forgotten these details, but now little snippets of information, gleaned through the years, flashed through my mind and just as I was remembering how she had once described the impressive entrance to Knight's Keep, there it was, with twin towers of stone standing like sentinels on either side of gigantic wrought iron gates. The gates bore a crest, picked out in gold.

They were opened wide, and beside them the lodge-keeper stood to attention, touching his hat respectfully as his lord and master drove through. It was all so impressive and so foreign to me that I had no time to feel triumphant; merely interested and curious and inwardly excited.

Lord Ashford said, "Welcome to Knight's Keep, Miss Bewleigh. I hope your visit will be a happy one. You know that we shall be delighted if you stay for a long time."

The drive must have been at least a mile long, winding between gigantic oak trees with trunks so vast that I knew they must have been standing there for hundreds of years. Lord Ashford saw my glance, and smiled.

"The good old British oak," he said. "It built many ships for Elizabeth of England. Did you know that when she called upon the Cinque Ports to equip her Armada the little town of Hythe built no less than eleven fine vessels? It was a flourishing little place in those days, and prior to that a haven for smugglers. We must take you to see the ancient church— I was married there," he finished negligently.

"But I thought Knight's Keep had its own chapel?"

"So it has, but my wife came from Hythe so we were married in her parish church. My parents would have liked the ceremony to take place in the family chapel, but what difference does it make? A marriage is a marriage wherever it is performed."

I was interested to hear that he had married a local girl, and wondered what she was like.

I hadn't long to wait before finding out, and when I did I got the surprise of my life.

CHAPTER SEVEN

Lady Ashford met us on the steps of the great house, and I don't know which made me catch my breath more—the beauty of the place, or the beauty of the woman.

She was very little younger than her husband, and since he had been fifteen at the time of my parents' runaway marriage, and I was born twelve months later, that made him thirty-six now. Lady Ashford could have been anything between thirty and thirty-four, but at any age she would be beautiful, for her looks were based upon wonderful bone structure, the cheek-bones high and well-defined, the brows arched, the mouth sensuous and full, the chin delicate and firm. But the most striking thing about her was her coloring. Her hair was dark as pitch, and her complexion had a hint of duskiness about it—tanned by the sea air, no doubt. Suddenly my blonde hair and pale complexion made me feel colorless and uninteresting.

I had come to Knight's Keep confident that my appearance couldn't be faulted. I had felt equal to meeting anyone, even the greatest ladies in the land. My clothes would pass muster in the salons of London or the drawing rooms of the stately homes of England. I'd been groomed until I had shed all sense of inferiority—and then in one instant my confidence was swept aside by a woman who walked down the wide steps of the Elizabethan mansion as if she were descending the staircase of some magnificent French château.

She walked superbly, and I realized why. She had a beautiful body, and used it well, the hips swinging suggestively and her long, rounded thighs subtly displayed beneath the tight skirt which, in the latest fashion, hung close and straight in front and swept into a train over a bustle frame at the back.

The dress lacked adornment, and so did she. A magnificent picture needed no ornate frame, and Lady Ashford knew it. Did she also know that she was lovely, and that men must find her desirable?

These thoughts whirled through my mind like leaves blown on a wind, troubling me. I had expected a gracious country hostess—not a woman so sultry and beautiful that a hot-house seemed a more fitting background. She reminded me of orchids, and heady perfumes, and sensual luxury, and with a great effort of will I jerked my mind away from the thought that her husband must find her very passionate in bed.

She held out a long, slim hand. Like her complexion, it was slightly dusky, and this surprised me. Evidently she went to no trouble to keep them lily-white, like the ladies I had read about in the feminine journals that old Tom Kelly had sold and allowed me to peep at from time to time. They had been full of hints about caring for the complexion, and whitening the hands, and protecting one's face from the sun or the heat of the fire; hints for all those pampered society women who had nothing to do all day but cream their faces and frizz their hair and prepare for the evening's balls and soirées. So I had expected someone of their kind—not an exotic creature like this.

"Welcome to Knight's Keep," she said in a voice that was as surprising as her looks—deep, husky, rather musical. She smiled as she spoke, revealing strong and even teeth. They were white against her amber complexion and I thought how wrong those elegant ladies' journals were. Lily-white skins were colorless and insignificant compared with this woman's.

I put my hand in hers with a strange reluctance, and curtsied: not too much, just the merest bend of the knee that I had seen smart ladies-about-town give to each other, and particularly to older women. And there was a regal touch about this woman that demanded it.

I was surprised by the strength of her hand. The skin was smooth and the flesh was soft, but the bones beneath were flexible. They closed about my own with a grasp as firm as a man's.

At my side, Lord Ashford said, "Miranda, my dear, this is Miss Bewleigh but I'm sure you and I will want to call her Jane."

Lady Ashford's smile became immediately more friendly, but I had the strange feeling that it lacked a certain spontaneity and only because her husband's voice commanded it did she extend to me anything more than polite courtesy. The feeling was illogical, for the next moment her arm was through mine and she was leading me up the steps and into the house, and I knew that there was absolutely no reason for me to feel that she was playing the courteous hostess and not really wanting to. If she felt that way, why invite me? I was no blood relation: there was no obligation on either her part or on her husband's to offer me hospitality.

I dismissed my foolish imaginings and responded to her welcome. I sensed that she was basically a reserved woman, which explained her inability to expand to a stranger so easily as her husband did. This made me appreciate even more the way in which she smiled and said with a touch of shyness, "I would like to call you Jane. May I?"

Nothing could have put me more at ease, and I answered warmly, "Please do!" Her touch of shyness added to her charm, and I liked her the more because of it.

As we mounted the side steps, I looked up at the great stone walls of the house admiringly. Knight's Keep had not been built in the timbered style of architecture which in the Elizabethan age had been confined to manor houses and yeomen's dwellings, but in the stately Italianate fashion copied by such men as Burghley and Hatton and other great families of the land. The result was a combination of elegance overlaid by English tradition.

In tracery and carving the Italian influence could be seen; the English tradition in battlemented coping, which had been retained simply for effect. The Elizabethan age had also dispensed with the moat and drawbridge of former centuries and replaced them with formal gardens and magnificent terraces, both of which Lord Ashford's beautiful house featured proudly. The windows were tall, with symmetrical use of bays and oriels, and some were even carried up the full height of the façade. The result was impressive, with mullioned panes adding mellowness and warmth.

I was a little awed by the immensity of the place, and as we walked through the arched double doors into the great chamber I could not repress a gasp of admiration, despite the sombre shadows cast by linenfold paneling and the great gallery which ran the length of three walls. The room must have been about two hundred feet in length, and the sweeping staircase of solid oak which mounted to the gallery above, was magnificent.

I saw Lord Ashford looking at me with a little smile of pleasure. He was pleased because I so openly admired his great house, but I colored a little under his scrutiny.

"It is useless for me to pretend," I said. "I've never been in a place so grand as this."

"Then I hope you will learn to love it as we do," Lady Ashford said warmly.

In my room, I unpinned my sable toque, and removed my coat. As I did so, there came an abrupt tap at my door. A maid entered carrying a huge copper jug of hot water. As she crossed the room the long white ribbons of her cap fluttered behind her. She didn't so much as glance at me, and there was a touch of insolence in her walk. She was followed by two menservants bearing my trunk.

The maid set the jug down, lit the lamps, and said with an attempt at respect, "May I unpack for you now, miss?"

I handed her the keys of my trunk, and as she lifted out my beautiful new clothes (did they look a little too new, I wondered suddenly) I sat on a window seat and gazed out upon the formal gardens to the distant park. Dusk was closing in, and gardeners were leaving their work. They wore leather jerkins and gaiters and even in the semi-darkness looked burly and ruddy-faced.

I had the sudden feeling that I was surveying a small kingdom, of which Lord Ashford was the beneficient overlord.

This was true, in a way. These gardeners, like the old family retainer who had stood by the front steps and hurried forward to open the carriage door for us, and the footmen who carried my trunk in between them, and the maids who went respectfully about their household tasks, and the unseen kitchen staff below-stairs, were all dependent upon Lord Ashford for their food and their livelihood and the roof over their heads, just as, once upon a time, my own family had been.

I opened the window and leaned out, wondering if I could see the stables over which my mother had been born, but all I saw was a wide sweep of terrace and a lawn sloping down to an ornamental lake. It was getting too dark to see more—tomorrow I would be able to.

I was about to close the window when something made me pause abruptly. Down below, within the shadow of an overhanging cedar tree, lurked the figure of a man. He was standing quite still and although I could not see his face I knew he was gazing towards the house—a silent, watchful figure. I shivered a little and closed the casement abruptly.

I was glad to turn my attention to my room. It had a fine tester bed hung with brocade, and a rich carpet, and elegantly upholstered chairs. It was the grandest room I had ever seen, and as I watched the maid hanging my clothes in a vast closet I thought: "She is doing what my mother must have done—perhaps in this very room," and I had an almost overpowering impulse to take the clothes from her and do the job myself, not because I was conscious that my ancestors had once been servants here, but because it suddenly seemed wrong to me that a mere accident of birth should demean someone. I was young and able bodied; I could unpack a trunk and hang up clothes for myself, and I felt almost ashamed to be sitting there, idly watching another girl do it for me. Not that she seemed to do it with any great willingness.

She was placing a dress of ocher-colored shantung on a padded hanger, and I said suddenly, "I will wear that tonight." She laid it upon the bed, finished the unpacking, and said sullenly, "Her ladyship gave orders that I am to serve you personally, miss. Do you wish to change now, or shall I come back later?"

"What is your name?" I asked.

She told me that it was Sarah.

"Thank you, Sarah, but I shan't need you any more. I can dress myself."

"But her ladyship said—"

"I'll ring, should I want you."

I had no desire to slight the girl, but there was something about her that made me feel uncomfortable. I felt she resented having to serve me. I disliked her manner very much, and was glad when she departed. She wasn't a warm, friendly creature like Dora Smee. Her face had a closed look about it, like a door shut upon secrets. There was also a suggestion of shrewdness. I felt she had assessed the quality of my clothes, and that beneath her forced politeness there was a probing glance. I decided to make use of her as little as possible during my stay.

Before leaving the room Sarah drew the heavy brocade curtains and the action shut out the picture of the lurking figure below. I told myself that it was probably no more than a gardener pausing after his labors, and so dismissed the incident.

In the soft glow the room looked cozy as well as luxurious, and I enjoyed undressing in a leisurely way, pouring the steaming water from the copper jug into a flowered bowl on the marble-topped wash-stand, and removing all traces of my journey, after which, since the dinner gong wouldn't sound for nearly an hour, I decided to rest.

Wrapping a quilted dressing gown about me, I lay down on the bed and gazed up at the brocaded tester. I had never before slept in a four-poster, and lying there gave me a strange sensation—almost of imprisonment. To sleep with the bed curtains drawn would be like sleeping in a cell, I thought.

Hard on that thought came another. Did Lord Ashford and his wife lie in a bed like this, enclosed in a passionate world of their own?

I had no right to wonder about such things, and was startled because I did so. Was it the yielding softness of the bed that conjured up sensuality in my mind, or was it Justin Ashford himself, with his handsome, friendly face, and the cultured voice and the arm that had drawn me close to him in the carriage so that he had spoken almost against my ear and set my heart thudding?

I flung off the quilted dressing gown and concentrated on my toilet. No sane young woman would allow herself to be attracted by a married man—and no sane young woman from a poor London district, even if she *had* come into money, should be foolish enough to delude herself that a man of title and estate would regard her as anything but an ordinary little creature whom he had befriended. Especially when he had a wife like Miranda Ashford.

Miranda. The name itself was unusual, and so was she. Her strange and lovely face floated before my eye. She was the most beautiful woman I had ever met—and, without reason, the most frightening.

CHAPTER EIGHT

I decided to wear my hair in a chignon tonight, but as I coiled it my hands were suddenly shaking. I could scarcely control them as I stepped into the ocher shantung which I had chosen because it was the simplest gown in my wardrobe and I didn't want to appear overdressed on my first evening at Knight's Keep.

The result was good. Even I could see that. I stood before a long cheval mirror and surveyed myself critically. The dull yellow seemed to deepen the gold of my hair; my skin looked clear and flawless against it and my eyes, deep-set and gray like my mother's, were certainly noticeable. I had made myself look as good as possible, and if the result, when I came face to face with Lady Ashford, was like the comparison between a field flower and a tiger-lily, it couldn't be helped. She was exotic. I was not.

When I stepped into the long corridor outside my room I was startled to find how dark it was. Candles flickered in alcoves, casting eerie shadows. There was no gas at Knight's Keep, and I had to admit that in such an ancient setting hissing jets would have been incongruous and unromantic, but the leaping shadows that advanced and retreated before me were vaguely frightening.

I shivered in my thin shantung, and was about to return to my room to fetch a shawl when a door opened further along the corridor and Lord Ashford appeared. He looked striking in a perfectly tailored dinner suit with the unmistakable stamp of Savile Row about it. I was aware once again of the quickening of my pulses. This man was too disturbing for my peace of mind. It would be wise to cut short my visit.

For a moment we stood looking at each other, and I knew that he was as aware of me as I was of him. I felt helpless, trapped, quite incapable of withstanding him. He was everything I had dreamed of in a man, fine and gentle and courteous and yet at the same time very masculine, and the sheer futility of my feeling for him emphasized the need for an early departure. The man had a wife. A very beautiful wife. There was no place for me here. I had to go.

He picked up a silver candlestick and came towards me. The easy, friendly smile was absent, but his compelling gaze mesmerized me. I was unable to do anything but stand there, waiting for him, and when he reached my side he didn't say a word: he merely extended his arm for me to place my hand within it, then led me downstairs.

After a few paces he said, "You look very lovely, Miss Bewleigh. No—I refuse to call you that, Jane, Little Jane. You scarcely come to my shoulder. Do you realize that?"

I realized it only too well. I realized how strong his arm was, and the height of him, and the power of him, and his nearness.

I nodded in reply, like a shy and embarrassed schoolgirl, and he smiled down at me, saying no more. And so we descended the stairs together, and beneath us the vast dining hall spread like a darkened ocean, lit fitfully by dim lamps which only seemed to emphasize the shadows. But a fire burned in an enormous dog grate, sending out much needed heat. Lord Ashford's arm pressed my hand imperceptibly nearer his side.

"You will be warmer now. Those corridors upstairs are drafty, but I trust your room is warm?"

I assured him that it was.

"If there is anything you need, you must ask for it. I want you to lack nothing. Lady Ashford has appointed a maid to look after you?"

"She has, and it was kind of her, but I'm not accustomed to being waited on. I hope your wife won't be offended if I tell her so. I would much rather—"

I broke off, for he was looking at me in surprise. "My wife?" he echoed. "Surely you don't imagine that Miranda is my wife?"

It was my turn to be surprised. "But she is Lady Ashford."

He threw back his handsome head and laughed. "Of course she is. She became so when she married my father. Miranda is my stepmother." When I could only stare in astonishment he laughed again. "Ridiculous, isn't it, having a stepmother younger than oneself, but there it is. My father met her in Africa and married her within a couple of months. Between you and me," he finished confidentially, his eyes alight with amusement, "my father was a bit of a roué in his old age. He had a weakness for young and beautiful women, and when he became a widower and was free to roam, he did so in more ways than one. You're not shocked, are you? He may have amused himself with other young women, but he did marry Miranda."

Shocked! I was relieved. Wildly and ecstatically relieved. But only briefly. If Miranda wasn't his wife, then I had yet to meet the woman who was.

He drew me nearer to the blazing fire. For a moment he seemed to study me in the glow of light, then continued, "My father was in failing health long before he took that final trip, but he would never admit it. He was the sort of person who liked to extract every ounce from life—not a lazy, country-loving man like me."

"You don't strike me as being lazy."

"Then how do I strike you?"

"As—as—" I hesitated, lost for words. It was difficult to sum up the impression he made upon me. "As a man," I finished lamely.

"Good," he said, and I found myself looking away in some confusion. Because of this I spoke at random.

"Tell me more about your father."

"There is little to tell. The doctors warned him that a journey to such a climate might kill him, but he only scoffed and went his way, as always. As it turned out, I was glad he did. My mother, poor soul, was never the right woman for him. She was neither gay nor vital enough for a man who never really lost his youth. He found the right woman late in life, but he did find her, and I shall always be grateful to Miranda for making those final months happy for him." He finished unexpectedly, "That is really why I invited you to Knight's Keep."

"I don't understand—"

"She is lonely, and shy—a stranger in a strange land. I suspect she feels alien here, and the local inhabitants have done little to make her feel otherwise. Country people are rather insular. They don't go out of their way to welcome strangers. Had Miranda been a local woman, it might have been different."

"Instead, she is beautiful and exotic, like some tropical flower."

"Beautiful?" he echoed. "Do you think so? I've always considered her striking, but personally I prefer a more English type of beauty. Miranda's father was Dutch—or a Boer, as they are called in Africa. Her mother was Spanish. She hasn't a drop of English blood in her veins, so you can imagine how alien she feels here."

"Then why does she stay? Has she never wanted to return home?"

"I've often wondered, but she is reserved—even with me. We are good friends, but I think she has only ever opened her heart to one man—my father. Marriages between people of widely divergent ages are never expected to be successful, but theirs was. She brought him back to England so that his final months could be spent in his home. She nursed him devotedly, and after he died she stayed at Knight's Keep because it was the place where he belonged and so, she felt, did she."

"She must have loved him very much."

"She did indeed. She is a selfless creature, and wasn't the least resentful because he had failed to change his will. There had been no time for that—and it didn't matter, she said. So you can understand why I consider her my responsibility. I want her loneliness to end. She needs a friend. When your solicitor's letter arrived and I learned that you too were alone in the world, you seemed heaven-sent." He looked at me, and added, "Something is puzzling you. What is it?"

"Your wife. Isn't she Miranda's friend?"

He answered quietly, "If I had a wife, it wouldn't have been necessary for me to invite someone to keep Miranda company."

"But you married. You told me so."

"And two years later my marriage was over. I'm surprised Daniel Firth didn't tell you."

"Daniel Firth?" I echoed.

"The man who was carrying your valise when I met you."

"But why should he tell me anything?"

"Because he usually wastes no time in letting everyone know how it happened—or how he believes it happened."

"And—how did it?"

There was a sound from the stairs. I looked up and saw

Miranda there, her foot poised mid-way between one step and the next, as if halted by the question.

She said, "Tell her, Justin. She is bound to hear sooner or later. It is better that she should hear now—and from you."

His face was dark with pain, and I wanted to cry out, "Don't tell me—don't talk about it if it hurts you!"—but instead I waited, because it was suddenly important that I should know.

He hesitated, then said tautly, "I killed my wife. That is how our marriage ended. I killed her."

CHAPTER NINE

Lady Ashford came downstairs swiftly and furiously, her taffeta skirts rustling. "Don't talk like that!" she commanded. "You know it isn't true."

"Our good doctor doesn't think so."

"The man was proved wrong! How can he continue with his monstrous ideas?"

Lord Ashford shrugged, then looked down at me and said, "Have I upset you, Jane? Frightened you, perhaps?"

I shook my head. Frightened wasn't the right word. Shocked, yes, but frightened, no, because I didn't believe what he said.

"I wish you would tell me more," I admitted. "You are both talking in riddles."

"It's perfectly simple. My wife caught a fever, and died, and it was my fault."

"But that wasn't murder!"

"It was my fault because I ignored the symptoms."

His stepmother said, "And no wonder you did! Dulcie was always unwell—or pretending to be. The doctors told you that it was mostly her imagination, but you wouldn't believe them."

"I did that night. I made up my mind to. I ignored her pleadings. I made her get dressed and go to the ball at Lympne Castle, wearing a flimsy gown on a bitter night, and all because we were expected to put in an appearance."

"My dear Justin, how were you to know that she'd catch a chill? And there were no signs beforehand, no trace of a fever. I can vouch for that, because when she began whining about feeling unwell, I took her pulse and checked her symptoms. You seem to forget that I have a knowledge of nursing."

"I know, I know—but if I had listened to her, it would never had happened."

Lady Ashford said with elaborate patience, "If Dulcie couldn't get her own way, she would run a fever, or develop a sick headache, or throw a fit of hysteria—as she did that night. *Anything* to gain her ends, or to win attention. You spoiled her to death, Justin. If a woman can be killed by too much indulgence, then guilty you were! But you were right to be firm with her for once. She didn't want to go to that stuffy ball—that was what she called it, remember?—simply because she wasn't in the mood. She didn't want to do all those duty dances—she said that, to. So she adopted her usual tactics and made a scene. You should have spanked her like a child—that was what she needed. Instead, as always, you began by soothing and petting her—"

"How do you expect a man to treat his wife?"

"Not like a spoiled, fragile little flower, or she quickly comes to believe that is what she is."

"I shall never forgive myself for making her go, or for suddenly losing patience with her."

"I'm not surprised you did, behaving as she was—screaming hysterically!"

I wanted to ask what caused the hysteria—surely mere petulance couldn't go that far?—then felt I had no right to probe.

Justin's stepmother changed the subject.

"Come," she said, "it is cozier in the small dining room than in this mausoleum."

As she turned, the glow of the candlelight touched her amber shoulders; the effect was beautiful against the vivid peacock blue of her gown. My own simple dress looked very ordinary by comparison, and I found myself wishing that I had worn something more elaborate after all.

Lady Ashford's dress was magnificent, and around her throat was a necklace of rubies, glowing richly. They seemed like a darker reflection of her lips, which were naturally warm in color. Justin had called her striking; to me she was very beautiful, but I was glad that he had disagreed with me on that point—glad, too, that upstairs in that long, dark corridor he had held the candles aloft and told me that I was lovely.

There was no gainsaying that this man had made a great impression on me. I had been aware of him from the moment he stepped down from the Ashford carriage outside the station, and within a few hours this awareness had increased, until now I was caught like a bird in passage—a bird he had suddenly captured and held. A short while ago I had been bent on escape, but now my tension had relaxed and my resistance with it. There was no reason to run from this place or from this man. My heart was free—and so, miraculously, was he.

As he opened a door across the hall and held it for us to pass through, Lady Ashford cast a comprehensive glance over her shoulder, taking in the paneled walls and the gallery above, and the Ashford coat of arms emblazoned above the staircase.

"Awe-inspiring, isn't it, Jane, but I'm sure you prefer something less pretentious, as I do. Like this."

She preceded me into the room, which was small and charming. It had an intimate, personal feeling about it: a room in which people could relax and enjoy themselves. Suddenly I felt more at ease than I had felt since my arrival.

A candle-lit table was set for dinner and the dancing light, coupled with the glow from the fire, was reflected back from brocade-covered walls that shimmered with a touch of gold. There was no dark paneling here; no gloom, no shadow.

Justin's stepmother smiled and said, "The perfect background for you, Jane. You couldn't have chosen a better gown tonight."

The compliment was sincere, and perhaps not unjustified, for the soft yellow of my dress harmonized perfectly with my surroundings. Above the fireplace a gilt mirror threw back my reflection—pale skin, shining hair, and shoulders that looked creamy compared with Lady Ashford's olive skin. No two women had ever looked more different, nor, perhaps, been more aware of it. I sensed that she was as conscious of it as I, and that she was not displeased, for my blonde looks acted as a foil for her dark beauty.

I found myself wondering if it would be possible to make a friend of her, as her stepson wanted me to. I felt it wouldn't be easy, for there was a wall of reserve about Lady Ashford and her loneliness might not be entirely the fault of the local inhabitants. Friendship had to be given, as well as received, and overtures shouldn't be one-sided.

I was glad that in between courses the servants withdrew, for I was unaccustomed to being waited on at meals, or to having flunkeys standing in the background. They made me self-conscious. Meals had been simple at home, but occasionally, at Christmas or on birthdays—and particularly after Uncle Silas joined us, for he loved a party—we would set the table as grandly as possible and pretend we were dining at the Café Royal. Thus I had learned how to cope with an elaborate row of cutlery, most of which I considered superfluous. It had been a game then, but now I had walked into a way of life where it was the normal thing, and if I stayed here I would have to get used to it.

Would I stay? The question troubled me. I wasn't wholly averse to the idea now, but wondered whether Lady Ashford would want me, or even if she knew what lay behind her stepson's invitation. The fact that a welcome had been extended from both of them meant nothing: that could be a mere formality, an expression of Lord Ashford's wishes, not hers. I hadn't forgotten the feeling I had had when she greeted me on arrival—that only because he commanded it did she make an effort to welcome me.

But "command," I realized now, was the wrong word. Then, I had been assuming he was her husband, but now I learned otherwise I knew she wasn't his to command. All the same, she had obviously been aware of his wishes, so presumably she also knew why he had invited me. I wondered if the knowledge antagonized or pleased her. With this woman there was no way of telling.

Despite the fact that the meal was companionable and conversation easy, I couldn't forget Lord Ashford's self-accusations. If a man blamed himself for his wife's death, he would live in torment for the rest of his life, and it was apparent, from the things Lady Ashford had said, that he could no more be held responsible for the tragedy than a man could be for accidentally startling a horse and throwing its rider.

I looked up, and saw him watching me. I noticed how deeply set his eyes were, and that they were hazel in color, flecked with green. It was a fascinating combination. I also noticed that although he gave an impression of being handsome, in actual fact he was not, for his features were irregular. Beneath his well-tailored dinner jacket his shoulders were broad and muscular. This surprised me, for my first impression had been one of elegance rather than of strength. The combination of indolence and vitality about him was fascinating, and I felt a swift pang of envy for the young wife who had been petted and spoiled by such a man. He must have loved her deeply, which made the very idea that he could have been responsible for her death quite ludicrous.

"You are troubled, Jane—I can tell. Your face is expressive, as I'm sure you've been told many times. I don't like to see a guest in my house looking worried. Come, tell me—"

I stammered, "It is nothing—nothing at all," and felt myself coloring hotly.

"Then *I* will tell *you*. You are wondering, if I was innocent of my wife's death, why Doctor Firth should believe otherwise."

Lady Ashford protested, "Really, Justin, you're not going to open that stupid subject again!"

"Jane must be told, otherwise, as you yourself said earlier, she will hear sooner or later—and not from us. The fact is, little Jane, that despite the medical testimony of the best doctors in Canterbury, Daniel Firth insisted that Dulcie had been poisoned."

CHAPTER TEN

"Poisoned!" I gasped.

"Did you ever hear of anything so ridiculous?" Miranda asked.

"But why? How could he make such accusations? On what grounds?"

"Absolutely none," Lord Ashford admitted, "except that chronic food poisoning sometimes produces similar symptoms —vomiting, high temperature, fever, even near-delirium. My wife had all those."

"And he believed that *you* poisoned her food?"

"Not necessarily her food, but certainly that I had poisoned her in some way or other."

"Then it was a good thing you called specialists from Canterbury to prove him wrong," I declared.

"It was after they had been that he made his outrageous suggestions. He was never in attendance on my wife. He never examined her."

"Then what right had he to pass an opinion?" I exploded.

"He claimed the right of a brother." Seeing my surprise,

Lord Ashford nodded. "Yes—Daniel Firth was my brother-in-law. Still is, I suppose, technically speaking."

Lady Ashford put in angrily, "The whole thing was a personal vendetta against you, my dear Justin. Matthew told me that Daniel was jealous of you even as a boy."

"He had no reason to be."

"Except that you were better off in every way than he—titled, handsome, and more popular. You lacked for nothing. Compared with yours, his people had little."

"On the contrary, they were comfortably off."

"Relatively speaking, but Dulcie did very well for herself when she married into the Ashford family."

"Her people provided for her," Justin defended.

"Only reasonably," Miranda conceded, "and of course she had the small inheritance from an uncle. Daniel coveted that too, as well as fearing that he was going to be patronized from then on by the pair of you. That was why he opposed his sister's marriage to you, and because he failed to stop it he wanted to hurt you."

"In that, he succeeded."

"But only for a while! You vindicated yourself. You turned the tables. It was he who was humiliated in the end."

Justin said sincerely, "I had no desire to turn the tables or to humiliate him. All I wanted was to prove my innocence which, as you say, I did. I bear him no malice and wish he could do likewise."

"Surely no man would accuse another of murder solely because he was jealous and wanted to hurt him?" I said aghast. "He must have had to produce a motive for such a crime."

Justin said painfully, "He hinted that I wanted poor Dulcie's money, little as it was. He seemed to overlook the fact that it could have become mine on our marriage, had I wanted to take it. I neither needed to, nor wanted to."

"He also overlooked the fact that she was extravagant and foolish. She squandered her modest fortune on clothes and fripperies. You should have told him that—*and* other things," Miranda put in.

"And destroy his illusions about his sister? I could never do that."

"You are too charitable by half, my dear."

"Why shouldn't I be? Nursing resentment only leads to bitterness, and I always remember that I liked Daniel as a boy. So did Uncle Silas. In fact, he rather favored him."

I said, "Uncle Silas had a kind heart and was naïve enough to like everyone."

"But it is true that as a boy Daniel was thoroughly nice," Justin defended.

I found it hard to imagine, and said, "Well, I hope he withdrew his abominable accusations when the specialists proved him wrong!"

"It wasn't the specialists who did that. They expressed their opinions as strongly as I but it made no difference to Daniel. Not even the signed death certificate convinced him. In the end, *I* had to do that. I asked for a post-mortem, and I shall always be glad I did. There was absolutely no trace of poison, for my wife died a natural death."

"And a fine fool that made Daniel Firth look!" Lady Ashford exclaimed.

"What are you thinking, Jane? That I should merely have ignored his accusations?"

"Good gracious, no! That you were wise. You have absolutely nothing to reproach yourself with."

"Except my selfishness and stupidity that night."

Lady Ashford pushed her chair back a little impatiently. "We have talked of this enough. Come, Jane—we'll leave Justin to his port."

He rose. "I want none tonight. I will join you both now."

We withdrew to an elaborate little salon, over-decorated and ornate. I wondered if Dulcie—spoiled, selfish Dulcie—had chosen the frills and the furbelows which were so completely out of character with the rest of the house. At Knight's Keep the furniture was preserved from the time the house had been built and equipped—carved court cupboards and joint stools and oak refectory tables—but in this little room there were frivolous papier-mâché tables and fragile gilt chairs which had begun to creep in of recent years, a fashion emanating from the Marlborough House set and the Prince of Wales's society friends.

I don't think anything could have conjured up for me a more vivid picture of Justin's wife. I could see her perfectly now—pretty and petulant, befrilled and becurled, an empty-headed little doll who had been indulged by her husband. I pitied her—how could I fail to?—but I pitied her husband more.

I said suddenly, "I agree with Lady Ashford. You cannot

reproach yourself with your wife's death. Any woman attending a ball in bitter weather can be stricken with a chill, or even pneumonia. We dress so senselessly for evenings."

He gave me a grateful smile, and I knew he was touched by my words. I even felt that they meant a lot to him, and my senses quickened.

It was then that I saw the look on Miranda's face—a mixture of contempt and amusement. But it was not for him. I knew that, because she had been hot in his defense.

It was I who amused her. She read my thoughts too well.

We retired to bed soon after that, and I was glad to escape the woman's too-seeing eyes.

My bed had been turned back, my nightdress laid out, and my bed warmed. I had never been so cosseted in my life, and reveled in the luxury. The brocade curtains of the tester bed and the matching curtains at the window glowed richly in the light from oil lamps. As I undressed I was aware that I was tired, but that underneath my tiredness was an excitement due to more than my arrival at this famous house, the luxury that surrounded me, or the welcome extended to me. It had something to do with Justin Ashford. Even to think about him was disturbing in a new and unfamiliar way. No man had ever made me feel like this before.

I don't know what made me draw back the window curtains and look out into the night before I went to bed. The gardens were bathed in moonlight and the beauty of the scene took my breath away, but it was on the immense cedar tree that my glance focused. Its gigantic branches overhung the lawn like a beneficent and protective god. No figure lurked within its shadows, watching the house. The whole episode had been a figment of my imagination. There was nothing sinister down there.

I let the curtains fall again, and went to bed.

CHAPTER ELEVEN

Life merged into a pattern at Knight's Keep, the calmly regulated pattern of life in the country. I was drawn into it quickly, and the days slipped by like beads on a string. I saw little of Justin, for he was always busy on his estate and had only one steward to help him, a good-looking and able young man named Gavin Rudge. On the whole, I was surprised by the small number of household and outside staff employed at the Keep. My mother had once told me of the vast army needed to run the place, so it was obvious that Justin's forebears had not been so hard-working as he, nor made themselves personally responsible for many of the duties he undertook as a matter of course.

There was no denying that times were changing. Until recently the landed gentry of England had lived like feudal lords, housing and feeding and supporting a small world of tenants and staff, but opportunities for skilled workers were opening up in towns and cities now, luring the young ones away from traditional country employment, but not yet giving them the same security and protection that the country squires or the feudal lords did. I decided that a farm hand was far better off than a man who sought employment in the town, for the farm hand was sure of a roof above his head and a good overlord saw that it didn't leak, and that beef and sometimes venison were provided by the gamekeeper from the estate's slaughter-house, and leather from the tannery for coats and breeches, and flax for the wives to spin into yarn for cloth, and that when they were too old for work they would still be fed and housed and looked after.

On the many walks I took—always alone, because walking was not one of Miranda's activities—I was enchanted by the well thatched roofs and the neat little gardens. It was obvious that Justin took care of his workers and their homes.

Knight's Keep was his world and his pride. Every morning he rose early and toured the estate. I would hear his horse gallop away and knew that he wouldn't return until long after Miranda and I had breakfasted. By that time he had inspected the fields and the crops, talked with his men, and given instructions for the day. Afterwards he would get down to the serious business of estate management with Gavin Rudge, in his study. Justin was an industrious man.

There was one accomplishment I lacked and which Justin said I would have to master if I was to enjoy country life to the full—I couldn't ride. "You must teach her," he said to Miranda at dinner one night, "and then you can show her more of our beautiful county."

Miranda's surprise because I had never ridden amused me.

"I'm city born, city bred," I told her.

"But surely you could have ridden in Rotten Row? I thought that was the fashionable place to ride in London."

I laughed. "So it is—for those who can afford it. Church Parade on Sunday morning is a highlight in the Park, but the nearest I ever got to it was as a looker-on. Sometimes, after Matins, we would go on a horse-drawn bus to Hyde Park Corner, and then walk along the Row, admiring the fashionable folk and the riders. Once I saw the Prince of Wales and Mrs. Langtry riding together. She is very beautiful, but I couldn't help feeling sorry for poor Princess Alexandra."

Miranda shrugged. "That is the way of the world, Jane. One must accept it. And it must be very trying for a man to be married to a woman almost totally deaf."

"Surely it is much more trying for her," I answered dryly.

As if to comfort me, Justin said, "You needn't fret for poor Alexandra. His Highness is devoted to her, despite his peccadilloes. He would discard a mistress, but never his wife. She comes first in his life, and she knows it."

But that wasn't the sort of marriage to appeal to me, and I suppose I showed it, for Miranda said in some amusement, "Poor Jane—you have a lot to learn!"

"An unfaithful husband would break my heart," I said.

"If he were unfaithful, very likely you wouldn't know," she answered, but Justin said, "I can't imagine any man being unfaithful to you, little Jane," and sent the warm color rushing to my cheeks again. His compliments frequently had this effect on me and although Miranda's inscrutable eyes appeared not to notice, I knew they did.

She agreed, amiably enough, to teach me to ride.

"I'll have to get the right clothes," I said. A riding habit was one item I hadn't bought.

"We will visit my tailor in Canterbury tomorrow," she promised.

We set off soon after breakfast. As I came downstairs, wearing the blue velvet outfit in which I had traveled from London, I met Justin in the hall.

"As long as I live," he said. "I shall remember you in that coat and gown. The blue matches your eyes. I noticed that the first moment I saw you."

"As a matter of fact," I said lightly, trying to still the ridiculous trembling of my heart, "my eyes are gray."

"But they have a capacity to reflect color. I've noticed that, too. You have an emerald evening gown that plays wonderful tricks with your eyes."

At moments like this, isolated moments when we were entirely alone, I could feel ridiculously shy with him. Even his lightest remark could seem intimate and personal, and yet he never deliberately made it so.

I was standing there, tongue-tied as a schoolgirl, when I saw Gavin Rudge standing at the open door of Justin's study. This was the hour they spent on estate affairs, and the steward was waiting. He was a well set up young man, educated, good-mannered, and attractive, but somehow he made me feel uncomfortable. I never met him without feeling that he was watching me. I felt it now, and suddenly had the wild notion that this might be the man who had stood in the shadows of the cedar tree that night. Perhaps he had even been watching my window! I dismissed the idea as absurd, but it was impossible to dismiss him as a person.

He smiled politely and said, "Good morning, Miss Bewleigh." I returned his greeting, trying hard to make my voice sound cool because I had the feeling that with very little encouragement he would try to get into conversation with me. His position at the Keep was a responsible one, but something made me wary of this young man, despite his open smile and frank eyes. I also felt that Justin wouldn't like me to be on too friendly a footing with his steward, although his own attitude to Gavin was companionable. The young man frequently joined us for lunch since his position was not that of a servant.

All the same, some instinct made me keep myself slightly aloof from Gavin Rudge, and when I saw Justin's eyes follow me now I knew why. The master of Knight's Keep, quiet and gentle as he was, could be capable of strong jealousy, and it was useless to deny that between him and me there was a deepening attraction. When he touched me, even to hand me into the carriage as he did now, my blood ran hotly.

Miranda was not down yet. Justin had walked with me down the wide front steps and Gavin had gone into the study. Apart from the coachman standing deferentially beside the open carriage door, we were alone. Justin took the rug from the man, leaned inside, and tucked it gently about my knees. "We must take great care of you, little Jane," he said, so softly that only I could hear. "You are becoming very precious to us."

"Not to Miranda," I said, trying to keep my voice steady. "I make no headway with Miranda."

"I wasn't referring to her, and I shouldn't have said 'us' when I meant myself. You are becoming very precious to me, Jane, and I think perhaps you know it."

I tried to speak, and failed. My heart was thudding wildly.

"Please, Jane—say you know it."

"I—I—"

Swiftly, he stooped and brushed my hand with his lips, and that was very nearly my undoing, for a rush of desire for this man swept through me in a quickening tide. I had never experienced intense physical desire before.

I clenched my hands beneath the rug to still their sudden trembling and Justin looked at me, and smiled. His eyes were eloquent. He knew how I felt, and was pleased.

It was a moment so exquisite that if Miranda hadn't appeared I must surely have betrayed myself in some reckless way—like leaning forward to press my lips against his, an impulse that was almost overpowering. I think perhaps he guessed this, for his mouth curved sensuously in response. Then he stepped back and greeted Miranda as if everything was perfectly normal.

"You look magnificent, as always, Stepmother."

She laughed at him, as she always did when he called her by that name and suddenly the magic of the moment was gone. Perhaps that was a good thing, for I was able to wave goodbye quite nonchalantly, but my heart was still hammering as we drove away.

It was a beautiful day for a drive to Canterbury, and my first sight of the magnificent cathedral, dominating the ancient and lovely city, took my breath away. We made straight for the tailor, who greeted Miranda with an elaborate show of welcome and respect. I think he was surprised when I ordered a very costly outfit, but as always Miranda's face remained quite inscrutable. I noticed that the tailor immediately transferred his gushing attention from Lady Ashford to me, and I guessed at once that I must have placed a far better order with him than she had ever done. I didn't regret this. I wanted to have the best and to look as elegant as possible now that there was a man in my life whose opinions and reactions were important to me.

When we were driving away, after long and rather tedious measurings and consultations, Miranda said, "I know it isn't my concern, but what made you be so extravagant? You don't even know whether you will make a rider or not."

I shrugged. "The expense won't kill me."

"Apparently not. It would me!"

I was embarrassed. I had been reckless and impulsive in not counting the cost for the first riding habit I had ever ordered but I had been thoughtless too, which was worse. Miranda always looked so well groomed that I tended to forget she was a young widow, dependent upon Justin for everything, and that her only assets were her looks and her title. These things, not her wealth, had earned the unctious little tailor's respect—so quickly transferred to the customer with more money. Now I felt ashamed.

Miranda gave a sudden laugh and said "Don't worry, Jane —think how elegant you will look when you fall off!"

I laughed too. "I'm sure to do that, but not too often, I hope. My father once told me that it took six falls to make a rider—or was it twelve? I suppose it was silly of me to be so extravagant, for if I prove to be no good in the saddle I will fall more frequently than that, and ruin my precious clothes."

"If I had your money, *I* would be extravagant too. At any rate, until I got used to it."

This subtle reminder of my sudden transition from poverty to riches was not intentional, but it made me most keenly aware of my background, and that but for a fantastic turn of fortune it would be my background still.

"I haven't hurt you, have I, Jane?"

Miranda spoke gently, and when I looked at her I saw that her eyes were kind. I was wrong to misjudge this woman. She was reserved and inscrutable, but not untrustworthy or cruel. I remembered that Justin had told me of her shyness and this, I felt, accounted for a lot. Shy people very often hid behind a mask.

Canterbury was a little more than fifteen miles from Knight's Keep, so to return home in time for luncheon was impossible. Miranda ordered the coachman to drive to Chilham, where we stopped at the Woolsack Inn at the entrance to the village, and were served in a small private room, for ladies could not visit the public ones. Afterwards we strolled up the winding street lined with timbered cottages. I was enchanted, for I had only read of such villages in books, and when we emerged into the market square, with the entrance to Chilham Castle at the far side, I couldn't suppress a cry of pleasure.

"It sounds as if you admire our Kentish villages," a man's voice said. "Lady Ashford must show you more."

I had recognized the voice even before we turned and saw Daniel Firth, looking as large and implacable as he had been on the train.

I looked at him coldly, bidding him a polite good-day but nothing more. I knew now why he had urged me to take the next train back to London and why he hadn't wanted me to visit Knight's Keep—because I would learn of his accusations against Justin, and of how effectively he had been proved wrong. It was a situation no man would want talked about.

I turned aside, knowing that Miranda would be as eager as I to get away from Daniel Firth, for she had condemned the man very thoroughly. To my surprise, she made no attempt to, but greeted him affably.

"I shall certainly show Miss Bewleigh more," she said. "I'm going to teach her to ride, then we can explore the countryside together."

I admired her courtesy toward a man who had every reason not to expect it. At the same time, I felt she was being disloyal to Justin. She seemed in no hurry to depart, and remained chatting to Daniel Firth while I stood aloof. I felt she was quite unaware of my disapproval; unaware of everything but the man himself. I was shocked, and tried not to see the way she looked at him, as if she were not only conscious of him as a man but determined that he should be conscious of her as a woman.

How could I ever make friends with someone I could never hope to understand? Miranda was an enigma; a beautiful enigma. I felt that she liked being that way, and that she wouldn't care if every woman in the world disliked her so long as men didn't.

Dr. Firth certainly didn't. His attention was wholly upon her. I sauntered away, ostensibly to visit the picturesque old church but really because I wanted to put as much distance as possible between myself and this couple.

"Did you know that the followers of Julius Caesar built the first castle in this village, when he camped here after invading Britain more than two thousand years ago?" the doctor's voice said at my elbow.

They had followed me. Miranda was holding up her skirts

as she walked, displaying slender ankles.

"Yes," I answered with polite indifference. "Are you ready to return home, Lady Ashford?"

I said "home" instinctively, and suspected that Daniel Firth noticed it.

"Whenever you like, Jane dear, but don't you want to see more of this place? We could call at the castle. There's always a welcome there for a member of the Ashford family."

"Some other time."

Miranda shrugged. "As you wish."

The doctor removed his hat, bowed, then walked back across the market square to a hitching post where his horse was tied. Within a minute he had ridden away, not looking back.

We walked down the hill to the Woolsack, where our carriage was ready and waiting.

"You are angry, Jane."

"Not angry. Shocked."

"May I ask why?"

I stopped dead and looked at her. "*Why?* You talk amiably with a man who has accused Justin of poisoning his wife, and then ask why I am shocked?"

She didn't answer until we were settled in the carriage and bowling along the highway, then she said calmly, "It is wise to be pleasant to one's enemies. Unwise to let them know how you feel."

"That's all very well in theory," I retorted, "but *I* couldn't bring myself to be pleasant to a man who had misjudged another so abominably—especially someone like Justin."

"I am well aware of that," Miranda answered, but when I looked at her there was nothing but friendliness in her face; no mockery, no suggestion that she knew why I championed Justin. "It does you credit," she continued, "but I believe it would be folly to maintain a feud with a man like Daniel Firth, even when one hasn't forgotten it. Wisdom lies in letting him think one has."

"I'm not convinced. In any case, he must know well enough that such a thing could never be forgotten."

She shrugged. "I still think my attitude is the right one."

"And I think mine is. There *is* such a thing as loyalty, after all."

Miranda looked at me for a long moment, then said, "And what loyalty do you owe Justin, pray?"

"The loyalty of a guest in his house. Of a friend, I hope."

"Is that all? Only of a friend? Or are you hoping to be something more?"

She had defeated me. I felt she would always defeat me. I found her question quite impossible to answer, and when I was silent, she laughed.

I think it was at that moment that I realized how useless it was to try to make a friend of her, or even to like her, for there was only one feeling I could have toward Miranda Ashford. Fairly or unfairly, I could only fear her.

CHAPTER TWELVE

There was one further encounter before we reached home. Turning into Lympne, we came face to face with Gavin Rudge.

He reined his horse and greeted us. I returned the greeting, but Miranda merely bowed and didn't order the carriage to stop.

"I don't understand you, Miranda!"

She answered coldly, "I know that you and Justin are on Christian name terms—in fact, the speed with which you accomplished this surprised me—but I don't recall suggesting that you and I should be."

I colored hotly. "I beg your pardon—Lady Ashford."

To my astonishment she threw back her head and laughed. "My dear little Jane, can't you tell when I'm teasing?"

"It didn't seem like teasing to me," I retorted, not a little vexed.

She patted my hand affectionately. "Well, I was, child, so chase that frown from your pretty face. And what is it you don't understand about me?"

"Your attitude to a man like Dr. Firth, a man who made the most terrible accusation against your stepson, and your attitude to an apparently honest young man like Gavin Rudge.

"My dear girl, Rudge is a servant."

"He is nothing of the sort. He's an Estate Steward—a position of responsibility and trust. More than that, he is well educated and a gentleman."

Miranda shrugged. "Oh, I'll grant you all that, but I know more about him than you do."

"That still doesn't explain why you should be amiable to your stepson's enemy, and cold towards his friend."

"His friend!" Miranda laughed mirthlessly. "That shows how little *you* know about Gavin Rudge. And do stop reminding me that Justin is my stepson. He happens to be five years older than I."

She sounded petulant, and I realized at last that the way to crack Miranda's guard was to upset her vanity.

"Listen to me, Jane." The petulance was gone and in its place was a confidential note. "There is something you must know. Justin blamed himself for forcing Dulcie to go to the ball against her will, but what he doesn't know—and what he will *never* know because I'm determined to keep it from him —is that her real reason was an assignation with Gavin Rudge. The man was her lover."

I was too shocked to speak.

"Nothing Dulcie ever set her mind on could be denied her," Miranda continued. "She slipped away from the ball, met that young man, caught a chill, and died. And in my opinion it served her right. She asked for punishment, and she got it."

Reaching home, I went straight to my room. I had been shocked by the news about Dulcie, but I was also shocked by Miranda's attitude. Justin's wife had been faithless, but her end had been tragic. To Miranda, however, it was merely justice, and it seemed to me that to consider death a suitable punishment was callous in the extreme.

Opening the door of my room, I was startled to find Sarah there. It was too early for her to be turning down my bed for the night and too late for her to be tidying up. She was standing near the huge oak cupboards that housed my clothes, and I had the distinct feeling that she had just shut the doors.

She didn't blush, or stammer an apology. Sarah could never be caught out. She was bold and self-confident, and I disliked her more than ever. I was convinced that she was untrustworthy and knew that if I were mistress of Knight's Keep, I wouldn't employ her.

She curtsied deferentially enough, but offered no explanation. Before she reached the door, I stopped her with a question.

"Do you want something, Sarah?"

"No, miss."

"Then why are you here?"

"I brought clean towels, miss. I forgot them this morning, begging your pardon."

Her eyes slid to the wooden towel rail standing beside the marble wash-stand. Both were near the wardrobe cupboards, so her excuse was feasible and made me look rather foolish.

"I see. Thank you, Sarah."

Her wooden face stared back at me, and I had the uncomfortable feeling that it mocked me. My dislike of her intensified, and I decided that the time had come to put her in her place.

I moved across the room, untying my veil, then unpinning my hat.

"Will there be anything else, miss?"

The question was purely automatic and she fully expected me to say no, because I had made few demands on her since coming to the Keep. In fact, she was already half-way through the door, so my reply pulled her up sharply.

"Yes," I said, negligently handing her my hat. "You can put this away."

The door shut with a little slam. She took the hat and marched across the room. The wardrobe door also slammed a little after she had put the hat carefully in its box.

"And now this," I said, shedding my coat.

She took it sullenly. I was learning, but so was she. One of these days, I thought, you won't dare to look at me like that.

"I'll have my robe—the Paisley one," I ordered. "Unbutton me, please."

Her heavy hands fumbled with the tiny buttons so clumsily that I would have preferred to do the job myself, but because I was determined to tame her I let her do it, then stood in my fine cambric petticoat, waiting for my robe.

"And what gown will m'lady wear tonight?" she asked as she slipped it over my shoulders.

I looked at her sharply, and she actually colored.

"Beg pardon, miss—I'm so used to waiting on her ladyship that I forgot. What gown, please?"

"The emerald green," I said at random, wondering if her slip of the tongue had been accidental, or a deliberate mockery.

"Then I'll take it and press it now, miss."

I sat at the desk between the two tall windows, taking no more notice of her. I took a sheet of crested note-paper from

an embossed rack, picked up a quill pen, and began to write
at random, fully aware that the maid's eyes watched me, fully
aware that *she* was aware that since coming to Knight's Keep
I had sent or received little or no correspondence. I had had
a couple of letters from Mr. Claythorne reporting progress in
executing Silas's will but no more, and right at this moment I
had the distinctly uncomfortable feeling that this knowing girl
was only too well aware of the fact.

Did she spy on me, and if so, why? Was she the type to
whom spying just came naturally, an inquisitive young woman
who couldn't keep her nose out of anything, or was she watching me for a reason and reporting on me—but if so, to whom?
It could only be to Miranda.

The idea was so ridiculous that I dismissed it. I heard
Sarah close the wardrobe door again and walk out of the room,
taking my emerald satin gown with her. I was glad when she
had gone.

My action in sitting down at the writing desk had really
been one of dismissal, but now I found that I was writing
instinctively to Dora Smee. *This is a beautiful place, and
everyone is most kind. I am to learn to ride, although I doubt
my ability as a horsewoman. . . .* I went on to describe Knight's
Keep, and the Park, and the countryside surrounding it. *And
far below, stretching towards Rye and Winchelsea in Sussex
are the Romney Marshes, which saw many a smuggler in days
gone by.* I could imagine her eyes, round with awe, as she
laboriously picked out the words, and suddenly I felt such an
overwhelming nostalgia for her warmth and kindliness that I
wanted to cry. I had been swept up in my new life to such an
extent that I had scarcely thought of my old.

Nothing could have been more evident of the change in me,
which wasn't merely due to my surroundings, nor the acqui-
sition of wealth, but to something fundamental in myself. I
had stepped into this great house and belonged to it at once,
and where I should go and what I should do when the time
came for me to leave, I had no idea. Suddenly the world outside seemed alien to me. I had stepped from poverty into
riches, and the step had been incredibly easy.

Now that I had started writing to Dora, the words flowed
on. *I have a maid to look after me. Her name is Sarah, and I
neither like nor trust her. She watches me all the time—or so
I feel. It is probably all due to my imagination, for there is
absolutely no reason why I should be spied on. And now, I*

suppose, you are thinking, 'Silly creature—she's getting fanciful, like her Uncle Silas, who thought someone was chasing him in a green carriage. . . .'

My pen stumbled, splashing the page with ink. Why should I remember Uncle Silas's fears now?

But they had come true. A carriage had charged at him out of the fog, and run him down, and killed him.

My hand closed on the sheet of paper, screwing it into a ball. I threw it on the fire and watched the dancing flames devour it, then I went back to my desk and finished my letter to Dora in a matter-of-fact way, giving her my news, but nothing else. What else was there to report? That my host was the most attractive man I had ever met, that I couldn't get him out of my mind, that my blood stirred at the sight of him and at the thought of him, that I was in love for the first time in my life? All this was real enough. Justin Ashford had taken possession of my heart and my mind, and I longed for him to take possession of my body.

So this was love, I thought, my cheeks aflame. It was obsession and desire. If I never saw Justin again after I left Knight's Keep, life would be empty, for all the money in the world couldn't replace him. How Dulcie could have been unfaithful to such a man was incomprehensible, but obviously she had not been a good wife in more ways than one. I had become aware of signs of neglect in this beautiful house, upholsteries in need of repair, window hangings that needed replacing, carpets that were worn but for the most part skillfully hidden beneath the heavy furniture. These signs of deterioration were not obvious at first glance; it was only after a time, when the lovely house became familiar and the rooms seemed less vast and formidable, that flaws became apparent and imperfections became visible. A diligent mistress would never have allowed them to develop, but Justin's wife had apparently been indifferent about her household.

The same couldn't be said of Justin. He maintained the place with pride and had only recently undertaken extensive repairs to masonry and woodwork. The stables had also been restored, carriages re-upholstered, and improvements to barns and outbuildings were still under way. Both he and Gavin Rudge were diligent in their care of the estate, and although I couldn't admire the young steward, I had to admit he was a good worker. No doubt he cherished his comfortable position here and counted himself lucky for never having been found out in his infidelity with Dulcie. I wondered how he would feel if he knew of Miranda's knowledge of it—and now mine.

At that precise moment hooves echoed on the drive below and looking out I saw Gavin riding towards the stable block. He was attractive enough, I supposed, but how Dulcie could have preferred him to her husband, I failed to understand. Obviously, she had not only been indulged and spoiled, but bored. Probably she had drifted into a cheap affair with Justin's steward for no other reason. Life at Knight's Keep was quiet and placid, and, unlike her husband who was a country-man at heart and content to be, Dulcie might have found the life tedious. Personally, I could imagine no existence more ideal than living here with Justin.

I watched Gavin out of sight, glad of the opportunity to study him unobserved. Too often it was the other way around.

When Sarah's rap sounded on the door I realized with sur-prise that it was dusk. When she saw me sitting there, just as she had left me and apparently unaware of the oncoming darkness, she said in her stolid way, "You'll be after straining your eyes, miss," and moved impassively across the room to light the lamps. Then she drew the heavy curtains, laid out my dress, and went to fetch a pitcher of hot water. I was address-ing the envelope to Dora when she returned.

"Would you like me to take your letter down to the mail-bag, miss?"

Some impulse made me decline. I said I would put it there myself when I went downstairs.

I let her dress me. I disliked it, but I let her. I disliked the touch of her heavy hands as she fastened the endless hooks and eyes of my gown, I disliked her brushing my hair, I dis-liked her very nearness, but because I felt my attitude to be unfair I endured her. All the same, I was thankful when she could be dismissed.

As she went to the door I noticed that she walked in the same hip-swinging way as Miranda; not so naturally or so gracefully, but self-consciously, as if she was very much aware of her sex and enjoyed flaunting it. When the door closed I felt that something unwholesome had left the room, and was thankful.

CHAPTER THIRTEEN

They say that love beautifies a woman; if this is true, then it explains why my appearance that night seemed to glow from my mirror. The change was evident even to myself. When I had first arrived at Knight's Keep I had been pretty enough, a young girl with moderate looks and a wardrobe of beautiful clothes, but it wasn't merely the clothes that made me blossom tonight. The emerald-green gown gleamed richly and my hair shone—but so did my eyes, and my skin had a bloom on it that had been absent when I first arrived from London. Country air—or the inner glow of love? Whatever the cause, I felt that my appearance had improved a hundredfold and tonight I hoped it would attract Justin more than ever.

From below, the dinner gong sounded. My heart leaped, for now I would see him. The evenings were the most precious part of the day to me, the hours I spent with him the hours I really lived for. Even though they had to be shared with Miranda, Justin and I were aware only of each other, and each of us knew it. Beneath the three-sided conversation there would be hidden undertones in his voice that only I could catch, for they were meant only for me. There would be secret glances, and the accidental touching of hands, and a longing to be alone together, but always Miranda was there, quite unaware that she was an unwelcome barrier between us.

Above her dark head Justin's eyes would meet mine, and I would know that he wanted to be alone with me, and knew that sooner or later he would somehow arrange it. When I went downstairs every evening I wondered—will it be tonight? Will he get rid of her somehow tonight? Will he make some excuse, *any* excuse, to be alone with me? But the opportunity never arose, and his beautiful young stepmother would remain with us until bed time, unconscious of our frustration, and Justin would be courteous to her, as became a dutiful stepson, and I would be courteous, as became a dutiful guest, until sometimes I felt that the situation would explode and that either he or I would betray ourselves—and if we did, how would Miranda react?

Not with jealousy, I knew. She was fond of Justin because he was the son of the man she had loved, but beyond that she displayed no interest in him. It was therefore impossible to look upon her as a rival, even though she often made me feel inferior as a person. All the same, she was mistress here and might well resent being replaced by another.

In the peaceful atmosphere of this old Elizabethan mansion everything was very orderly and serene, and it was the easiest thing in the world to go right ahead and fall in love with Justin. Everything went smoothly, as in a fairy tale, with the happily-ever-after ending waiting just around the corner.

And that night, it came.

After dinner we always withdrew to what I now called Dulcie's Room, the overbedecked little salon that seemed to conjure up her image more and more. It was so frivolous that it seemed in keeping with the flighty, petulant, unfaithful young wife who now mattered so little to me that I couldn't even be jealous of her. She had made Justin unhappy, and although he had not openly admitted it, it was obvious that his love for her had rapidly changed to patient forbearance and nothing more. They had been married precisely two years, a tragically short time in which to experience the death of love, so its basis, I felt, couldn't have been very deep.

I never questioned him about her. All I wanted was to help him achieve forgetfulness. So far, he had sought this in work, but such a man needed more than ceaseless labor. There were depths of tenderness in him that deserved not only some outlet, but reciprocation. He needed love, and I had an abundance to give.

We were sitting as usual, drinking the strong black coffee that Miranda made in her own special way in an ornamented Arabian coffee pot over a spirit lamp. She carried out the ritual every night on a small side table. The method was slow and meticulous, but the result delicious. "Matthew initiated me," she told me tonight. "We used to make coffee in our sitting room upstairs, sitting alone together every evening. Poor Justin—you felt shut out, I think—and the tea Dulcie brewed for you down here was horribly insipid."

"She never acquired a taste for coffee," Justin answered tolerantly.

"You should have made her."

"I don't believe in forcing anyone to do anything. Why should one person's will be imposed on another?"

"You're too tolerant, too lenient, my dear."

"So you've told me before."

But it was this tolerance and kindness in him that I loved. He was considerate towards everyone; to his stepmother, his staff, and his tenants—and particularly to me. It wasn't in my imagination that his smile revealed a special quality when we met. It was there at this moment as he looked across at me, and the fascinating curve of his mouth moved as if in a soft caress. I had watched many times to see if he smiled in this way at anyone else, too afraid to believe that it was reserved only for me, but not once had I seen it. It was his substitute for a kiss, and I knew it. I also knew that I couldn't be content for much longer with anything but the real thing.

Miranda said quietly, "Your coffee, Jane."

I jerked to attention, my cheeks aflame. She was holding out to me one of the beautiful Crown Derby coffee cups in which she took great pride. They had been a gift from Matthew shortly after he brought her home. "I never saw anything so lovely in Africa," she had once told me. "England is the place for rare and beautiful things."

Something made me remember the remark now—perhaps because she was looking so lovely tonight that she outshone anything in the room. Matthew had found in Africa something far more rare than anything in his own country.

I wondered if she had noticed my interest in Justin, and to cover my embarrassment I said at random, "Did you all live here together?"

"Of course. Matthew was mostly confined to bed, but our sitting room was next door. Justin and Dulcie had the rest of the house to themselves."

"Knight's Keep is big enough to house an army," Justin put in. "Too big, I sometimes think."

"But you wouldn't change any of it, would you?" Miranda said. "No matter how much work it entails, or how costly it is to run, you won't shut up a single wing, or a solitary room." She handed him his coffee, then sat down on a gilt chair beside the fire and spread her skirts. She wore a gown of ruby red tonight, and her dark skin looked exotic in comparison. I was able to view her with detached admiration and absolutely no jealousy now, and I knew that my own emerald gown did as much for me, in my different way, and that Justin couldn't take his eyes off me tonight.

"I can understand Justin's pride in Knight's Keep," I said. "If it were mine, I would feel as he does."

"And what do you intend to do when your affairs are settled?" Miranda asked. "Live in the country, or go back to London?"

I had given the matter no thought for a long time. Now Miranda was forcing me to, and I answered, "Mr. Claythorne advised me to buy a small house in Belgravia or some similar district, and engage a companion. Perhaps I shall do that."

"Companions are for old ladies," Miranda protested. "Not for young ones like you. Of course, I agree you will need a chaperon—"

"Not thinking of yourself, are you, Miranda?" To my surprise, Justin's voice was a little sharp. "I know you've fancied a London season for a long time, and now your period of mourning for my father has passed, I suppose you deserve it."

She answered indignantly, "Nothing was further from my mind! If I want to visit London, I can do so at any time. My concern is entirely for Jane. She is young and pretty, and when she finally comes in to her inheritance she could be a target for many a fortune-hunter in town. There is less chance of that in the country, I think. If she bought a house near here, I could keep an eye on her and see that no undesirable suitors pestered her. I'm more experienced in the ways of the world than she is. Older, too. Therefore I imagine I am a better judge of men."

It was the first time I had sensed any antagonism between Justin and his stepmother. The moment passed quickly enough but I saw Justin frown as he stirred his coffee. Something in what Miranda had said, displeased him.

"It's kind of you to be concerned for me," I told her, "but I'm sure that when the time comes, and it shouldn't be long now, Mr. Claythorne will help me find the right home."

"What do you mean—'it shouldn't be long now'?" Justin asked quickly. "You're not thinking of leaving us, are you?"

"I must eventually, and I heard from Mr. Claythorne the other day that things are proceeding normally. Those were his words." I smiled. "He is always very precise."

"Solicitors are. Pompous, wordy, and slow, but as far as I am concerned the slower he proceeds in this instance, the better. You've brought new life into this old house. Hasn't she, Miranda?"

"She has indeed, but if I were Jane I should be very impatient for affairs to be settled. I can never understand why probate always takes such a time to put through. It was just the same when Matthew died, remember?"

"Mr. Claythorne has been very kind," I said. "He advanced money against the estate, so I can't feel any urgent need."

"Hence your beautiful clothes," Miranda commented.

"You are quite right. The only ones I had before were those I made myself."

Justin put down his coffee cup with a sharp little clatter.

"I hate to think of you ever having been in need. I hate to think of you suffering, or being unhappy in any way."

"But I never was! My home life was wonderful, and the only time I really suffered was when I lost my parents. Uncle Silas helped me over that."

"I never met him," Miranda put in, "and from all Matthew said about him, I never wanted to."

"They quarreled," Justin said curtly. "You've heard all about that, and so has Jane, so let's not talk about it." He moved restlessly about the room. I knew he was wanting to end the conversation, but Miranda persisted.

"But what did they quarrel about?" she demanded. "Matthew would never tell me."

"How should *I* know?" Justin's voice was impatient. "It is ancient history, finished and done with. Besides, I knew nothing about it until it was all over. Even then, I paid no attention, apart from feeling a little sorry that my friendly uncle had gone out of our lives. I was rather fond of him." Suddenly he added, "Has Miranda ever shown you over the house, Jane?"

"Most of it," she told him.

"I was asking Jane."

His stepmother made a little grimace of amusement, "You're touchy tonight, Justin!"

"Would you like to see it now?" he asked me.

"At this time!" Miranda exclaimed. "In the dark!"

He picked up a lamp. "You won't miss this, and it will light our way very well. Come, Jane."

Miranda shrugged, and picked up a tapestry she was embroidering. As we left the room I saw her dark hair gleaming as she bent over it.

Once outside the door, Justin took hold of my hand and led me rapidly across the hall. Neither of us spoke, but the clasp of our fingers sent messages that had no need for words. He took me up the wide staircase and along the minstrels' gallery, opening doors and closing them, giving me time for no more than cursory glances inside. The rooms were big and well proportioned and beautiful, but I saw nothing of them—only Justin's handsome face looking down at me all the time.

He didn't speak until we reached the second floor, then he gave a sudden laugh.

"This is farcical—a pretense, and we both know it. You can explore the house any time, but it was a good excuse to get you to myself. I've been wanting to for days. You've known that, haven't you?"

I nodded, unable to speak. He opened another door and led me inside. The room was small, and furnished as a writing room. I knew he had brought me here because in the corridor some servant might come along. He set down the lamp, then turned and looked at me. I went into his arms as if it were the most natural thing in the world.

His lips on my hair were inexpressibly gentle. So was his hand as he turned my face upwards for his kiss. I had always known that he would be a tender lover, and that first embrace confirmed it. Then he picked me up like a child, carried me to a couch, and sat down, cradling me. My head fell on his shoulder and I knew such contentment that it seemed as if I had been waiting for this moment all my life. I wanted nothing to intrude on it—not even words. Perhaps he felt the same, for we remained there silently, his lips touching my face and my throat, his arms holding me as if he would never let me go.

I had always known that real love would be like this— deep and quiet, with no undertones of violence such as I had heard of in my father's stark parish. Justin could never be cruel. I remembered how I had once seen him carrying an injured lamb from one of the fields, cradling it tenderly, as he cradled me now.

Suddenly he put me aside.

"I want you too much," he said. "I want you so much that we must be married soon. I refuse to wait. You're never going to leave Knight's Keep and to make sure of that we'll be married as quickly as possible. Promise me, Jane. Promise."

"I promise!" I cried. I was wildly in love and knew now what it was like to be filled with desire for a man.

Later, alone in my four-poster bed, my cheeks burned at the remembrance of that moment. I had never before suspected my capacity for physical passion, but no man before had ever stirred me as Justin did.

I was on the verge of sleep when a voice startled me. It seemed to come from below my window. I lay awhile, thinking I must be mistaken, for no one would be in the grounds at this time of night. Then I heard it again—a man's voice. I flung back the bedclothes and crossed the room. The moon was full and beneath the cedar tree I saw him once more—the man who had watched the house on the night of my arrival. But this time he was not alone. As I looked, a woman broke away from him. She wore an enveloping cloak with a hood that concealed her face, and she gathered it more closely about her as she ran towards the house, heading apparently for a side entrance. For a moment the man stood watching her, then turned on his heel and vanished. I had a brief glimpse of the height and breadth of him, and the tall, upstanding collar of his coat, but his face was completely in shadow.

Who could be keeping an assignation at this hour, I wondered. Certainly not Miranda, for she had retired to bed by the time Justin and I returned to the little salon. And who would she be meeting furtively, like a guilty servant? Not Gavin Rudge, whom she disliked, and surely not Daniel Firth who she professed to—although when they met at Chilham she had seemed by no means averse to him, despite the excuse she had made later about hiding her dislike.

I dropped the curtain and went back to bed, but not to sleep. The possibility that Justin's stepmother might be having a secret affair with the doctor troubled me. It would be logical for her to keep such a thing secret, for the man was Justin's enemy, and since she was dependent upon her stepson's generosity as a means of support she would obviously run no risk of jeopardizing it.

But the whole idea was so distasteful that I preferred to think that the cloaked woman had only been a guilty servant —Sarah, perhaps. Sarah was the type to be promiscuous, and secrecy was part of her nature. To be having an affair with one of the married footmen was also in character, and good reason for a surreptitious meeting in the dark.

But servants had no right to meet down there, so close to the private apartments—not that that would worry Sarah. She was as bold as brass beneath her deferential front, also wise enough to make sure that she was not spied on from the servants' quarters.

There was a logical explanation for everything, but I didn't like it. And I particularly disliked that lurking figure beneath the cedar tree, and could not forget my conviction that the first time I saw it it had been spying on the house—too close to my window for comfort. The thought was a sinister one, and made me shiver.

CHAPTER FOURTEEN

I was awakened by the sound of horses' hooves. In an instant I was at the window again, but now it was daylight and I was watching Justin ride off as usual. His departure was so normal, so much the everyday routine, that for a moment I wondered if last night had been a dream until he turned and looked up at my window. He lifted his hand and I waved in return, quite oblivious of the fact that I was in my nightdress and that the morning sun shone full upon me, until another rider came into view and I saw Gavin Rudge follow his master's glance.

I dropped the curtain abruptly. The steward must have been surprised to see me standing brazenly in my night attire waving to his employer, but I was too happy to care about the opinions of others and hoped very much that once Gavin heard of my engagement to Justin he would stop watching me the way he did. He would find that Justin's second wife was very different from the first.

To return to bed now was impossible. I rang for Sarah, but had to summon her twice before she appeared, heavy-eyed and disgruntled.

"You rang, miss?"

Her tone was sullen, and so were her eyes. I didn't care. Very soon I would get rid of this young woman and replace her with someone of my own choice. Someone I could trust. Someone like Dora Smee.

Dora! Would she come, I wondered. Would she leave London and make her home here? She had once promised to think about it, so I decided to write and remind her of that promise—I would add it to the letter I had written last night, and which would still be in the mailbag downstairs. The village postman called at eleven each morning to collect.

"You want something?" Sarah demanded harshly. She looked tired and heavy-eyed—as well she might, I thought. I was sure now that she was the woman in the garden late last night.

"Yes," I answered. "I would like some tea."

"At this time?" she muttered.

"Yes—at this time." I was aware of a new note of authority in my voice. She apparently noticed it too, for she looked at me sharply, opened her mouth on a swift retort, shut it again, and turned to the door.

"It's Tweeny's job to make morning tea, miss. I doubt if it'll be ready yet."

"Then perhaps you will be good enough to make it yourself."

She looked back at me insolently, and suddenly I felt that this young woman was altogether too sure of herself.

For an imperceptible moment our glances met and did battle. I won. Hers was the first to waver and then look down. I looked down, too, and noticed that she had not had time to dress.

"I'm sorry if I roused you too early, Sarah. I will wait for the tea—"

I broke off. Her large hands were drawing a dowdy robe about her, but I noticed to my surprise that beneath it she wore a nightdress of fine lawn, trimmed with lace, an elegant and quite costly garment that could surely not have been bought out of her wages. What was more, it was new.

She saw my glance, and I thought I detected a faint smirk on her face, but couldn't be sure. Her heavy, well-formed features were adept both at hiding her thoughts and at being uncomfortably suggestive. I thought with satisfaction that when she heard I was to be the new mistress of Knight's Keep she would get an unpleasant shock.

"I'll fetch some tea," she said grudgingly, "seeing as how I'm up."

"You may get dressed first."

"Well thank you, miss, I'm sure."

Sarcastic, sneering, insolent, detestable. Oh yes, she would have to leave Knight's Keep. I had had enough of Sarah.

When the door closed behind her I pulled on a wrap and went downstairs to recover my letter to Dora. My encounter with Sarah had settled the matter once and for all. It would be wonderful to have someone like Dora Smee around—warm and lovable with her cockney good nature and kindness, ever willing to lend a hand, good with her needle, motherly and loyal. I hoped she wouldn't refuse to come, but uprooting a cockney from her native city might be asking a great deal. I would have to use all my powers of persuasion, and hope that when she heard of my forthcoming marriage she would be so excited that nothing would keep her away.

Even in daylight the corridors were shadowy. The house was very quiet and my slippers seemed to echo loudly on the wide oak stairs and across the great hall. The leather mailbag was in its customary place on a carved table against the wall. I put my hand inside and withdrew the letters waiting for collection. The one I had written to Dora wasn't there.

Ridiculous. Impossible. I had put it there myself on my way down to dinner last night! I searched through the little pile again, most of which were addressed in Justin's flowing hand, or in Gavin Rudge's surprisingly strong one; business letters to timber or grain merchants, harness suppliers and stone-masons, all concerning estate affairs for they were written on the paper that Justin used for business matters—all except one, which matched my own note-paper but wasn't addressed in my hand. *I* had not been writing to an apothecary in Rye. The name and address leaped out at me—Leo Van der Heul, Esq., Apothecary, Dolphin Street, Rye, Sussex. A strange name Van der Heul—perhaps that was why it caught my eye. The handwriting was feminine—Miranda's no doubt—but I wasn't really interested. I picked up the mailbag and shook it, but nothing more fell out.

There was a sound behind me. It was Carter, the under-footman, wearing a green baize apron for his early-morning duties and obviously surprised to find me here.

"Has the mailbag been emptied, Carter?"

He looked at the little pile of letters in my hand, obviously thinking I had taken leave of my senses.

"One is missing," I explained. "I wrote it last night and put it here before dinner."

"Then it should be there now, miss."

He was right. It should be.

"Perhaps I left it on my desk after all." I turned towards the stairs, feeling rather foolish. Carter was searching the floor beneath the table. "It isn't there," I told him. "I've looked."

"If I find it, I'll see that the postman takes it when he collects, miss."

"Thank you, Carter. It was addresssed to Mrs. Dora Smee, at Blake's Dwellings, Long Acre. London. If you find an envelope bearing that address, you'll know it is the right one."

"I'll look out for it," he promised.

I could see that he thought I was making a mistake, and I was almost beginning to believe it myself. The only logical explanation was that I had forgotten to bring the letter down. All the same, I felt an inexplicable uneasiness.

Back in my room, I searched thoroughly—my desk, my dressing table, my reticule, the gold-mesh bag I had used last night and even the linen basket, but my letter to Dora had disappeared into thin air. Somewhere, somehow, I had mislaid it. I shrugged the matter aside. I would write another, and post it in the village on my morning walk, and it would be a more exciting letter than the other anyway.

Sarah brought my tea, dumping it unceremoniously. She had dressed, but not in her uniform. She wore a rather unbecoming wool frock that was very much in contrast with the fine lawn nightdress.

"If you want anything more, miss, you'll have to ring for Tweeny. It happens to be my day off."

This young woman had a genius for making me feel uncomfortable. I was glad when she marched out of the room, hips swinging arrogantly as usual. I should have remembered that it was her free day, and I fancied she enjoyed reminding me. However, I was too happy to be troubled by people like Sarah, and while I sipped the tea I wrote excitedly to Dora, giving her my news.

And please say you will come to live with me. As my maid if, as you said, you would feel happier that way....

I went on to tell her about the beauty of Knight's Keep, and the home she would have, and that neither of us would ever be insecure or worried again. *No girl was ever so lucky as I, and I want you to share my new life,* I finished.

My happiness was so great that I could think of nothing so mundane as breakfast. I wanted action, movement, people. I wanted to shout my news to the world and felt frustrated because it was far too early in the day to disturb Miranda, who rarely rose before mid-morning. I wanted to rush along to her room to tell her, but I had never been invited there and hesitated to tap on her door. I would have to control my impatience and wait until Justin returned, then we would tell her together. I hoped she would be pleased. I saw no reason why she shouldn't be. As Justin had said, Knight's Keep was big enough to house an army, and some arrangement could be made about Miranda. She could have the sitting room upstairs that she and Matthew had shared: her own private suite again. In my happiness, I wanted everyone to be happy, and felt that in this way Miranda would be. Her elderly husband would have wanted us to take care of her.

I was out early that morning, relishing the sharp clean air and noticing that everything seemed to have taken on a new loveliness. The park was carpeted with early-falling autumn leaves and in the winding lane to the village, children were gathering glossy-skinned chestnuts and stringing them together as conkers. I found a giant, a real King Conker, and presented it to a delighted small boy who promptly became the envy of all—whereupon, of course, I fell to with the rest to search for more. I must have spent a good half-hour there, enjoying every moment. One day Justin and I would have children of our own to go on conker-hunts with. The thought added to my pleasure.

After that I stepped out briskly. I posted my letter to Dora and decided to take a different route home. I had seen a road leading towards the Romney valley, which I had never been down. Glancing at my fob watch, I saw that there was more than an hour to spare before Justin was due back; I had time to explore this lane and still be home in time to greet him. I knew that he would stride into the house, looking for me impatiently, as eager to see me as I was to see him.

I thought the road would lead straight to the hilltop above the valley, but instead it wound like a maze between high hedges and giant sycamore trees. There was an occasional cottage, but nothing more, and I was on the point of turning back when I saw a pillared gateway leading to a house. I remember thinking, "I'll walk as far as those gates, and then turn back," not really interested in where they led to. But when I reached them I stood still.

The gates were small compared with the massive ones leading to Knight's Keep, but the delicate tracery of their wrought-iron was beautiful. Even more beautiful was the house beyond, an Elizabethan manor built in the traditional style, half-timbered, gabled, lattice-paned. It looked mellow and warm, a welcoming house. Despite the admiration I felt for Knight's Keep I knew that this timbered manor was more to my liking, and that it was the sort of house in which I would have preferred to live with Justin and our children, for it was a real family house with a charm of its own.

I stood for a while, looking at the smooth green lawns beyond the gates. They were surrounded with trees and rhododendron bushes, and shrubs which must have been planted a long, long time ago, kept under control by an efficient gardener. The timbered house was approached by a short drive, and I knew that in spring daffodils and hyacinths and crocuses would dapple the warm earth, and in summer the garden would be a blaze of color. Perhaps there would be children romping on the lawns, and a mother calling them in to bed, and a father swinging the youngest shoulder-high to carry him, protesting, indoors.

I knew without a doubt that this was a house of happiness. I believed that some places were like that, just as others could be doomed.

I turned away, wondering who it belonged to, and if I would ever meet them when I became mistress of Knight's Keep. It would be nice to have friends here, to entertain them in my home, to visit them in theirs. I decided to ask Justin who owned it, and if he knew them—as surely he must —and as the thought passed through my mind I saw the name of the house carved into the stone pillars beside the gate.

Beechwood Close.

My heart leaped. This had been Uncle Silas's house, and fate had led me straight to it.

It was impossible to turn away now, so I opened the gates and took a few steps inside, peeping around the curve of the drive to get a closer look. I had no intention of trespassing further, and found myself walking almost on tiptoe in case I was discovered. There seemed to be no one about, so I became bolder and took a few more paces forward. It was even lovelier inside than the view from the lane suggested, and I remained where I was, gazing around and wondering how Silas could have brought himself to leave such a home, and why he had sold it when he really had no need to.

I was so lost in thought that I was quite unaware of anyone's approach until a voice said, "Welcome, Miss Bewleigh. How nice of you to call."

I spun around, startled, and saw Daniel Firth standing there.

CHAPTER FIFTEEN

I didn't believe it. Not this man, of all people, in Silas's old home. The thought outraged me.

"You look surprised," he said. "I'm disappointed. Am I to take it that you didn't come to see me?"

"Most certainly not!"

"Indignant, too," he said reflectively. "Even more disappointing! But how do you think I feel, seeing you open my front gate and walk into my drive, only to learn that you have no desire to see me?"

"I was curious—no more than that. I wanted to take a look at Uncle Silas's home."

"You mean Silas Bedell?"

"Who else? He became my uncle by adoption. He lived with my parents and myself until the time of his death."

Daniel Firth said in surprise, "I didn't know that. I understood he was under medical care somewhere."

"That was long ago." I looked at him in speculation. "You remember him, then?"

"I knew him as a boy."

"And you didn't recognize him that night in Long Acre—the night he was run down and killed?"

He stared at me in what appeared to be genuine astonishment.

"Was *that* Silas? I hadn't seen him since my schooldays, so of course I didn't know him—" He was pensive for a moment, then exclaimed, "I am being ill-mannered! Pray come inside. You must forgive my thoughtlessness. A bachelor living alone isn't always the best of hosts."

"I should have expected the reverse, sir. Most bachelors entertain guests—particularly women guests—quite frequently."

He laughed. I didn't want to stand there talking to him, but somehow his smile made me linger. He was audacious and cunning, no doubt, but I could be a match for him. And the cards were decked in my favor—I knew quite a bit about his past, and not merely as far as it concerned Justin. I had heard in a roundabout way of this man's reputation. He was no respecter of women. I tried to recall whom I had heard that from—Miranda, wasn't it?—but it didn't matter. I could sum the man up pretty thoroughly for myself.

I turned towards the gates.

"Forgive the intrusion, doctor—"

"But I don't forgive it. I welcome it. And it isn't an intrusion. If you want to see Silas's old home, I should be happy to show it to you."

I hesitated. The temptation was strong.

"You're not afraid, are you—a spirited girl like you, who isn't scared of driving through a dark tunnel in an empty railway carriage, alone with a man who might be intent upon robbery with violence—or worse?"

There was laughter in his voice. It challenged me.

"I can spare a little time," I said. "I was taking a morning walk—"

"As you so frequently do. You are a great walker, Miss Bewleigh. I have seen you many times—most weekends, in fact, when I return from London." At my glance he explained, "My work is there. Come, let me show you the house. I know you want to see it, otherwise you wouldn't have troubled to walk in."

He was right. I wanted more than anything to see the house where Uncle Silas had lived, but I disliked the idea of seeing it with this man—Justin's enemy. Even more, I disliked the idea of his living in it.

Daniel Firth said calmly, "I know you don't like me, but let us call a truce for ten minutes at least. After that you can walk out and never see me again, if you wish." He took hold of my arm and led me towards the house: it was useless to resist, for his grip was firm.

"I can't stay long—"

"Do you call ten minutes a long time? And why the hurry?"

"Lord Ashford will be back at eleven."

I felt his attention, but he made no comment. He led me across a circular brick porch and through studded doors of weathered oak, into a small and welcoming hall, and then into a long drawing-room with windows at both ends. The house more than fulfilled the exterior promise of beauty, but it seemed to me to lack a feminine touch. Had it been mine, flowers and foliage would have been massed in great copper bowls and the place would have been gay with chintz.

He had an uncanny way of sensing my thoughts, for he

said, "When Dulcie was here, the house looked very different."

I could imagine that. There would be frills at the windows and flighty touches everywhere.

"Your sister lived with you?" I asked politely.

"For a while. Our home was originally in Hythe—if you come to this window, you can see it." He drew me across the room, maintaining his hold on my arm as we looked across a rear garden to wild fields and the sea. "On the hillside over there—beyond Saltwood," he said. "The road is called Blackhouse Hill, after a notorious monastery that Henry the Eighth closed at the time of the dissolution; the wickedest monastery in all England, he called it, and it was the first to be dissolved. Dulcie and I grew up nearby. The house is now gone. I bought this place from Silas's successor, who decided that the Kentish climate was too harsh for him and sought warmth in the South of France. Dulcie came here with me, until her marriage—"

"Which you opposed," I said.

"So you heard about that. I might have guessed. And what else have you heard?"

"Everything."

He shrugged. "Well, you were bound to sooner or later."

"You sound as if you don't care."

"Why should I? Do you wish to see more of the house, or shall we go?"

"I would like to see more," I admitted, "but not with you, so I'll take my leave."

"You'll do nothing of the sort. You came to see Silas's house, and see it you will." He marched me firmly from the room.

He showed me the dining room and a small morning room which he used as a study, then led me upstairs, antagonism flaring between us all the time.

"I think it abominable that a man like you should live in this house," I declared. "It is far too lovely. You don't deserve it."

He laughed aloud.

"And who does deserve it?" he demanded. "Your precious Ashford?"

"Yes—my precious Ashford."

He stared at me, then said slowly, "Good God—not you, too?"

"Yes—me, too. I am going to marry him, and what is more, I'm glad you are the first to know. That proves how little I heed your dreadful accusations about Dulcie's death."

He didn't answer. He merely turned and walked back towards the stairs, leaving me to follow. He walked straight across the hall and through the front door.

Outside, he said curtly, "I will drive you back."

"There is no need—"

"There is every need. You've been here more than half an hour and the walk back to Knight's Keep is a long one. You won't be there in time to greet Ashford on his return, and I can imagine how important that is to you. Wait while I fetch a carriage."

You couldn't argue with a man like Daniel Firth. I waited beside the timbered porch until he brought a carriage around the side of the house and stopped before me. He leaped down to hand me inside, but I stood rooted to the spot.

The carriage was green.

But what of that? There were hundreds of green carriages in England, and it could merely be coincidence that a green four-wheeler like this had run Uncle Silas down and killed him very shortly before this man had walked into my life. . . .

CHAPTER SIXTEEN

"Is something wrong, Miss Bewleigh?"

"Nothing at all," I answered with an effort, and stepped into the carriage, and drove away from Uncle Silas's house with the man I now thoroughly mistrusted.

For a time we were silent. Then I said sharply, "You must have lost many patients in this part of the world when you accused a man of murder, and were proved wrong."

"I lost friends—not patients. I accepted an appointment in London after qualifying. I was working there when my sister died." He turned and looked at me, his mouth tilting wryly. "Sorry to disappoint you, Miss Bewleigh, but I suffered nothing more than the loss of friends who counted for little. Real friends have understanding and loyalty—like your friends, I imagine."

"Mine?" I echoed, surprised.

"I pushed my way through a little knot of them on the

platform at Charing Cross depot, remember?"

"You must be very observant. You arrived in a great hurry."

"I am observant—I have to be. And I was in a hurry because I'd been browsing in the medical library of my present hospital—"

"From which you borrowed that dull-looking volume?"

"It might have looked dull, but to me it wasn't."

"You said your present hospital. Did you leave your old one?"

"I did, althought everyone thought me mad to do so. I had reached a good position there."

"Then why did you?"

"I had my reasons."

We were bowling along at a good pace and I noticed that his hands were strong and sure upon the reins. To my surprise, they were the kind of hands I liked in a man. This annoyed me a little. I felt that a man I disliked shouldn't possess them.

Turning a bend as we approached a row of cottages he was forced to slacken pace, and it was at that moment that a young woman came out of one of them, with a child in her arms. To my surprise, it was Sarah.

Daniel Firth reined in the horses, and stopped.

"How is she now?" he called. "Sleeping more normally, I hope?"

"My mother can answer that better than I can, sir, seeing as how I have to live-in at the Keep. I only get home on my day off."

I knew that Sarah was interested to see me driving with the doctor. I even thought there was a touch of secret amusement in her eyes, but I turned my attention to the baby, a little girl of about two years. As Sarah held her up I could see that the eyes were vacant, and my heart moved in pity.

An old woman came shuffling out of the cottage. She was a replica of what Sarah would be like later in life.

"Aye, she be sleeping better, doctor, thanks be."

"No more colic?"

"No, sir. That medicine you gave her stopped all that, thank'ee, sir."

Daniel Firth touched the child's cheek.

"I'll call and see her on my way back," he promised, and drove on.

Leaving the cottages behind he said, "You see, I have *some* patients down here Miss Bewleigh. Those who cannot afford to pay for a more respectable man from Canterbury."

It was so obvious that he was treating the child purely from charity, that I felt uncomfortable. "Don't talk like that," I said.

"Why not, if it's true?"

"Is that Sarah's child?"

"Yes."

"I didn't know she was married."

"She isn't. Children are born illegitimately in the country as well as in the town, you know."

"Who is the father?"

"I have never bothered to ask. Why should I? The child is my concern, not her mother. Sarah is well able to look after herself."

"I could imagine that."

"Well, at least she visits the poor little thing on her free day," I said.

The sight of that pathetic child had saddened me. I noticed too that the day had clouded over.

"When are you to be married?" he asked casually.

"As soon as possible."

"An impatient man, Ashford. I can't say I blame him."

"*I* am impatient, too."

He turned and looked at me. We were passing beneath the shadow of overhanging trees and I couldn't see his face very clearly.

"You must love him very much," he said.

"I do. More than I thought it possible to love a man."

"And you are sure it is real love? Not just passion and desire?"

"Passion and desire are part of love."

"Yes—but they can also be something separate."

Because I wanted to change the subject I asked at random, "What hospital do you work at now?"

"A medical training center—the College of Tropical Medicines. The country sends missionaries and soldiers and doctors to all parts of the globe, and someone has to do research into possible diseases and train the doctors in handling them."

"Can you do that effectively from a distance? Don't you have to go overseas to do research on the spot?"

"In many cases, yes, but one particular thing I am working on is proceeding very satisfactorily at the moment." He changed the subject suddenly. "They were a mixed little lot, your friends at Charing Cross."

"They were good people, kind people."

"I could see that. Particularly one woman who looked aghast when I leaped into your compartment—the woman who took care of you on the night poor Silas was killed."

"You mean Dora—Dora Smee. That was her house in Long Acre. Uncle Silas and I rented rooms from her until he died. I had no idea that Silas had any money, until then. He left it all to me, and a staggering amount it was. Or will be."

"So it isn't actually yours yet?"

"Mr. Claythorne, his solicitor and now mine, is handling it. He has been very kind and helpful. The estate hasn't been wound up, but will be soon. Meanwhile he advanced me more money than I have ever possessed."

"And meanwhile you are invited to stay at Knight's Keep."

"It was a kind and generous invitation. Mr. Claythorne was pleased, and advised me to accept at once. I think he was a little anxious that I shouldn't be pursued by fortune hunters. He said that a girl with so much money could be the target for a man in need. He worried quite unnecessarily. When he hears that I am to marry Lord Ashford he will be very relieved."

"I can imagine that. The Ashford family has always been rich. I take it Mr. Claythorne was the elderly gentleman who also saw you off?"

I nodded, and Daniel Firth smiled.

"He looked very annoyed when I barged in. I shall have to look him up and apologize. I'll find him in the Law List."

We had reached the gates of Knight's Keep. I expected to be put down, but Daniel drove calmly up the long drive.

"There is no need for you to come further," I said.

"What you mean is that you don't want me to. You are even surprised at my audacity. You think I should be ashamed to show my face here. Well, I'm not. Ashford and I have met occasionally since my sister's death."

"Your meeting at Sandling Junction being one of them," I answered dryly.

"True. We are polite when we meet, but hardly affable. In the circumstances, it isn't surprising."

"In the circumstances, I am surprised Lord Ashford greets you at all!"

"But he enjoys it. It gives him scope for condescension and the opportunity to gloat."

"I won't allow you to talk of him like that!"

"You can't stop me. And I don't give a damn how besotted you are with the man."

"You hate him, don't you? Really hate him."

"How do you expect me to feel?"

He cracked the whip so that the horses surged forward at a gallop. He was now anxious to be rid of me, and I knew it.

"You hate him because he proved you wrong!" I cried. "He was completely vindicated."

The carriage wheeled to a stop before the great entrance to the house.

"Oh yes," the doctor said bitterly, "he was completely vindicated. There wasn't a trace of poison in my poor sister's body, and absolutely no suggestion of foul play."

He climbed down from the carriage, and it seemed to me that he was suddenly weary. He came around to my side and helped me down, and as I looked into his face I felt a stirring of pity. Grief had made this man hurl his terrible accusations at his brother-in-law, and no doubt Justin understood that. He was incapable of bearing malice.

Unlike this man, I thought as I turned my back on him and went indoors, saying goodbye politely but coldly as I walked away.

Justin met me in the hall. He was beside me in a couple of strides and swept me into his arms.

"I came back early. I couldn't keep away from you—and you weren't here. I thought you would be waiting for me!" His lips upon mine were hungry and demanding, and I felt a leaping response. We clung together and he said almost angrily, "*Why* weren't you here?"

"Darling, I always take a walk in the morning—you know that."

"But today of all days! How could you? Surely you knew how impatient I would be to get back?"

"I'm sorry—"

He kissed me again. There was a touch of savagery in it, a hint of uncontrolled passion.

"You must always be here—*always*, understand, so that I can come to you whenever I wish."

"But I must go out sometimes," I protested with a laugh. "What do you want to do—lock me up like the Lady of Shalott?"

"If I could, yes. Then no man would be able to look at you and you'd be all mine!"

I was so much in love that his possessiveness thrilled me, but I declared, "If you tried it, I would break out! My father always said I was a rebel at heart."

"Like your mother?"

"She never rebelled against *him*."

Justin said with emphasis, "And you must never rebel against *me*."

"Why should I?" I answered, and he swept me close again.

At a sound from behind I tried to draw away, but Justin merely held me tighter, and said, "You can be the first to congratulate me, Rudge. Miss Bewleigh and I are to be married."

For an imperceptible moment the young man was silent, then he said, "I congratulate you indeed, sir."

That was all. It was polite, but lacking in surprise. I was disappointed, and hoped Miranda's reaction would be more satisfactory. I wanted to see delight on people's faces when they heard the news. Daniel Firth's had been dark with anger, the Steward's completely expressionlesss. It was almost as if he were taking good care to reveal nothing. I didn't understand it, but neither did I care.

"Come," Justin said, tucking my hand in his arm, "we must find Miranda—"

She wasn't in the morning room, nor in the flower room where she usually spent an hour or so each day. There were signs that she had been busy there, for clippings of stems and leaves were scattered about, waiting to be cleared up. I wondered how she would feel when I became mistress here and took over the flower arranging myself, for I had very definite ideas on it. I found her displays over-elaborate, even bizarre. There was a touch of flamboyance about them that was incongruous against the mellow background of this ancient house. I had heard her complain that it was impossible to get the exotic blooms she was accustomed to in Africa, and sometimes I felt that the loveliness of an English garden was quite lost on her, although she had once conceded that our roses couldn't be beaten.

"Perhaps she's upstairs, or in Dulcie's Room," I said.

Justin said in surprise, "Dulcie's Room? What do you mean?"

"I mean the little salon where we sit each evening. I always think of it as Dulcie's Room. I don't know why. . . ."

"Neither do I. Dulcie never liked it. You look surprised, my love. Why?"

I was about to tell him that I imagined the over-elaborate decoration and the fussy embellishments typical of his first wife, when Miranda came downstairs.

Her tone was pleased and her smile was vivid, but at the sight of my hand within the crook of his arm the smile was wiped away instantly.

She looked from him to me, then back again. I saw apprehension in her eyes, but Justin apparently saw nothing for he said proudly, "You can congratulate me too, Miranda."

"Too?" she jerked.

"Gavin has already done so. He was the first to hear."

"The second," I said without thinking. "I've already told Dr. Firth."

"And when did you do that?" Justin asked.

"An hour or so ago. I didn't know he lived in Uncle Silas's old house."

"You've been there? You've visited Firth? Why did you do that?"

"Only by accident." I could see that Justin was a little annoyed and was anxious to placate him. "I came across the house when out walking, and when I saw the name I wanted to see inside—that's all."

"Well, I can't say I'm sorry that he was the first to hear."

"Hear what?" Miranda asked tautly.

"About our marriage. Mine and Jane's."

Justin was so proud and happy that he didn't see what I saw—the swiftly controlled shock in his stepmother's eyes.

I said, "I know this is unexpected, Miranda, but please be happy about it, for our sakes."

"Why shouldn't I be?" she said, and came towards us, and put her hands upon Justin's shoulders, and reached up and kissed him. But not me.

"It is Jane I should congratulate," she added, and she smiled down at me as she said it. I had always been conscious of her height, but at this moment it made me feel small, insignificant, and unimportant: a creature who had dared to rise above her.

She put out her hand and patted my cheek.

"Well done, Jane. Life is being very generous to you, isn't it?"

"Very generous," I agreed, and held even more tightly to Justin's arm. When he put his hand over mine, I was grateful.

Justin said, "To me, Miranda. Life is being generous to *me*. Remember that."

I knew he was displeased by her attitude and that this was his way of reproving her.

"And when is the wedding to be?" she asked pleasantly.

"As soon as possible. Before Christmas, definitely."

"Before Christmas!" I cried. "But, darling, it is nearly November now. That scarcely gives me time to get ready!"

"Do you need to get ready?" There was impatience in his voice.

I laughed and shook my head. "No—not really. I am ready any time!"

"But there are things to be done, preparations to be made," his stepmother pointed out. "A man in your position cannot marry secretly or quietly. The whole county will expect to be invited."

He waved an impatient hand. "I'm prepared to skip that nonsense. Jane and I can be married quietly in the chapel."

"And who will officiate? We have no family chaplain now."

"Some visiting clergyman will do, or the local Deacon. As for having a lavish affair, no one will expect a widower to make a big show of his wedding. We can do all the necessary entertaining afterwards." He smiled down at me. "I shall enjoy it more that way—presenting my wife to everyone personally. You'll like that, won't you, Jane? You don't want a big affair, do you? That sort of thing takes so long to get ready for and I don't want to wait. I *won't* wait. I don't care what you wear to be married in—you'll look beautiful, whatever it is."

All the time Gavin Rudge had stood aside. Now he said, "If you will excuse me, I have work to do," but as he turned away, Miranda's voice halted him.

"Wait, Gavin! Isn't this a nice surprise? Don't you find it delightful to think of another young mistress at Knight's

Keep? And such a pretty one, too. As pretty as Dulcie, I would say. Perhaps even more so."

"I have already congratulated Lord Ashford," the young man said evenly. "I wish them both happiness."

"As I do," Miranda said softly, looking directly at me. But there was no softness in her eyes. Only hatred. It was gone in a moment, but it had definitely been there.

CHAPTER SEVENTEEN

Things moved quickly after that. I was full of plans for my new home, replacing curtains and upholsteries, buying new carpets, adding improvements. Justin couldn't see the necessity for it, but I knew he was pleased by my enthusiasm.

It wasn't until I pointed out deficiencies that he even noticed them. "I've lived too long in the old place—I've become used to the general shabbiness, I suppose."

"It is a wife's task to take care of such things," I said.

"And Dulcie didn't."

"She was a sick woman," I reminded him. "That was probably the reason."

"No, my love, it wasn't. I had to face up to the truth about Dulcie, but I've never openly acknowledged it until now. She was lazy and indifferent. She didn't like Knight's Keep —she told me so often enough—and took no interest in the place. The servants became slack; an idle mistress breeds an idle staff. She didn't mind in the least when Miranda took over. She was glad to let her. That's why Miranda may find it a little hard to take a back seat now. You'll go gently with her, won't you?"

"I'll try not to hurt her, if that is what you mean, but surely she won't be hurt if I add to the comfort of the house? And there's something else—she won't actually live with us, will she? She'll have her own sitting room upstairs again, the one she used to share with your father?"

"A good idea. It was made into a sitting room only because he was ill and couldn't get downstairs, but it hasn't been touched since his death."

"Then it will make a nice suite for her."

"A suite?" he echoed.

"She still occupies the bedroom, doesn't she?"

"No, darling. She gave it up when my father died, and moved into one on the floor above. Wouldn't it be better if she remained there? I don't want her on the same floor as us. I want the main part of the house to be ours exclusively."

I agreed. Remembering the look in Miranda's eyes when she heard of our marriage, I would have preferred her out of the house altogether. It was a pity there was no dower house at Knight's Keep, although it was ridiculous to think of anyone so young as Miranda retiring to a dower house.

But I was far too busy and far too happy to think of anyone but Justin and myself. I wrote to Mr. Claythorne asking for a further advance—a lavish one, too, because I was determined to make Knight's Keep the most magnificent home in Kent. Meanwhile I went ahead and ordered whatever I wanted, sweeping Justin's protests aside.

"It is my job to pay for the upkeep of this place," he pointed out. "Inside *and* out."

"But you can't object to your wife spending her money on her home!"

"Not when she is my wife and it is her home, but all the same, I'd rather you didn't. I don't need your money."

"I know that! But what else am I to spend it on? Clothes? Vanities? I've all sorts of plans, Justin. I want to do the whole house over. How long is it since it was redecorated inside?"

"Frankly, I can't remember. I've always been too absorbed in the estate, and keeping the buildings in good repair, and running the home farm, and looking after the tenants' cottages—"

"I know. I've seen for myself all you do. And speaking of tenants, did you know that Sarah has a child?"

Justin shrugged. "I've heard about it, yes. A boy, I believe."

"No, a girl. A tragic little thing. She's mentally defective, poor mite."

He didn't shrug this time, but he didn't seem very interested. "These things happen in villages," he said. "They breed indiscriminately—they've nothing else to do!" He stooped and kissed me. "I must be off. I want to inspect the new barns with Gavin. As for the house, go ahead and do what you please, my love. I can refuse you nothing."

But apparently Mr. Claythorne could. His reply came almost by return. Unfortunately there were delays in settling my affairs.

. . . but rest assured that everything is proceeding smoothly

and that by January you will be in complete possession of your fortune. Moreover, the new Act comes into force then, which means that in the event of your marrying you will retain all you possess. Meanwhile, the advance you ask for seems somewhat extravagant. It would be difficult for me to advance so large a sum in addition to that you have already received. May I suggest that you wait a while before spending too liberally?

I was vexed, but what difference did it make? I could order whatever I liked, confident that everything would be paid for in the very near future. So I hid the letter from Justin, knowing that he would agree with the solicitor. Calmly, I went ahead with my plans, for I refused to be thwarted. In Justin's absence I explored the house and was shocked by some of the servants' rooms, although Miranda could see nothing wrong with them.

"The staff get their board and keep, plus wages," she said. "What more would you give them?"

"A few comforts, at least. Coverings for their bedroom floors, and fires too."

"Country folk are spartan folk," she told me. "They don't need pampering. Still, I will say this for you—you're obviously going to be a more conscientious housewife than Dulcie."

Miranda seemed to have accepted my forthcoming marriage with equanimity, after all, probably because she was reassured about remaining. I began to wonder if something couldn't be done to help her financially, for I knew that Matthew had left her entirely dependent on her stepson. From her clothes, it was apparent that Justin didn't stint her, but what sort of an allowance he made her over and above that, I had no idea. When we were married, he would take me into his confidence over many things, I knew.

So I continued my plans for the house. Only two rooms worried me—the first was Sarah's, which was more comfortable than any of the other servants', with a carpet on the floor and curtains at the window and even a wardrobe for clothes instead of the open shelf with a hanging rail which was all the others had. What was more, she had a room to herself, an unheard of luxury for someone below the level of housekeeper.

No improvement was needed here, but if Sarah enjoyed a room such as this most certainly Dora Smee should be given something even better. I was determined on that. As yet, I'd had no reply from her, but I knew that she would have to get someone to write on her behalf, since she could scarcely sign her own name, and that would cause delay.

Sarah was absent from her room when I visited it, and I noticed the general untidiness of the place. Comfortable as it was, she took little pride in it. Clothes were littered everywhere—far more clothes than one would have expected a housemaid to have—and I wondered who the man was who had fathered her child, and if the money for these things came from him. Someone in the village, perhaps—a farmer, or a tradesman, or even one of the footmen at Knight's Keep. It was no business of mine, so I turned away, and as I opened the door the current of air caused the wardrobe door to swing wide open.

I stopped and stared. It was full of clothes, good clothes, and one item in particular caught my eye—a gown of deep ruby red that I had seen Miranda wearing.

I went across the room and slammed the door shut. If Miranda was giving things to Sarah, it must be for reasons of her own. I didn't want to know what those reasons were, although I now suspected that Sarah's constant observation, that feeling I had of being spied on, had a basis in reality. Miranda had delegated Sarah to me. Miranda had given me the feeling of being unwanted. Miranda had looked at me with hatred when she heard of my coming marriage to Justin. Everything always came back to Miranda—whom Justin wanted me to befriend, and who was anything but a friend to me. When we were married I would tell him how I felt about his stepmother, but not before.

The other room that surprised me was down a corridor off the first floor. My present bedroom was on this floor, and the one I would share with Justin was at the opposite end, overlooking the front drive. A long corridor ran the full length, with two short ones at either end, like an E without the central branch. The room that puzzled me was in the middle of the short corridor on the north side, and it puzzled me because it was the only room in the house that was locked.

After supper that night I asked Justin about it. We sat as usual in the frilly little salon, and Miranda had gone to bed. She had tactfully adopted this practice since our engagement.

We were sitting before the fire on a small couch, and

Justin's arms were about me. Within a week we would be married and this tormenting hour before we said goodnight would end. I felt happy and content. Justin was stroking my hair and talking desultorily.

"I hear you've been busy, darling, going all over the house, making plans."

"All sorts of plans," I agreed, nestling closer. "But I'm not going to tell you about them yet. I want to surprise you."

"You mustn't be too extravagant. I've told you, I—"

I put my hand over his mouth.

"I know, I know! You've told me that I mustn't spend my money on Knight's Keep, but I *want* to! I've already had our bedroom redecorated—"

"Yes—I've seen it."

"You like it?" I asked eagerly.

"It's beautiful, but I would like any room that I slept in with you. You don't expect a man so much in love as I to care what the walls are like, or the curtains, or the furnishings, do you? Except the bed, of course," he added his lips against my ear.

"Don't!" I cried, half laughing, half trembling.

He moved to the end of the couch.

"Very well—I'll behave." He gave his light-hearted laugh, the one that endeared him to me so much. "Tell me what else you want to alter."

"This room. I'm going to get rid of all these frilly lampshades and things. You won't mind, will you?"

"Why should I? But Miranda will."

"*Miranda?* But it isn't her type of room at all!"

"It is very much her type. She furnished it. She wanted a sitting room down here and chose this one."

"But it's completely out of character!"

"You think so? I wouldn't know. But if you want to do this room over, darling, let her keep all this stuff, won't you?"

"Of course. It can go in her room upstairs. And talking of rooms upstairs, there's one I can't get into."

He lit a cigar. He drew on it and exhaled slowly. "Which one, my love?"

"It's along that corridor at the north end of the first floor, about half way down—"

"Yes?"

"Well—it's locked. I tried the door and I couldn't get in.

It is the only room in the house that is locked. Have you a key?"

"Somewhere."

"May I have it?"

"No, my love, you may not. In any case, I don't know what has happened to it."

"But, Justin—"

"Forget about that room. It is full of nothing but junk— things my father collected on his travels. Miranda stored them there after his death and won't hear of them being disturbed."

"But they'll collect dust. Surely the room must be aired and cleaned occasionally? And why lock it up, if all it contains is junk?"

Justin threw his cigar stub on the fire, put his arms around me, and swung me on to his knee. He was smiling again, his eyes alight and warm.

"Forget about that room," he said again. "No one but Miranda ever goes there. The things may be junk to me, but not to her. She treasures them because they belonged to Matthew. Perhaps one or two of the souvenirs are valuable— I don't know. Maybe that is why she keeps the room locked, but I'm more inclined to think she looks on it as a sort of secret shrine. What does it matter? I'm not going to sit here talking about storerooms and attics and household matters which can very well be left until after we're married. Now kiss me."

His mouth found mine. His kiss was as tender and loving as always, and I forgot about the locked room, and spying Sarah, and Miranda who made me so uneasy, and even the shadow of Dulcie whom he had once loved, for she no longer existed and I knew that my life with Justin Ashford was going to be very, very different from hers.

CHAPTER EIGHTEEN

Justin had his way. We were married quickly and quietly, and it mattered nothing to me that I had none of the traditional white wedding and orange blossoms. Instead, I wore a gown of parchment-colored brocade that I had not yet worn, and because it was an autumn wedding I went to the chapel with a sable cloak over my shoulders. It was Justin's wedding present to me and was truly magnificent, made of perfectly matched skins and reaching to the ground. It must have cost a fortune, for he had ordered it from the best furrier in Canterbury.

I coiled my hair in a coronet on top of my head, surrounding it with a bandeau of ivory moss roses, and I carried an ivory-backed prayer book that my parents had given me at the time of my confirmation.

The simplicity of my wedding made it all the more impressive, for it was far more personal than a lavish affair would have been. I knew that Justin wanted a ceremony in complete contrast to his former wedding, when guests from far and near had crowded to the service and the reception.

There was nothing like that this time. I had no bridesmaid and he had no best man. The vicar of Lympne Church came to officiate, and since I had no relative to give me away I had to fall back on Gavin Rudge to do that.

Miranda sat at the back of the chapel and departed for a month's visit to Hastings afterwards. It was a tactful gesture, for Justin and I were foregoing a honeymoon until the summer, when we planned to sail across to France on the start of a continental tour.

The idea of going straight from our marriage to our home, and of spending our wedding night in our own bedroom instead of a strange one in some hotel, appealed to both of us. It was a beautiful room, with tall mullioned windows from floor to ceiling, and I had had it redecorated in record time, in shades of turquoise and silver, with thick-piled carpets of soft gray and new window drapes of turquoise satin. There was a small boudoir for me opening off the room, and a dressing room for Justin. It was a private world of our own in which no unhappiness could possibly intrude.

Only one thing caused a slight dissension before our marriage. Daniel Firth drove calmly up to the front door one day and asked to see me.

It was shortly before the wedding—a Friday, I remember. I had first arrived at Knight's Keep on a Friday, and the carriage that brought Daniel was the plain black one that had met him at Sandling that day—not the green one in which he had driven me home from Beechwood Close. (*Did he ever have that with him in London*, I wondered.) Every weekend he returned to Kent by that train, and was met by his man at the station, but on this particular day, instead of going straight home, he came to Knight's Keep to see me.

Justin was out. Miranda received him, and her surprise was as great as mine when he asked for me. He was waiting in the long drawing room and when I entered he didn't beat about the bush.

"I wish to speak to Miss Bewleigh alone."

Miranda, who had come to fetch me, raised questioning eyebrows.

I said, "Whatever you have to say can be said in front of Lady Ashford."

"It could, but I would prefer it not to be."

Miranda was looking at him with her strange sloe-eyes, her expression unreadable. She shrugged and said, "The choice is Miss Bewleigh's."

"Then I choose that you should remain. What is it, Dr. Firth?"

"I have a message for you from Dora Smee."

"*Dora!*" My delight was so great that I forgot to be on my dignity. "How did you come to meet her?"

"I called at the house in Long Acre on my way back to my lodgings one evening."

Miranda put in quickly, "And who, may I ask, is Dora Smee?"

"You've heard me talk about her!" I protested. "She was the woman Uncle Silas and I lodged with."

"I remember—a seamstress, I believe."

"A dressmaker," I corrected, "and a very good one." I turned back to the doctor and asked eagerly, "Did she say anything about my letter? Did she receive it safely?"

"She did indeed and that is why I am here. Being unable to read anything except her name, and knowing no one else who could, the poor soul was wondering what was in it. It was lucky I dropped in—I read it for her."

"Unable to read!" Miranda's voice was aghast. "What poor sort of creature is this?"

No one was allowed to belittle Dora before me, and I rounded on Miranda pretty thoroughly. "If you are going to sneer at my friends, please go!"

"Your friends?" she echoed. "I doubt if Justin would approve of his wife having illiterate friends."

I turned my back on her.

"What is Dora's message?" I demanded eagerly.

"That she will come to you as soon as you wish."

"Wonderful! It must be very soon, as quickly as possible!"

It was then that I saw Justin standing in the doorway.

"Who must come as quickly as possible?" he asked pleasantly.

"Dora Smee. I want her, and she has agreed to come."

Justin closed the door quietly, walked across the room, and said, "You wrote to this woman, my love? You offered her employment at Knight's Keep without consulting me?"

A faint chill touched my delight.

"You don't mind, do you, Justin? I asked her to come after my marriage. Surely I can engage a maid for myself then?"

"You have one already."

"Sarah—whom I don't like."

"She has worked here for years. Miranda gave her up, for your sake."

"Then Miranda can have her back. If the choice were mine, she would go. I don't like her."

"One doesn't have to *like* servants, my love. One has to make use of them and see that they work efficiently, that is all."

"Like machines?" I flared. "Well, Sarah is nothing so inhuman, believe me. She's a young woman and very much aware of the fact. She is sullen and unpleasant into the bargain and I will *not* have her as my maid after I am married. I give her back to you, Miranda, with the greatest of pleasure."

Justin said with a laugh, "I do believe you have a stubborn streak!"

"And why not? Would you have me meek and docile? You must take me as I am."

"My sweet, I do, with the utmost delight—but I wish you had told me about this Dora Smee. Employment here is by tradition. For generations my family has engaged staff from the ranks already working here. Sarah's parents and grandparents were at Knight's Keep—"

"As mine were," I said involuntarily. Justin's face went momentarily still and I wondered if he didn't like to be reminded about that. Since my arrival he had not referred again to my mother's family, and I knew that he had only let it be known that he was marrying the granddaughter of a prominent Bishop. This hurt a little, but when I told him so, he had kissed the hurt away.

"My dear Jane," he said now, "I am merely trying to make it clear that an outsider will not be welcomed in the servants' quarters. It would be kinder to this woman to dismiss the idea of bringing her to Knight's Keep. If you don't want Sarah, you can choose another maid from the household staff."

"I want Dora, and no one else."

Justin then explained patiently that the Keep was completely staffed and the payroll full.

"I shall engage her myself and pay her wages myself," I insisted. "You cannot object to that! What is more, I shall decide which room she shall occupy and see that it is comfortable. If Sarah can be favored, so can Dora."

"Sarah?" he said a little sharply. "In what way is Sarah favored?"

"You are probably unaware that she is the only maid here who has her own room, with comforts none of the other servants enjoy, but I am sure Miranda knows." I nearly added that Sarah had a wardrobe full of clothes that Miranda herself had provided, but refrained.

"She is so favored because she has been my personal maid since Matthew brought me to the Keep," Miranda said calmly, "but how did you know she has her own room?"

Justin laughed. "My dear Stepmother, I am marrying the most efficient young woman. She has already gone all over the house, carrying out a thorough inspection and planning improvements. Getting back to this Dora Smee," he finished, "just where does Daniel come in?"

"I am bringing her here. I have promised to accompany her on the train and deliver her safely to Miss Bewleigh." Daniel bowed to me. "Good day to you. Please let me know the date you want Mrs. Smee to arrive."

Justin went with him to the front door. I heard him saying amiably, "This is kind of you, Daniel. Don't think I fail to appreciate it. If having Dora Smee here makes my Jane happy, then she is most welcome as far as I am concerned. I only hope the servants will welcome her too."

We were married on a Monday, and the day dawned fine and clear. I lay in bed late, for the ceremony was to take place in the afternoon. Sarah brought me a tray late in the morning, but I had been awake long before that—awake and too excited to think of food, or even to ring for tea. I had let the household believe I was asleep, for I was anxious to be alone. I felt as every bride must feel on her wedding morning, tremulous with excitement, as if standing on the brink of a new horizon, or a threshold she longs to cross.

Sarah drew back my curtains and let in the morning sun. Her manner towards me had changed since the announcement of my engagement. She was respectful now—or as respectful as it was possible for a girl of her nature to be. The surface politeness was there, but what lay beneath? The old, smoldering resentment—of that I was sure.

She put a bed-jacket around my shoulders and settled the tray on my lap. As usual I disliked her near me, and, as usual, she walked out of the room swinging her hips in that suggestive way of hers, a way which must have attracted many a man. Sarah's sexual awareness was blatant.

I was glad when she had gone, and that I should have to put up with her no longer. Until Dora arrived I could well look after myself.

When it was time for me to dress, Miranda tapped on my door.

"I told Sarah not to bother you. I knew you wouldn't want her."

"That was kind of you, Miranda."

"May I help you?" There was almost a touch of diffidence in her voice, and certainly there was a touch of sadness. For the first time since we had met I was able to hold out my hands to her without fear of rejection.

"Only by being my friend," I said impulsively. "By trying to like me—"

She took my hands, but she didn't answer. She seemed to be battling with some emotion.

I said impulsively, "You know that Knight's Keep will always be your home, don't you?"

"Oh, yes—Justin has told me that."

"Then what are you afraid of?"

As unpredictable as ever, she flung back, "Afraid? *Me*—afraid? I am afraid of nothing, let me tell you. Nothing! Life has taught me not to be."

She dropped my hands, and the sense of communication between us snapped. Whenever I was remotely in touch with Miranda, a shutter slammed between us.

"I'm sorry," she said brightly. "This is your wedding day and nothing must spoil it!"

"I don't think anything could. I am much too happy to let it. Thank you for your offer of help, but—"

"But you don't need me. Not me, nor Sarah, nor anyone. Only Justin. Well," she said, moving to the door, "he will be yours soon enough. Are you sure you can cope with all those buttons?"

"Quite sure, thank you. I've not only fastened endless buttons in my time, I have also sewn them on."

"If you take my advice, you won't remind Justin of that. You are marrying a man of title. You will bear that title yourself, remember. You don't want to shame him, do you?"

I didn't know if she was taunting me, or simply warning me—the enigmatic look was back on her face and she was again unfathomable.

"I shall never shame him," I told her.

She smiled a little.

"In *that* gown you certainly won't. Nor in those magnificent sables. Justin is a most adoring bridegroom, I must say. What does it feel like to be marrying a man so rich?"

"I should feel just the same were he poor," I said honestly.

"I actually believe you would." She closed the door softly behind her.

A shadow seemed to have been cast on the day, but I refused to heed it. I lingered over my toilet, and knew when I was ready that I had made myself as lovely as possible. The parchment color of the gown and the bandeau of ivory roses encircling my hair—roses I had chosen from the hothouses of Knight's Keep—subtly emphasized my blondeness.

Justin was waiting at the foot of the stairs. He took one look at me, then lifted my hand and kissed it.

Neither of us spoke as we walked through the grounds to the old family chapel. The walls were crumbling and there was a smell of disuse about it, which wasn't surprising since the place had been neglected for years. It had been cleaned and aired occasionally, but even so the mustiness of centuries remained.

And it was cold. So cold that I drew my sable cloak about me and Justin put his arm around my shoulders in concern.

"My darling, you're shivering!"

Gavin Rudge was waiting for us. He explained that the old stove used for heating the chapel had completely rusted and would no longer function, but he had placed braziers at strategic points and kept them alight throughout the night, and certainly, as we reached the nave, the first chilling impact had gone. I was able to remove my cloak and stand like a bride before the altar. It was a tiny altar, and someone had placed flowers on it, and in the flickering candle flames the desolate chapel assumed a certain beauty, as if brief life had been infused into it after years of death.

The service was short, but moving. My wedding ring was an Ashford heirloom, rather heavy and a little too big, but beautiful. As I walked back down the aisle with my hand on my husband's arm, I could feel the weight of that ring on my finger.

Miranda kissed me. On my cheek, of course, and briefly. Gavin Rudge stooped above my hand, and wished me happiness. Justin was proud and smiling, a triumphant groom. We all walked back to the house, and the vicar came with us. Our health was drunk, but there was no feasting. Justin and I were to have a bridal supper alone upstairs.

The vicar made a fatherly speech, and wished us well, and said what an honor it had been to join us in Holy wedlock, and drank yet another glass of champagne without any persuasion at all, and after that became so gay that Gavin offered to drive him home. I felt that Gavin was glad of the opportunity to leave, for Justin's impatience to be alone with me was obvious. After that, the coachman brought around the carriage to take Miranda off to Hastings, and when she had gone Justin had his wish. We were alone at Knight's Keep: husband and wife at last.

The light was a thin white line slicing the curtains. Like the white edge of a cloud, I thought through mists of pain. Like the pale emergence of the sky out of darkness. Like my consciousness, returning to reality from the stunned recesses of shock that had converged and drowned it.

Very carefully, I moved. I had been unable to for a long time. For hours I had lain there, exhausted and battered and spent, racked by violence I had never imagined or dreamed of—the violence of a man carried away by passion.

I had known that sex could be tempestuous, and love demanding. I had not expected it to be so brutal that it left a woman barely conscious at the end. And the end had been long in coming.

Beside me, Justin slept. I had not slept at all, but lain in a state of semi-consciousness through which pain was an un-receding tide. He had spared me nothing. He had taken me ferociously, and for such ferocity I had been totally unprepared.

There had been no tenderness, no gentle approach, no wooing, no love-play to awaken a bride's response. There had been no softness, no kindness, no wonderful fulfilment. Only unleased passion which had in it nothing but wild and insatiable desire.

There had been other things, too. Things which had bewildered and stunned me. Things I had not known a man could do to a woman. But my husband had done them to me.

Slowly, softly, I pushed away the bedclothes. My body was naked and the marks of his attack were like weals left by a savage. Was this love? Could anything that called itself love leave a bride's body so abused?

I covered myself and lay still again. Turning my head slowly, I looked at him. In sleep his handsome face was calm and reposed and gentle, the face of the man I loved.

I closed my eyes, and darkness descended mercifully.

I must have slept for a long time, the deep sleep of exhaustion, for when I wakened I knew at once that the morning was far advanced. We had come to bed early and it had been dawn before a merciful oblivion had overtaken me. Now that I emerged I was calmer, but shock lingered and the memory of certain things leapt back into my consciousness so that I shuddered.

"Don't—don't, my darling!"

The voice was Justin's. It was stricken and remorseful. He was sitting beside me on the bed, wearing a robe with gold dragons embroidered all over it. I remembered it well for he had been wearing it when he came towards me from his dressing-room—how many hours ago? My mind went searching back to the day before, to the moment when we had been left alone and he had lifted me and carried me upstairs . . .

I drew away instinctively, and he reached towards me with a gesture that was at once pitiful and beseeching.

"Dearest—forgive me. Forgive me, please."

I lay still, knowing there was now no reason to shrink from him, for he was himself again. Quiet and gentle and kind.

"Was that *love*?" I demanded, and pushed back the bedclothes, and let him look at me.

He closed his eyes, and I saw a spasm of pain cross his face.

"Yes," he said at last. "You won't believe it, but that was love. I've been nearly demented with longing for you ever since we met. You can't blame me. You must understand."

I said with an effort, "You must make me understand."

"You are young—so young!"

"I am old enough to be married, so make me understand."

"Now you are hating me," he said in a low voice.

"No, not hating you. Just bewildered and stunned and unbelieving. So make me understand," I repeated yet again.

He said harshly, "I'm not an inexperienced boy who doesn't know how to bed a woman, but I'm not a sadist, either. A passionate man if you like, and one who has been denied a woman for longer than he can happily endure. I thought I had become accustomed to living like a monk, until you came along. Do you realise how much I've been wanting to make love to you? Being polite to you, talking to you, looking at you, *wanting* you—and never being alone with you! Night after night Miranda was there, watching us secretly, guessing how I felt, and enjoying keeping us apart—"

"Sometimes she left us alone, after we were engaged."

"Do you think I'd have taken you furtively, like a servant girl? *This* was what I wanted—to be man and wife. You're not a slut to be seduced on a couch."

He touched my cheek with his long fingers.

"Don't hate me," he said humbly. "Try to understand how a man like me feels when he suppresses every normal instinct."

"Normal?" I echoed.

"You excited me too much. Dulcie never excited me as you do. She was cold and indifferent and unresponsive. We ceased to be lovers very quickly and since then I've made love to no woman. Then you came along, so warm and alive that I wanted you more than I've ever wanted any woman. I rushed our wedding because I couldn't endure the waiting. I meant to be patient and to woo you gently, but it was impossible, impossible . . ."

He buried his face in my shoulder. I couldn't bear to see a man so ashamed. I put my arm about him, and we lay for a long time, not speaking. I had to understand. I did understand. But not everything.

It didn't happen again. No one could have been more kind than my husband during the rest of our honeymoon month. After that first night, it was a true honeymoon. He left estate affairs entirely to Gavin, and spent every moment with me, driving about the countryside, showing me the county, letting me choose a new place to visit each day—or staying at home together like husband and wife. His solicitude helped me to forget the shock of our wedding night, and the memory of it receded as my bruises faded and the marks on my breasts disappeared.

He was considerate too, and made no physical approach until I was ready for it again. I slept peacefully in his arms at night, and then slowly he initiated me into the ways of love, and because I was young and healthy, my body responded. I gave and received delight.

But sometimes I sensed suppressed violence, like a dangerous undercurrent from which I shrank, and at such moments a barrier would come between us until he broke it down with his ardour. Then I would love him as before, and the shadow would disappear, and only later would I feel that despite the intimacy of our bodies I had been making love to a stranger, and that even at the peak of our consummation he had been mentally apart from me. And then I would be frightened, and not know why, and not knowing why was the worst part of all.

CHAPTER NINETEEN

It was wonderful to see Dora again. I drove to Sandling to meet her. I now had my own trap and Justin had taught me how to handle it. It was an elegant little affair which had once belonged to his mother, but Justin had had it remodeled for me. All the carriages at Knight's Keep were well maintained and smartly turned out, and all had recently been repainted and overhauled—part of their annual refurbishing.

My trap bore the Ashford crest on either side and was drawn by a pair of grays. I was very proud of my turn-out, and Justin told me that not only did I look well at the reins, but I handled them well, too.

Perhaps I wanted to show off a little, and for that reason

drove to the station. Or perhaps I didn't want Daniel Firth arriving on our doorstep again. Whatever the reason, I was there, and my heart leaped at the sight of Dora's spritely figure bounding along beside Daniel Firth over the footbridge.

She had dressed herself up for the occasion. Her costume was vivid scarlet, adorned with a black feather boa. She had given her hair a bright henna rinse, an unfortunate combination with her pillar-box red costume, and perched on top of her head was an enormous black hat with floating black ostrich feathers. She wore two-toned boots in black and cream, with high black heels, and the whole outfit was capped by a long-handled cream umbrella with an enormous black frill around the top.

She was a startling figure, but a welcome one. Before I went running to meet her I noticed the broad smile on Daniel Firth's face. She had his undivided attention, and was chattering nineteen to the dozen. Something told me she had done so the whole way, not in the least awed by him, and that he had thoroughly enjoyed himself. He seemed to be doing so still.

I flung my arms around her, and only at that moment did I realize how much I had missed her. She was part of a life I had no desire to forget; part of my childhood and my girlhood; she had known my parents, and Uncle Silas; my happiness and my sorrows. She was almost a part of me.

As I embraced her, I saw Daniel Firth watching. There was an expression in his eyes I would never have expected to see there: compassion and friendliness mixed with an understanding that was quite out of character with such a man.

Dora held me at arm's length and said loudly, "Let me look at you, miss! My, but I've missed you, that I 'ave! Blimey, I can't call you miss any more can I? What is it now? Your lidyship?"

"Call me anything you like!" I cried. "I shall always be the same person to you, as you are to me."

"I'll settle for ma'am," she said. "I useter take you to the zoo when you were a little 'un, and wipe your nose when you needed it, so you can't go all uppish on me now, that you can't!"

Daniel Firth laughed, and so did I.

"Has she chattered like this all the way?" I asked.

"Non-stop!"

"Well, sir, you 'aven't minded, 'ave you? Leastways, you never told me to shut up."

"I would never tell a lady to shut up," he answered solemnly.

"'Ark at 'im!" said Dora. "Well, thanks for looking after me, sir. You're a gent, that's wot."

Daniel Firth put her luggage—one shabby grip—into the trap, removed his hat, and bowed over her hand.

"The pleasure has been mine, believe me."

He handed her into the trap and as she settled herself, spreading her skirts and patting the upholstery and forgetting all about us in her excitement, the doctor turned to me and said, "I am only sorry about one thing."

"And what is that?"

"That by meeting Mrs. Smee you have cheated me of the opportunity to congratulate your husband."

"Then you may congratulate me, instead."

"On what? On gaining a title? I can't believe that sort of thing means much to you."

"On marrying the man I love," I answered.

It must have been my fancy that saw a fleeting pity in his eyes.

"Indeed I wish you every happiness—but congratulations, no. Don't expect those from *me*."

"I would hardly have expected even your good wishes, doctor."

"So you think as little as that of me? I suppose it's inevitable. The new wife of Justin Ashford could hardly be expected to feel goodwill towards his enemy."

"You can cease to be his enemy," I said impulsively.

"And how?"

"By retracting everything. Being proved wrong isn't enough. My husband bears you no malice, but he is a proud man. I know that your suspicions still hurt him." Without thinking, I put my hand on his sleeve in a gesture of pleading.

"And how do you want me to retract? In public, on my bended knees, doing penance?" He shrugged my hand aside.

I turned on my heel, climbed into the trap, and picked up the reins. I saw Dora's sharp eyes on me and knew that she had noticed my flaming cheeks. I flicked the horses and we drove away quickly. I didn't look back, but Dora did. She waved the end of her black feather boa merrily, and I knew that Daniel Firth was waving goodbye in return.

"And wot was all that about—ma'am?"

"All what?" I answered evasively.

"That carry-on with the doctor. Looked to me like a flamin' row!"

I stared straight ahead, saying nothing. Dora shrugged.

"All right, miss—sorry, ma'am!—I'll mind me own business. Gotta keep me place now, I 'spose."

"Don't talk like that, Dora. You have always been my friend and always will be. It's just that there are things I don't want to talk about."

"To do with the doctor? But 'e's a gent, dear. A real gent. I can tell wot a bloke's like soon as I meet 'im, so you can take it from me."

How little she knew, I thought wryly. But I said no more. Daniel Firth had been kind to her and I had no desire to belittle him in her eyes.

"My love, she's a *horror!*"

"She is nothing of the sort! She's a dear, kind woman."

"With Pearly Queen written all over her! I can just see her dancing on Hampstead Heath on a Bank Holiday! Well, one thing is certain—she won't stay here for long. She'll be hurrying back to her winkle barrow in Stepney as fast as those dreadful boots will carry her—heaven be praised."

Justin's reaction to Dora had shocked me. I hadn't expected him to be bowled over by her, but nor had I expected him to recoil.

He had seen us driving through the main gates. He had also seen the Lodge Keeper's reaction to Dora, but whereas it had amused me, it had shamed Justin.

"If you *had* to bring such a creature here, the very least you could have done was to drop her at the servants' entrance and leave her to find her own way to the kitchen quarters."

"A half-mile walk up the side drive, carrying a heavy grip! I'd do no such thing. Dora has been my friend since my childhood."

Justin's mouth tightened.

"You may have had some unfortunate friends in your childhood, my love, but let me make it absolutely clear that my wife doesn't associate with skivvies, nor count them among her friends. Driving to the station to meet this woman was undignified and unnecessary. There are wagonettes for the servants to travel in. All you had to do was send one to the station. I see I must begin to educate you, and when Miranda returns I will ask her to initiate you into the kind of behavior expected in Society."

I blazed, "You'll do no such thing! You found no fault with my behavior when I was here as your guest!"

"Ah—but you didn't bring your cockney friends to keep you company."

I couldn't really believe this was happening. Justin and I were quarreling, and doing it violently. I was now so angry that nothing would stop me.

"I won't allow you or anyone to be unkind to Dora! And, what's more, she never lived in Stepney, nor kept a barrow, and as far as I know she never ate a winkle in her life, and even if she did it would make no difference to me. And if the 'education' you want to inflict on me is how to look down on people less fortunate than I, I'll have none of it! I was never a snob."

"My sweet, you were never in a position to be."

The difference between Justin's anger and mine was that mine was hot and strong and his was cold and smooth. Like ice.

"I could hate you for that!" I cried.

He laughed and tried to take me in his arms.

"My darling Jane, you could never hate me. You adore me, and you know it. You are besotted and bemused by me. All I have to do is make love to you, and you forgive me anything—and always will."

I pushed him aside. "Not always. Even you could go too far!"

The self-confident smile on his face was replaced by a frown of displeasure. "You must never do that again—push me aside, I mean."

"Then don't anger me! Don't cast slurs on my friends. Dora's been a friend all my life, and a very great one when in need."

"You are not in need now."

To my own astonishment as much as his I answered swiftly, "But I am! I need a friend here very badly."

Justin's surprise overcame his anger. He protested in concern, "But you have me!"

"You won't always be here. Not when this month is over."

"In my absence you'll have Miranda."

"Miranda! She is no friend."

"What do you mean?" He looked at me with sharp speculation. "What makes you think Miranda isn't your friend?"

"Instinct, if you like, but mainly it is something in her attitude to me."

"Her attitude has been friendly right from the start. She welcomed you."

"Only on the surface. Underneath, she didn't. She doesn't want me at Knight's Keep—and nor does that maid of hers, Sarah."

"You're talking nonsense, my dear."

"I hope I am."

He put his arms about me, and this time I didn't resist. I was glad to feel them there. I wanted reassurance, comfort, and more than all a feeling of safety.

"You're fanciful, my sweet. I didn't realize you were so imaginative." He shook me fondly. "Stop all this nonsense about needing a friend. The whole county has welcomed you—"

"I haven't met the whole county yet."

That was true. Since our marriage Justin had taken me calling upon a few local families, even to places as far distant as Tenterden and Ashford and Romney, and the few people I had met, I liked. I felt they liked me in return, but brief acquaintanceship didn't make a friend.

Justin argued reasonably, "My darling, what time have we had—or, more truthfully, how have we spent it? Making love, or just being together. I didn't know you were wanting to admit the outside world yet. When Miranda returns we'll begin to entertain at Knight's Keep."

"Why when Miranda returns?" I demanded indignantly. "Do you think I don't know how to act as hostess? If so, you are mistaken. My mother had to entertain a lot of parishioners—some were rich, believe it or not. I learned from her. Miranda can teach me nothing."

I tried to withdraw, but he wouldn't release me.

"And what has angered you now?"

The patience in his voice didn't lessen my resentment one bit.

"This harping on Miranda! The suggestion that I have a lot to learn from her! What, pray? How to be sly and evasive, how to win over the maids with gifts of clothes so that they will be on *my* side?"

All Justin's anger had gone. Now he looked merely puzzled and concerned.

"Jane, my love, I don't know what you are talking about."

"I'm talking about Miranda—your stepmother, who doesn't want me here. I doubt if she would want any other woman to be mistress here. She has put on a front, and wished us well, and tactfully withdrawn—but for how long? How is she going to behave when she returns? I don't trust her."

"I can see that, but much as I love you, my darling, I'm going to ask you to end this nonsense."

"It isn't nonsense! Go upstairs and take a look at Sarah's wardrobe—it is full of clothes no housemaid could afford, and some of them are Miranda's. Or were."

"The domestic staff always receive our cast-off clothes."

"*When* they are cast-offs, yes, but not before."

"What Miranda does with her clothes is no concern of yours or mine," he said firmly.

"That puts me in my place," I answered lightly. "Very well, I accept the rebuff, but not the suggestion that I've a lot to learn from her. I suppose you think that with my background the social graces are beyond me. You shall see."

He laughed and hugged me. "You're an idiot, but an adorable one. When I'm in a temper, you must take no notice of the things I say."

"Do you often get in tempers like that?"

"Only when I'm goaded."

"And bringing poor Dora here, goaded you? I can't see why. She is staying, you know. I insist on that."

"Now *I* accept the rebuff! You're a stubborn little witch, my Jane, and as usual I can refuse you nothing. But it's a good thing you married me—a girl like you needs firm handling and someone firm to do it."

"Like yourself, for instance?"

"That's right."

We kissed and made up. I was appalled to think that we had quarreled so early in our married life.

"My father sometimes called me a firebrand," I admitted guiltily.

"Your father was right! He'd have been glad to know you have a husband to keep you in order now and handle your affairs. And talking of your affairs, you mustn't rebel against a little guidance from me. It is my job to take care of you and advise you."

"Advise me on what?"

"On how to use your fortune, for one thing. I fear you are frittering it away, my love. I've noticed the things you've had done to the house—all very charming and acceptable, but not *all* necessary. We can do better things with your money."

"Such as?" I snuggled up to him and kissed the end of his nose.

"Don't distract me!"

"I want to distract you."

He put me aside, laughing but firm.

"All right," I said. "Let's be businesslike. Such as?"

"Such as enlarging the estate, buying more land—"

"Buying more! But surely we've enough? Gavin tells me that the park alone is well over a hundred acres. Then there's the home farm—acres and acres more! Not to mention the house and the grounds."

"It isn't enough," he answered shortly. "Less than fifty years ago the Ashford family owned all the land as far as Elam. My ambition is not only to get it back, but to extend until we own the whole of the Elam valley. *Then* the name of Ashford will be something to reckon with again! Come here—" He led me towards the window and thrust aside the heavy drapes impatiently. "As far as the eye can see, and far beyond, once belonged to us—and could again! Times are bad and are going to be worse. There's many a landowner will be glad to sell—at my price."

I asked uneasily, "What do you mean—'at your price?' Not that you would underpay them?"

He laughed and pinched my cheek. "That shows how little you know about business, my love."

"Perhaps, but I'd have no part in unfair dealing."

"I'm not asking you to. Financial affairs are a man's territory. They are not and never will be a woman's."

"So you don't want me to spend more money on the house. How about outside?"

"That depends on what you want to do outside."

"There's a sunken garden, terribly neglected. I'd like to restore it. It has an arbor with a view of the sea. It would be nice to sit there on a summer's day."

"Oh, that. Yes, you can have the place cleaned up, if you wish."

I smiled secretly. "As a matter of fact, I've already started.

Mr. Claythorne won't be pleased when he receives the bills."

"Claythorne? Why should he receive the bills?"

"Because he couldn't increase the advance I asked for?"

"He couldn't what?"

"Wouldn't, then. He said it would be difficult until my affairs were settled." I shrugged. "I was annoyed, which was silly of me I suppose, so I just went ahead and ordered what I wanted and had the bills sent to him. They can all be met in January."

"Why January?"

"Because everything will be concluded then."

"You mean he hasn't settled your affairs yet!"

"These things take time, he says. He is investing the capital, to make it secure. The interest will be ample for my needs. In the New Year everything will be mine, and if I want to draw on the capital at any time he will arrange it for me."

"Providing he approves of its use?"

"I suppose so. He won't let me spend it unwisely, which is a good thing because never having had any money, I've no head for figures! Invested this way, the principal will be there for me to leave to my descendants. I laughed when he talked of my having descendants, because at that time I didn't even think I'd get married, and now, before the New Year is even up, I am not only married, but rich!"

I put my arms about my husband. He embraced me in return, but then said something that took my breath away.

"The one thing I am thankful for is that Silas left his money to you and not to Daniel Firth."

"*Daniel Firth!* But why he?"

"My father used to say that Silas was fond of the boy because he had never had a son of his own, and that Daniel used to curry favor with my uncle, with an eye to the future. Of course, it was all nonsense. Daniel was too young to think of the future then."

I asked against my will, "But when he grew up?"

Justin shrugged.

"Silas had gone out of our lives by then, so I'm quite sure Daniel had forgotten him. In any case, the promises which my father declared Silas had made were probably incorrect. As you may have gathered by now, my father was a bit of a rake—a romancer and even a reprobate in some ways. And he never liked Silas. They were always quarreling."

"But these promises—promises to whom?"

Justin dismissed the matter indifferently.

"Nothing but the wildest notions, my love, and as I said, probably untrue. You and your parents were the only people in the world who looked after Silas when he was lost and alone, and you deserve to have everything. That was the way he wanted it."

"But not always? Not years ago, when Daniel was young and Silas looked on him as a son?"

"My dear Jane, all that is ancient history and for all I know it was merely one of my father's outlandish tales. He was always suspicious of Silas—at any rate, he disliked him. The feeling was mutual, and in one of their quarrels Silas hinted that he intended to leave everything out of the family. The Firths were his closest friends in those days. When Daniel's parents died he sold their home on Blackhouse Hill and bought Beechwood Close. My father said it was the nearest he would ever get to owning Silas's estate after all, but I have to admit that my father had a caustic tongue at times."

I was thoughtful. I didn't believe that Daniel Firth was the sort to curry favor with anyone, he was too downright and must have been the same as a boy, but without doubt he was the sort to remember things. The way he had stuck to his story about Justin proved that—*and* how malicious he could be. Wouldn't it be characteristic of such a man to remember promises made to him in boyhood, and wouldn't a man so relentless in purpose sweep aside obstacles such as old men who tiresomely refused to die, old men without dependents who would never be expected to bequeath everything to some unknown girl from a poor London district? If Daniel's parents had been Silas's close friends, it would have been easy enough for him to learn what Silas's investments were, and to have kept one eye on the stock market and another on the future; easy enough for a man so tenacious to trace Silas's whereabouts, to watch and to wait and then to strike; easy enough to follow him in those foggy London streets, run him down with that hateful carriage, and then appear on the scene full of concern, to check on his victim's death.

And what of me? He had heard me call the old man "uncle" that night—and remembered it. The term would have suggested a fairly intimate relationship and possibly a dangerous one as far as his own interests were concerned. And while he watched and waited, he could somehow have found out that Silas had switched his promise from himself to me. I didn't underestimate Daniel Firth. The man was clever and would know how to go about these things, deviously learning all he wanted to learn.

Suddenly I felt sick. I was remembering a cab wrecking mine on my way to the solicitor's office. A hired assassin? If I had never got there, I would never have come into my inheritance.

But I was not killed and I did get there—and on the way back a sinister figure had tried to catch up with me in dark and deserted streets.

I tried to clutch at logic, telling myself that I was letting my imagination run away with me. If anything *had* happened to me, surely Justin, being Silas's next of kin, would have inherited?

Not if there had been a previous will, leaving everything to someone he once regarded as a son.

And the figure hiding in the shadows of the cedar tree on the night of my arrival—had that been Daniel Firth, awaiting his chance?

But he had his chance in the train. We had been entirely alone then. I had been completely at his mercy as we rushed through the darkened tunnel.

The answer to that was obvious. There had been witnesses at Charing Cross, people who had seen him get into my carriage and steam out of the station alone with me—one of whom was Dora, who had met him before and obviously recognized him.

Suddenly I clung to Justin. "Hold me close," I begged. "Hold me close!"

"My darling," he said in concern, "what is the matter? What has frightened you?"

His nearness quieted me. I was safe now; safely married to Justin. I had a husband to protect me, and anyone desiring my death had left it too late, for whatever I had would now go to Justin—not automatically once the new law came into force, but because at the earliest opportunity I would will it to him. I determined to write to Mr. Claythorne tomorrow and make sure.

Justin stooped and kissed me. Normally I forgot everything when he did that but now, unbidden, a picture floated through my mind—the picture of a cloaked woman meeting a man in the dead of night, out there in the shadowy garden.

Now I was convinced that the man had been Daniel Firth, so his assignation would not have been with one of the servants. Whatever he was, I knew he wasn't the type of man to carry on with a girl like Sarah. So the woman could only have been Miranda, and her professed dislike of him merely a cover-up for an association she did not want Justin or anyone to know about.

The inference was frightening, suggesting that these two were in league in some way. I had always mistrusted Miranda —now I thoroughly mistrusted them both. If Daniel Firth was my enemy, so was she—his ally, right here in this house.

CHAPTER TWENTY

My riding habit was delivered from Canterbury the day of Miranda's return. It fitted perfectly and I looked well in it. I primped before a mirror, turning around and around for Justin's benefit.

"You like it?" I asked gaily. "Don't I look grand?"

"Very grand, my love."

But he wasn't looking. He seemed remote, lost in thoughts of his own. I watched anxiously. This mood had lasted for days; longer than any before. In the short time we had been married I had learned that besides having a passionate man for a husband, I sometimes had a moody one. Occasionally it worried me, but the moods usually passed so quickly and his light-heartedness and affection in between were so welcome that they overcame my bewilderment.

I put the hard hat back in its leather box, changed out of the habit, and hung it away. When I came out of my boudoir, Justin had gone. A few minutes later I saw him riding away from the house. He was absent a long time and when he returned his humor was unchanged.

He told me he had ridden over to the Elam Valley.

It was a clear, sunny day. "The valley must have looked very beautiful," I said.

"Too beautiful!" His voice was harsh. "It angered me to think of my father allowing it to be sliced up and sold piecemeal."

"Why did he do that?" I asked, surprised.

"Why does anyone sell anything? Because they want money. My father was an extravagant man; a man with a wanderlust. Traveling is an expensive pastime, especially when done in style, the way he did it. And he could pull up his roots easily because they never went down so deep as mine. But for his extravagance, our estate would be much larger than it is."

I still couldn't understand Justin's desire to expand, but it was obviously a long-cherished dream.

"We have so much," I said. "Can't you be content?"

He didn't answer. I saw his glance wander through the window to the vast expanse of the park, but I knew that he was looking beyond that, like a king searching for a lost kingdom.

I tried again.

"We have a wonderful home, Justin, and to me the estate seems big enough. You maintain it well. When I first came I noticed how hard you'd been working on the place. Even if your father did have a wanderlust, he left Knight's Keep to you and the money to maintain it. Be grateful to him for that."

He gave his sudden, light-hearted smile. "I am grateful for more—for you, my sweet. No man could have a lovelier wife, nor a more sensible one. You bring me down to earth when my dreams threaten to carry me away." He reached for my hand, and squeezed it. "Content? Of course, I'm content!"

Miranda returned late that afternoon. She looked well and said the change had done her good. "It's wonderful to be home!" she declared.

But with her return Knight's Keep seemed less like home to me. There were three of us now, no longer two. After dinner we retired as usual to the frilly salon, and Miranda picked up her needlepoint from the stool where she always left it, and we all sat around the fire. I wondered how I could raise the question of her having a sitting room of her own upstairs. I should have coped with the problem before, of course. I should have removed all this furniture and installed it elsewhere, and then she would have found the whole situation changed on her return. But there had been no time. Besides, I had had the idea of letting her choose which room she would have.

At ten-thirty, as always, tea was brought in. She put down her needlepoint and reached automatically for the silver pot. I was too late to forestall her, and since Justin didn't seem to notice, there was nothing I could do but let her pour, and accept the cup she handed to me, just as if I were still a guest and she still mistress here.

Suddenly she said, "That little table has been moved. I always keep it beneath the window."

"I moved it the other day. I found it useful to put the tea tray on, close to the fire." As she opened her mouth to protest, I hurried on, "I intended to refurnish this room after you've decided which one you would like."

"I don't understand, dear."

She was smiling, but frowning too in a puzzled sort of way, so that my task was made all the more difficult.

"We thought—that is, I thought—you would like to have a sitting room of your own again. . . ."

"But I have one already. This one. I have no desire to change." She looked from one to the other of us. Justin was intent on his cigar, and her glance returned to me.

"*You* thought?" she said softly. "Well now, that was very kind of you, Jane dear, but I would hate to sit alone in some upstairs room day after day. Was that what you had in mind? But not Justin—I'm sure it wasn't in *his* mind, because, after all, I am his stepmother, and one of the family. And this is my home, isn't it? Justin assured me that it always would be."

"Of course—"

"Then that's settled!" She smiled and held out her hand for my cup. "More tea, dear?"

"No—no, thank you—"

She took Justin's cup and refilled it, handling the heavy silver teapot with her customary grace. Ridiculously, I wanted to cry. I felt shut out, an intruder who had tried to usurp Miranda's place. I glanced across at my husband for reassurance, but he was leaning back in his chair, blandly smoking, totally unaware of any undercurrent and certainly of my distress.

"And as for moving this furniture to another room," Miranda continued, "it just wouldn't be suitable for any other."

She added hastily, "Of course, I realize it was a sweet

thought on your part, but believe me, I'm quite happy for us all to share this room, as before."

And everything else went on as before, except that Justin and I now went to bed together, and that Miranda taught me to ride. Every day she had me out in the paddock, going through my paces, and whether I enjoyed it or not made no difference. It seemed that riding was a necessary accomplishment for a countrywoman, and an essential for the wife of the master of Knight's Keep.

"You'll soon be able to go out with the Hunt," Miranda said encouragingly after my first long ride in the park. "I won't say you'll ever make a great horsewoman, but you ought to be able to follow the Field."

"I don't want to make a great horsewoman and I don't want to go out with the Hunt. Blood sports have no appeal for me."

I spoke a little sharply, but Miranda didn't mind. She was a very patient teacher. Even when I became frustrated to the point of anger, she just went on calmly teaching me, so that I always finished up feeling ashamed, and tried harder to make up for my rebellion. By the time Christmas came, I was just able to stay in the saddle at a canter. A great horsewoman? I would never make a horsewoman at all!

Justin watched my progress with a critical eye. One day he said, "You must start taking her over the jumps, Miranda."

"No, thank you!" I cried. "A nice gentle trot will satisfy my ambitions!"

"But not mine, my love. Ashford women have always been good in the saddle."

I swept indoors, biting my lips to keep back the tears. These riding lessons were becoming an endurance test, and Justin's determination that I should master them only increased my tension. I was anxious to please him, but inwardly rebellious, and when I watched the pair of them gallop neck and neck across the park, I felt worse. There was a bond between these two, the bond of mutual tastes and background. They belonged to Knight's Keep, and I did not—yet.

But Christmas was enjoyable. We had a tree for the estate children, and a party in the great hall, and I stood beside Justin and handed out the presents as he took them from the branches, and then we joined in the games, and later I saw my husband present braces of pheasants to his workers, and Christmas boxes to the servants, but despite all this unbending he still seemed like a lofty chieftain mixing with the peasants.

The thought shamed me. He was a good and generous employer and it was evident that both the household staff and the estate workers thought so too. The women bobbed curtsies and the men touched their forelocks, and I could see that each and every one of them respected him. They were even a little awed by him—all except Sarah, who accepted her Christmas box with the merest bob of the knee and a self-confident smile which, fortunately, Justin didn't notice. I was glad of that in one way, but not in another. The touch of insolence wouldn't have pleased him, but it would have proved that I was right about her. He had pooh-poohed my ideas about Sarah. If he had paused to take a look at her, he would have seen that I was right, but he was unaware of her as a person, as he was of all the domestic staff. "Servants, my dear, are there to serve us—not to be noticed." He had said that many times.

Dora hadn't been at the Keep long enough to qualify for a Christmas box, but I was determined that she shouldn't be left out. I put an envelope with her name on it along with the rest, containing the usual money. It came last in the line because she was the last to be employed, and when Justin picked it up I saw his displeasure. All he could do was hand it to her, for she stood there before him, perky as ever. She bobbed a curtsy, and said, "Thank you, m'lord," just like the rest, but there was no subservience in her manner, and I knew why. They had been antagonistic since the day they met, but much as this distressed me, I could do nothing about it, except see that Dora kept out of his way, and I had a strong suspicion that she did so of her own accord.

But I was more glad than ever that she had come to Knight's Keep. It was good to talk to her occasionally, good to feel that I had a friend to turn to when Justin was not around. He was an attentive husband, but estate affairs took him away for hours at a time, and during those hours, apart from the daily riding lessons, I began to avoid Miranda, going for solitary walks as before, and visiting the sunken gardens daily to see what progress was being made.

Winter was merging into spring when the garden finally began to take shape. The last job of all was being tackled—

stripping tangled ivy from the stone walls of the little arbor. It was tough ivy and years of growth clung there, but one day the stones were finally revealed, gray and mossy, but beautiful in their age.

Late that afternoon, the head gardener came to report to me. "That danged ivy be all cleared away, m'lady, and a right pretty little arbor it is. You'll be pleased, I reckon. Mighty pleased.

Flinging on a cloak, I ran to see it eagerly. Although it was twilight I was too impatient to wait until morning. The garden was approached through a wrought iron gate set within a stone arch. I stood on the threshold, delighted with the results. The little sunken garden was clean and newly-planted, and the arbor was rid of its strangling growth. In the dusk I could see letters carved in the stones and went forward curiously to examine them. When I did so, something froze inside me.

Repelle, Domine, virtutem diaboli. Drive back, O Lord, the power of the devil. . . .

I turned and hurried away. I ran unseeingly, but from what, I had no idea. I only knew that suddenly the sunken garden was a frightening place, as if haunted by ghosts. I was vaguely aware that the gardener stared after me in astonishment, but I did not care. All I wanted was to run away as fast as I could.

Perhaps that was why I didn't see the man until he stepped out from the shadow of the cedar tree, and grabbed me. I gasped, struggled, and stared briefly into a face which looked dark and saturnine beneath a sweeping hat brim. Even in that moment of terror the thought flashed through my mind that he had pulled it well down to hide his features.

"*At last!*" he said savagely.

I screamed. Beneath my terror I was aware that the gardener was already lumbering after me in concern. He was old and slow but his heavy tread echoed loudly on the gravel path behind a tall yew hedge. The man released me abruptly and dived into the undergrowth.

I was standing petrified with shock as the gardener rounded the corner. I pointed with a shaking hand. "A man—a trespasser—he went that way! Catch him!"

But I knew the stranger would be speedier than the old man. His movements had been stealthy, but agile: he would take no chances on being caught.

My legs were trembling as I stumbled back to the house. Mercifully, Justin was in the hall. He had just come in and was shedding his riding jacket. He took one look at me and was at my side in an instant.

I clung to him, still shaking.

"There was a man out there—a man beneath the cedar tree? He grabbed me—"

Characteristically, Justin wasted no time. Servants gave chase, but the intruder had disappeared. I even felt rather foolish when they came back to report no sign of anyone. By then the lamps were lit and the curtains drawn, Justin had given me a brandy to steady me and Miranda had come downstairs. They were both concerned, but I couldn't help feeling that neither really believed my story. "You're getting fanciful, my sweet—conjuring bogies out of shadows," Justin said indulgently. "You mustn't go walking in the dusk alone."

Miranda said nothing. She merely looked at me with a little smile that was meant to be sympathetic but which I took to be mocking. For the first time, I looked back at her challengingly, trying to let her know what I thought—that the man was her lover, meeting her clandestinely. Probably he had been waiting for her impatiently and, hearing me come along, had mistaken my cloaked figure for hers. She was a voluptuous woman, the kind to attract men, and couldn't be expected to mope in widowhood forever. The fact that the man had gone to some pains to obscure his face with sweeping hat brim and upturned collar signified guilt and certainly an anxiety not to be recognized. He was probably a local resident, respectably married, who couldn't afford to be found out. Distasteful as the idea was, I was surprised to realize that it was far less distasteful than my previous conviction that the man had been Daniel Firth.

Perhaps after all I had nothing to fear. As Justin said, I was getting fanciful, conjuring bogies out of shadows.

CHAPTER TWENTY-ONE

All the same, I knew I would never visit the sunken garden again. I would be unable to sit in the little arbor, enjoying the sea view. The place would hold no peace for me with those sinister words carved in the stones—the words that

Uncle Silas had penned so inexplicably at the end of his letter.

Justin laughed when I told him about the Latin inscription. I asked who had put it there.

"How should I know, my love? For as long as I remember that arbor had been covered in ivy. You're not going to be upset by a little thing like that, are you? Places as old as Knight's Keep have Latin mottoes carved everywhere."

"You could hardly call those words a motto!"

"Superstition, then. In days gone by, when the country was riddled with religious fears, fanatics carved such sayings in the way that some people would write sermons, or prayers." He looked at me anxiously. "You're becoming morbid, Jane. You're quieter than you used to be. Is something bothering you?"

I wanted to tell him, but couldn't, because I didn't know what it was. I had been married but a few months, and fancies or no fancies, uneasiness troubled me like a nagging tooth.

I said vaguely, "We have so little time alone together—"

He gave his light-hearted laugh. "Not even at night—in bed?"

"I mean during the day. We never even dine alone."

"We can't shut poor Miranda out."

"I know—I know—"

But I wanted to. How badly I wanted to!

"I tell you what I'll do," he said suddenly. "I'll leave everything to Gavin today and take you for a trip to Canterbury, just the two of us. Would you like that?"

I was delighted.

"You can visit the shops, and we'll go to the Cathedral, and then we'll lunch at one of the old pilgrim inns near the Butter Market. The landlord knows me well—we'll have his best private room."

"Everyone knows you well!" I cried gaily. "You're rich and famous, with a name the whole county looks up to!"

I was myself again. It didn't take much to restore my spirits.

Spring was in the air; the leaves were sprouting green; the swallows were returning from their winter migration and swooped overhead as we bowled along the road to Canterbury—the long, winding road that Bishop Becket's murderers had cantered along centuries before. It didn't seem possible that such a sylvan setting could have formed the background for one of the greatest crimes in history, or that men could have ridden along this leafy lane with murder in their hearts. Nor, as the beautiful cathedral came into view, did it seem possible that men could commit such a foul deed within its great walls, then plunder the sacred place before galloping away. But so it had been.

Justin showed me the Pilgrim Steps leading to where Becket's shrine had stood. They had been made concave by the feet of worshipers who for three hundred years had come from all over Europe, and before the place of the shrine the stone floor was also worn hollow.

"They fought to touch it, believing Becket's relics wrought miracles. The lame had been made to walk and the blind to see—or so legend had it. Mere superstition, of course," Justin finished contemptuously.

"But not to the pilgrims. To them it was faith."

"To the credulous, superstition is always a form of faith. Legend becomes fact to those who want to believe it. This is the power that witch doctors have. My father made a study of primitive tribes; he was fascinated by their rituals and their rites. With the aid of tricks and a lot of mumbo-jumbo the witch doctor convinced his patients that they were cured, or that a devil had cast a spell on them that only he could cast out, and in nine cases out of ten it worked."

"And if it didn't?"

Justin laughed. "That was the fault of the patient, of course. His soul was damned, or a curse was upon him because he was evil, but whatever the reason, *he* was to blame —and so he became an outcast, shunned by his tribe, who believed every word the witch doctor said. Power over the mind—that was the devil's skill."

"How horrible!"

Justin shrugged. "It achieved his aims and the people were happy. And so long as people are happy does it matter how they achieve it? To every man his own method—that's my belief. Primitive people enjoy themselves in ways that would shock so-called civilized folk."

I didn't like this conversation, particularly in a sacred place, so walked ahead, lingering before the pictures of the Poor Man's Bible, and trying not to feel distressed by my husband's skepticism, or to think of what he meant by primitive enjoyment.

I felt his hand beneath my elbow. "Down these steps, my love, we come to the martyrdom."

He led me to the spot where Becket had been murdered. He knew the place well, and its history. "You see this stone?" he said. "This marks the spot where he fell." He knelt and touched it, then rose and laid his hand against a nearby pillar. "And this is where he clung, fighting for his life. The power of the man! Think of it, Jane—it took three men to slay him, and the tip of Breton's sword broke in the fray and later was found nearby—bloodstained, like the stones."

I shuddered a little and wished we hadn't come.

"Is something wrong, my love?"

"I want to go."

His manner changed at once. "Did I frighten you?"

"Not exactly, but you told it so vividly."

"I see it vividly! Don't you? Can't you imagine the triumph those men must have felt when they finally slew him? To overcome such an enemy—think of the satisfaction in that!"

He took my arm again. "Come, I'll show you the cloisters. Nothing sinister there—unless either of us sees the ghost of Nell Cook in the Dark Entry."

His voice was gay. He was teasing me.

"If you're trying to frighten me with that old Ingoldsby Legend, I refuse to heed you!" I declared.

"You know it, then?"

"Of course I know it. You seem to forget that my father was a scholar and coached me in many subjects."

"Including Latin—"

"And French. I am not the ignoramus you sometimes think."

Within the Dark Entry, he stooped and kissed me. "I'm a bully and a tyrant," he teased. "You've married a dreadful man, haven't you, dear Jane?"

"I married the man I loved," I told him.

"And do still?"

"Of course."

"Good. Then if we meet Nell Cook we'll pay her no heed. Neither of *us* is going to die within the year!"

Of course, we didn't meet her and the rest of the day was everything I had hoped it would be. We lunched well at the Chequers, and the landlord produced his finest wines, and as Justin had foretold, offered us his best private room.

"I'd love to eat in that paneled dining room downstairs,"

I said after Justin had ordered. "Do you think the day will ever come when women will be allowed to dine in restaurants with men?"

"If it does, I won't let you, my darling. You're much too pretty to be put on public view. You're mine—mine completely. Remember that."

It was on the way home that we found the dog. I saw it first, huddled by the roadside. It was nothing more than a puppy, and its pitiful whimpering distressed me. I begged Justin to stop, and he reined in the horses, then climbed down. I clambered after him and in a minute was on my knees with the puppy cradled in my lap.

"It's half-starved!" I cried. "See how thin it is. It must be lost."

"Or thrown out, more likely."

"Thrown out! Who would do such a thing?"

"Many a farmer, my love. When a bitch has too big a litter the weakest are often thrown out or destroyed. There are enough animals to be fed on a farm without rearing those that may be useless."

"It's wicked! *Wicked!*" I fondled the poor little thing, and it whimpered gratefully. "I shall take it home. There's a shawl in the carriage—will you fetch it for me?"

"My dear Jane, it's a stray—a worthless mongrel! You can't keep a creature like that!"

"Why not?" I carried the puppy to the carriage and wrapped it in the shawl, not looking at Justin. Perhaps he was a little ashamed, for he put his hands on my shoulders and said, "I'm sorry, I didn't mean to be callous, but you must admit he's a wretched little creature."

"He won't be when I've cared for him."

And as we drove on, Justin said, "You can hand it over to Gavin when we get home. He'll see that it's cared for. One of the farm laborers can give it a home."

"*I* am giving it a home!"

"Not at Knight's Keep, my love."

"Certainly at Knight's Keep—with me."

I could tell that Justin was exasperated by my stubbornness, for he didn't say another word until we reached our front door. I carried the puppy up the wide steps, wrapped in my shawl like a baby. Justin hurried after me.

"Jane, I forbid you to bring that creature indoors. It's filthy."

"It is *not* filthy—just neglected and wet and miserable and starved. I'll wash him and feed him and *no one* is going to stop me!"

"Miranda will be as disgusted as I am."

"And what has it to do with Miranda?"

"Nothing—I suppose."

I marched upstairs. Justin followed me. "You're stubborn and willful. I won't have it—understand?"

"I'm afraid you'll just have to put up with it," I said over my shoulder. "I can't change my character, any more than you can change yours."

He caught my arm and spun me around. To my astonishment, his eyes blazed.

"And why *should* I change?" he demanded.

"I didn't say you should. I merely said that you couldn't —any more than I can." I pulled away and walked on to our bedroom. He didn't follow me. I heard him march angrily downstairs. I sighed and let him go. There was nothing I could do about his anger, and I knew how quickly Justin's moods changed, anyway. I was becoming accustomed to his lightning switches.

I rang for Dora, and at the sight of my forlorn little puppy she was as distressed as I. She brought a big crock of warm water and we bathed him together. She found a wicker basket and a blanket, and while she went to fetch a bowl of bread and milk I rubbed the puppy dry and gently brushed his coat. Already he began to look a different creature, and by the time I'd given him a tiny sip of brandy and wrapped him warmly in the blanket the misery had almost disappeared from his eyes.

I carried the basket to my boudoir. I was determined to keep the puppy near me day and night, and Justin couldn't possibly object to its presence there. My boudoir was my own private chamber, and the puppy would be my own private pet. I decided to call him Ruffles, because he'd been a ruffled little creature when I found him, though he looked very different now. Mongrel he might be, but his coat was handsomely marked in black and tan, with one black ear and the other a light brown. The black extended from the ear over half his eye, like a pirate's black eye patch pushed awry. He was a comical creature and I loved him. I felt he already loved me a little, as he sipped feebly at the bowl of warm bread and milk that Dora brought. He cocked an eye at both of us before he suddenly curled up and fell asleep. We were his benefactors, and I knew he would never forget it.

Justin didn't like the idea of Ruffles sleeping in the next room, but he made little protest when he saw that my heart was set on it. He was even a little amused.

"You're a soft-hearted soul, Jane. I suppose I should be glad. It shows you have a capacity for love."

"No more than any normal person, surely."

"More than some," he said, "though I suspect you haven't given your capacity for it full rein yet."

"I don't know what you mean."

"Then I'll show you."

That was the second night that he was violent in his love-making. When he made love to me normally I responded normally, but when he was sadistic, I shrank from him. I did so that night, and he was angry.

The next night, for the first time in our marriage, he didn't come to me at all. I was disturbed and frightened. There was a side to Justin's character that I neither understood nor liked very much, and at last I admitted it.

CHAPTER TWENTY-TWO

Ruffles soon blossomed from a pathetic little scrap into a healthy, bouncing puppy. He also became my devoted slave. I never went for a walk but he followed me, and very soon he took it for granted that wherever I went, he went too. When I rode, he followed behind, barking furiously if I went too fast. My riding was improving, but I still didn't enjoy it as much as walking.

Miranda gave up riding with me. For one thing, I was too slow for her, and for another Ruffles annoyed her. His barking and his friskiness irritated her, and once she even stooped from the saddle and took her crop to him when he raced alongside. I reined in sharply, gathered him up, and carried him home. I couldn't bring myself to look at Miranda, nor could I trust myself to speak. I had never felt such anger in my life.

At lunch, she had the grace to apologize, but she did it in her usual way.

"Your wife is angry with me, Justin. I've done something

unforgivable. I suppose I must beg her pardon."

"Why?" my husband asked. He even sounded a little amused, as if he thought that Miranda's offense could be only trivial.

"I saved her puppy's life," she said. "Or tried to."

"You did no such thing!" I declared. "You attacked him with your riding crop!"

"The puppy ran between Firebrand's hooves," Miranda said calmly. "The only way I could save him was to drive him away."

"That's a lie! He was racing alongside you and you leaned from the saddle and lashed out at him! That's the truth, and you know it."

Miranda sighed. "Poor Jane. She dotes on that puppy so much that it can do no wrong in her eyes. But if that is what she imagines, it's useless for me to say anything. You'd like me to apologize, would you, Jane? Very well, I do—but for what, I've no idea. Certainly I flicked my crop at him, but not to hurt him—to save him, as I said."

"Then it's Jane who should apologize to you."

I stared at my husband. I couldn't believe that he would take someone's side against me, much less accept their word against mine. My glance went from him to Miranda, and back again. They were both smiling at me indulgently, but suddenly I felt as if there were a barrier between us that I could never break down. I had felt it before, but never so strongly as now. It was as if I had stepped out of my social sphere, only to hover on the edge of a charmed circle into which I could never be truly admitted.

I pushed my chair back, and walked from the room. I wanted to slam the door behind me, but I didn't. I closed it quietly, and as I did so I saw Dora watching me from across the hall. She was polishing a big copper jug that stood on a carved oak chest. I ran straight across to her. She put her motherly arm about me and stroked my hair, just as she had done when I lost my parents and again when Uncle Silas died.

"There, there, ducks. What's the matter? Tell Dora, love, that's wot I'm 'ere for."

"I don't know—I don't *know*," I said unhappily.

"The best thing *you* can do is to put your bonnet on and go for a good brisk walk with Ruffles. Why don't you go and say hello to the doctor? 'E's 'ome today."

"And why should I do that?"

" 'Cos 'e's a friend, that's why."

I drew away from her. "No, Dora—he isn't a friend. I can't tell you why."

"You mean you won't. But maybe I know already—ma'am."

I should have guessed that gossip would have reached her ears. Nothing was ever secret from the servants' hall.

"Then if you know already," I said, "you know why Daniel Firth is no friend of ours."

"That don't stop 'im being a friend of mine," she retorted.

For a moment there was antagonism between us, then I held out my hands to her. I couldn't bear the thought of anything coming between me and the only friend I had at Knight's Keep.

I took Dora's advice and went for a good brisk walk. I even found myself at the gates of Beechwood Close, but fortunately there was no sign of its owner. I hadn't meant to walk so far, and had definitely not intended to go in the direction of Daniel's house. I turned away and hurried home. I walked so quickly that Ruffles whimpered in protest, and I gathered him up with a swift rush of affection. He licked my face eagerly, and I laughed, and was happier than I had felt all day.

"He's looking fine and healthy now," a male voice said. It was Gavin Rudge. I was passing the gate of his cottage and he was clipping the hedge. He wore an open-necked shirt and breeches. His sleeves were rolled up and his arms were strong and sinewy.

"I apologize for my clothes," he said.

"They seem very sensible to me. What else would you wear for gardening? White-tie-and-tails?"

He laughed, and fondled my puppy's head. Ruffles licked him as eagerly as he had licked me.

"I'm jealous," I said. "I thought I came first in his affections!"

"It's quite obvious that you do—I've watched him following you around like Mary's little lamb, but not so meekly. He's a lively little pup." Gavin ruffled his head again.

"He likes you—I'm glad. But I musn't interrupt—"

"I've finished, and just in time. I expected rain, and here it is!"

It came in a sudden downpour. Gavin took my arm and ran me to his cottage door. I accepted his shelter gladly.

The cottage was bigger than I expected, with a large sitting room lined with books and charmingly furnished. Gavin sensed my surprise and said, "It isn't what you expected?"

"No—"

"Why not?"

"I thought you were an outdoor man."

"So I am—but even an outdoor man has an indoor life."

I smiled, and let him take my cloak. He carried Ruffles off to the kitchen for refreshment, urging me to make myself at home. I found the room so charming that I was content to —even glad to, for I was strangely relucant to return to Knight's Keep. I sat down in an easy chair and tried to analyze this reluctance. The reason could only be Miranda. I was allowing her to dominate the place, and me, too much. It would have to stop.

I rose, and moved about the room, examining Gavin's things. If possessions were any indication of character, his was interesting. Everything here pointed to a man of intellect and good taste, untypical of a philanderer who seduced his employer's wife and even after her death had the effrontery to remain in his comfortable position without any sense of embarrassment or guilt, which was the picture Miranda had drawn for me.

I paused beside the photograph of a middle-aged couple, the man so like Gavin that it could only be his father. A pleasant, honest-looking man, I thought—and so was his wife, who had a kind and humorous face. They were a nice pair, the kind of parents who would bring up their children decently and well.

There were other photographs—two of girls who also bore a striking resemblance to Gavin, and one of a boy very much younger. These could only be photographs of the Rudge family, but one other, standing alone on a desk near the window, was of a young woman who bore no resemblance to them at all. I picked it up and studied it with interest, for the face was appealing. The girl was dark, with hair parted in the middle and drawn smoothly down each side of her face. Her mouth was wide and generous, the eyes calm. There was a serenity about her that I found restful. I felt that here was a young woman I could like and trust, whom I could talk to and make a friend of. I also felt that I had seen her before.

The door opened, and Gavin entered carrying a tray.

"I made some tea—"

He broke off. He was looking at the photograph in my hand, and then back at me, inquiringly. I put the picture in its place and said, "I was wondering who she was, and why her face is familiar—"

Gavin put down the tray and answered calmly, "That's easily explained; she resembled her brother closely."

I knew at once that the photograph was of Dulcie.

"Again you look surprised. May I ask why?"

"I didn't imagine her—like that."

"She was exactly like that. Would you like milk or lemon in your tea?"

"Lemon, please—"

The strange thing was that it was I who felt embarrassed, not he. As I stirred my tea I found I couldn't meet his eyes.

"I know what you are thinking," he said quietly. "You wonder why I'm not ashamed, and how I can stay here, working for your husband, after all that happened—or all you *heard* had happened. I can only say that I have my reasons, and if you ask what they are, I won't tell you."

"Then I won't trouble to ask."

The downpour had stopped as suddenly as it began. I drank my tea, set aside my cup, and said, "Thank you for giving me shelter. Now I must go—"

He didn't try to detain me. He helped me on with my cloak, went out to the kitchen to collect Ruffles, then walked with me to the front gate.

I held out my hand to him. Despite everything, I liked this young man, and I knew that nothing would change that liking. My father had once called me a creature of instinct, and I was following that instinct now.

"Goodbye, Gavin. Thank you once again—"

The sound of approaching hooves interrupted me, and around a bend in the lane came Miranda. Her immaculate riding habit was soaked through, but she looked exultant, as if she enjoyed battling with the elements.

She halted beside us. I saw her eyebrows lift, and knew what she was thinking.

I said calmly, "You must have ridden a long way, Miranda. You're drenched."

"And you are not," she answered, significantly.

"Gavin was kind enough to give me shelter."

"How very nice of him. I suppose you were out on one of your solitary walks?"

"I was. And enjoying it—as you enjoy riding."

I went calmly on my way, refusing to heed the inference in her words, which had said all too plainly that she now knew where my destination had been.

Since we were both heading for home, she overtook me. She passed me without a glance, and I fully expected her to tell Justin that she had seen me coming out of Gavin's cottage. If he hadn't accepted her word rather than mine at lunch that day, I wouldn't have worried, but I found myself feeling apprehensive as I went indoors.

There was no need. Justin greeted me affectionately, asked if I had enjoyed my walk, and even patted Ruffles on the head. The puppy snapped at him.

"Bad-tempered little beast! I can't understand your fondness for that animal."

I rubbed my cheek against Ruffles' ear.

"He's sweet, when you get to know him."

"When he'll let you get to know him."

I let the remark pass, and the rest of the day was pleasant and uneventful. Throughout the evening Miranda's manner was pleasant, and I felt that she had said nothing to Justin, after all.

She retired early. Justin was lost in a book and didn't even notice her departure. I was working on a sampler, but the afternoon's walk had tired me unduly, and I soon followed Miranda upstairs. As I kissed Justin's forehead he said absently, "Just to the end of this chapter, my love, and then I'll come. . . ."

Everything was calm and peaceful and unalarming. I slept at once, then suddenly wakened, apparently without reason. I immediately thought of Ruffles. Sometimes he wakened in the night, like a restless child. I decided to get him a drink of water, settle him, and go to sleep again. Lighting my bedside candle, I saw to my surprise that Justin had still not come to bed.

What the hour was, I had no idea. He must have forgotten it too, deep in his book. Perhaps he had fallen asleep over it. As soon as I had settled Ruffles I would go downstairs and see.

To my surprise, the puppy's basket was empty. Nor was he anywhere to be seen. Then I saw that the corridor door was slightly ajar. Evidently it had not been properly closed and my frisky young puppy had nosed his way through. I went out into the corridor, calling him softly. There was no response, and I walked the full length of the passage before I heard him scratching furiously against a door and whining to be let in.

It was the door of the locked room, and from beneath it a light shone.

I ran to him, my bare feet soundless on the thick carpet. He was scratching away vigorously but whoever was inside took no notice. I picked him up, stared for a moment at the slit of light, then turned the knob.

The door was still locked.

I called, "Is someone there?"

There was no answer. I put my ear against the door, and could hear nothing. The room was completely silent, and the light from beneath the door stared back at me like an unblinking eye.

CHAPTER TWENTY-THREE

The next day I told Justin about the incident.

"What of it, my love? Miranda grieves for her husband. Sometimes she goes in there and sits with his possessions. I've known about it for a long time. It's a morbid thing to do, but understandable. No one has ever taken his place in her life, and no one never will."

I didn't tell him that I believed Miranda to be consoling herself with another man—a man she met secretly in the garden. I felt that was her concern, not mine, but that Justin might not take so lenient a view of an affair which had to be conducted clandestinely. It was more than possible that Miranda's secret liaison had grown out of her loneliness, and her yearning for the husband she had loved.

I wondered why I hadn't guessed that it was Miranda in that room. Justin had told me that she kept it as a sort of shrine to Matthew's memory. Had I thought of that last night I would not have returned to my bedroom feeling perturbed and vaguely frightened. Justin had joined me a minute or two later, yawning and apologetic, and to atone for neglecting me he made love very tenderly that night. This was the Justin I adored, and these moments of happiness made up for all the rest.

So it wasn't surprising that I soon forgot all about the locked room, and in any case other things drove it from my mind. The first was the realization that I was pregnant. I had suspected it for the past two months, and now that the third had passed I was certain. Nevertheless, I decided to visit the family physician in Hythe for confirmation before breaking the news to Justin.

It was about three weeks after Ruffles had scratched at the door of the locked room, and since then life had been calm and untroubled. So I was quite unprepared for the next thing that happened.

I had waited for Justin to leave the house before ordering the carriage. He would be sure to ask where I was going, and a visit to the doctor might alarm him. I thought it better to keep it secret until I returned.

I felt happy and serene as I walked downstairs, buttoning my gloves. Even the voices in the hall didn't alarm me, although one was raised aggressively. There was a man on the doorstep demanding to see my husband and refusing to be turned away.

I paused at the foot of the stairs and said, "What is it, Bailey?"

The butler turned.

"This—gentleman—refuses to leave, m'lady, although I've told him his lordship is not here."

"And *I*'ve told this fellow that I'll wait till he returns," the man said belligerently through the open door.

I looked at him. He was a burly man, well enough dressed. His voice dropped a tone when he saw me and he removed his hat respectfully enough, explaining that he had driven over from Canterbury especially to see my husband.

I told Bailey to show him into the morning room, and waited until the door was closed before I said, "You can state your business to me. Whatever concerns my husband, concerns me too."

To my surprise, the man looked uncomfortable.

"Come," I said impatiently, "what is it?"

He took an envelope from his pocket and handed it to me. "Begging your pardon, m'lady, it's this. I'm a debt-collector appointed by this firm to follow up their approaches to his lordship. They've rendered accounts in the usual way and followed them up with letters, but everything's been ignored. In view of his lordship's name, ma'am, they don't want to cause embarrassment by taking legal action—yet."

"Legal action!" I took the envelope with a feeling of alarm mingled with disbelief. Justin would be incapable of doing anything that called for legal action.

I opened the envelope, glanced at its contents, and froze. It was a bill—a staggering one, for a costly sable cloak. Slowly, I put it back in the envelope.

"You have my assurance that this will be paid," I said, then walked to the door and opened it. The man hung back.

"I had instructions to collect—"

"And you have mine to return to Canterbury and tell your employers that the full amount will be settled."

"Either because I was a woman, or because of the authority in my voice, the man's aggression disappeared. Nevertheless, he still hesitated.

"M'lady, I don't want to cause embarrassment, but I was told to take the cloak back if—"

"The cloak is mine," I said sharply. "I can arrange for payment to be made without delay."

I wondered how long it would take for a letter to reach Mr. Claythorne and for the sum to be released. It was too big to be paid out of income. For the first time I felt that my solicitor was keeping a too-tight hand on my expenditure, and wondered why. Uncle Silas's fortune was now completely mine. Surely I should be able to draw upon it when and how I wished?

The man decided to accept my word. He even seemed glad to get away. I watched him march down the front steps and clamber back into his carriage. Mine was waiting there, with the coachman holding the horses' heads, and a brief altercation broke out as the visitor wheeled by, scraping the side of my carriage. He flung a bad-tempered remark over his shoulder at the coachman, and bowled off down the drive.

It was a few minutes before I could compose myself sufficiently to walk out of the house. The shock of discovering that Justin hadn't bothered to pay for my magnificent wedding present almost made me change my mind about going, but I pulled myself together.

The coachman was studying the side of the carriage, and I saw a slight scraping of the paintwork.

"Not much harm done, I hope, Jenkins?"

The coachman straightened up, his lips pursed disapprovingly.

"Nothing that can't be patched up, m'lady, but some folk shouldn't be allowed at the reins."

His hand touched the damaged paintwork. I glanced at it idly as I stepped into the carriage. The shining coat of maroon was only lightly scratched, but in one place another color showed through.

I stepped down again.

"Was that the original color?" I asked, and touched the spot with my finger.

"Yes, m'lady. It was done up only last spring. Not that it needed it, but his lordship didn't like that shade of green."

"Nor do I," I said, and stepped reluctantly into the carriage again.

I was waiting for Justin in the morning room. He strode into the house full of self-confidence, and announced proudly that his prize herd of Jerseys promised to yield good stock next season.

"That's fine," I said. "If they do well, you need run up no more debts."

He stopped dead and stared at me.

I took the bill from my pocket and handed it over. His face went an angry red, then he tore the bill to shreds, tossed it aside, and laughed.

"Tradesmen!" he scoffed. "Let them wait."

"This one has waited long enough."

"Are you sitting in judgment on me?" he demanded.

"No. I merely want to know why you haven't paid it. My wedding present, of all things!"

"Why should that worry you? You have the cloak." His glance shifted away from me.

"Justin—tell me the truth. *Couldn't* you pay for it?"

"In time," he blustered. "I would have paid for it in time."

"You've had plenty! They rendered the account several times and followed it up with letters. You ignored them all."

"Well—what was I to say? That I couldn't settle up—*me*, the Earl of Ashford?"

"Does being the Earl of Ashford justify ordering things you can't afford?" When he didn't answer I cried, "You told me you didn't need money! All along, you've said you had plenty! Now I find that you can't even meet your debts. How many more are there—and did you think they'd all be settled if you married me?"

I was so shocked by what I had said that I clapped my hand over my mouth. I was trembling and Justin saw it. His confidence returned.

"Well, a marriage is a marriage, isn't it? 'With all my worldly goods I thee endow'—remember?"

My throat ached as I said, "Is that why you stooped to marry a coachman's granddaughter?" I gave a mirthless laugh. "I suppose I should have guessed."

"I loved you," he said. "That is why I married you."

"But Uncle Silas's money made me even more desirable? Or was it the money in the first place? Let's have the truth. For the first time, let's have the truth!"

"I've given it to you. I loved you. I do still."

His sincerity was so obvious that I felt ashamed.

He said gently, "Don't you realize that if I had wanted money I would have accepted your offer to share the inheritance? I turned it down remember?"

I nodded mutely. "Forgive me—"

"My love, it is I who should beg forgiveness. I've hidden things from you, but only because I didn't want to worry you unnecessarily. Knight's Keep is my life. Every penny from the estate is ploughed back into it. That doesn't mean that I am financially in need—only that essentials have to be dealt with first and sometimes there isn't a margin for other things."

"Luxuries, you mean?"

"Yes."

"Then you shouldn't have ordered that costly sable cloak for me."

He said angrily, "Do you think I would give my bride anything less?"

It was useless to argue with him. I had been brought up one way, he another. I had been taught to pay cash on the nail, to keep one's head above water, to owe no man a penny. He had been taught to live according to his station, to keep up appearances no matter what the cost, and that tradesmen who could wait should be allowed to. Above all things, the estate came first. Cattle and grain and other essentials had to be paid for before luxuries, but the luxuries shouldn't be foregone. Two such different codes for living couldn't hope to reach understanding or even compromise.

I had to learn to understand this man I had married. He wasn't the paragon I had believed—he was a human being with faults and weaknesses and virtues and vices. No—not vices, I corrected hastily. Faults, human faults, no more than that. I would have to accept them as I accepted him—as he, in his turn, accepted me.

I said, "I have written to Mr. Claythorne asking him to draw on my capital. The debt will be paid at once."

Justin blazed, "Damn that man! Your self-appointed guardian angel—that's what your blasted solicitor is!"

"Perhaps I need one," I said without thinking.

To my astonishment Justin's hand shot out and struck my cheek. I recoiled under the blow, stunned by pain and shock. Immediately, he was penitent. He tried to take me in his arms, but I pushed him away. He pulled me to him roughly, took hold of my shoulders, and shook me.

"Listen to me, Jane—*listen to me!* I won't allow you to go running to your solicitor for everything. *I* am your husband. *I* should run your affairs. You are too inexperienced and too incompetent to handle all that money, and it's humiliating for me to even think of having bills paid by someone else."

"I didn't mean to humiliate you!"

He released me abruptly.

"Well, you certainly succeeded," he said bitterly.

I turned blindly to the door, unable to control my sobs.

"Jane, you're behaving like a child! Pull yourself together! You can't go in to lunch like that."

"I'm not going in to lunch. You can make my excuses to your stepmother. Tell her I'm not well. Tell her anything you like!"

I wished Dora hadn't seen me racing along the corridor to my room, crying bitterly. I heard her call my name in concern, but I ran into my boudoir and shut the door. Ruffles leaped at me, and I gathered him up, burying my wet cheeks against his soft coat. He licked my face in a mute desire to comfort me, but it was a long time before my grief was spent. When I stopped crying I felt immeasurably older, no longer a girl deluded by a dream, no longer Cinderella who had married her fairy prince.

I lay down on a chaise-longue, and Ruffles curled at my feet. I slept for a long time, and when I woke I remembered that I hadn't told Justin about the baby. There'd been a horrible scene instead of a happy one.

I touched my cheek gently. Even now I could feel the sting of his blow, and the memory of it curbed my immediate desire to make things up with him.

But he was my husband. I had married him for better or worse, which meant that I had to make something of this marriage, and bearing resentments wouldn't help. I now knew Justin to be an emotional, unpredictable man, a man who could be gentle as well as harsh, a man whose tongue could both charm and abuse me. On the other hand, I was stubborn and fiery-tempered, and some of my remarks must have stung him deeply.

The door of my boudoir opened. It was Miranda and she carried a tray.

"The last time I looked in, you were asleep," she said. She was smiling and her eyes seemed to hold genuine concern. "Justin told me you weren't well and wouldn't be down for lunch. I thought you might fancy something now. . . ."

She had brought me a cup of consommé and some toast. I wasn't hungry, but nibbled a bit of the toast. Miranda lingered a moment. "Don't take any of it if you don't fancy it," she said.

"I'm really not hungry—"

For a moment she looked at me thoughtfully.

"Is it a baby?" she asked bluntly.

I nodded. I hadn't wanted her to be the first to know.

"Have you told Justin?"

"Not yet."

"Do," she said urgently. "Tell him soon."

She left the room abruptly. I was a little surprised by her sudden departure, but glad to be alone again. I ate a piece of toast, but left the consommé. Ruffles stood upon his hind legs, begging comically, and with a laugh I put the bowl before him. He gobbled it all up.

As usual, I sought refuge in activity. Putting on my bonnet and cloak, I set off with Ruffles for a good brisk walk. Exercise, Dr. Mayfield had said, would be good for me. Apparently he was one of those new-thinking doctors who were against expectant mothers sitting with their feet up.

I'd found a short cut across the park to the village, and went that way this afternoon. Ruffles scampered along eagerly at first, but quickly tired. Part of the time I spent urging him along, and part of the time carrying him. "You're growing fat and lazy," I reprimanded. "You've got four strong feet, so use them. I've only got two!"

We were near the lane leading to Beechwood Close when it happened. Suddenly I missed him, and after calling for a while, went back to look for him. "Ruffles, you lazy thing—where *are* you?" I called.

The twittering of birds and the rustle of trees were my only answer.

I found him a little way back, lying in the middle of the lane. At first I thought he had curled up and gone to sleep, but when I picked him up his head lolled unnaturally and I felt a sharp suspicion and alarm. Gently forcing the lids open, I saw that his eyes were blank and dull. His heart was beating, but only faintly.

My suspicion hardened and became ugly. A healthy young puppy didn't suddenly collapse in this unnatural way. But there was no time for speculation or question—I lifted my skirts and ran with him to Daniel Firth's house. He was not a man I wanted to turn to for help, but I had no choice—and now I found myself praying that he would be there. Dora had told me that he wasn't in London so much these days—Dora seemed to know quite a lot about Doctor Firth—so with luck I would find him in.

I did. But the minute he felt my puppy's tiny heart, then looked at me compassionately, I knew that what I feared was true.

Ruffles was dead.

CHAPTER TWENTY-FOUR

"But how—how?" I entreated as soon as I was able to speak.
"It seems like normal heart failure," Daniel said.
"Seems?" I echoed.
"I can't be sure until I've examined him thoroughly."
"You mean you want to—"
"Yes, if you'll agree."
The thought of a post-mortem being carried out on poor little Ruffles distressed me, but I said, "If you think it necessary, yes. But why should it be?"
"For the same reason that we examine human beings

after death, if the cause is in doubt. When you set out for a walk, was he well?"

"Absolutely, and very frisky—but he did tire quickly. I couldn't understand why. He raced along at first, then began to flag, and after a while I even had to carry him. I scolded him, I remember—"

My voice broke. Daniel put his hand on my shoulder and said reassuringly, "I'll find out why he died—I promise."

"Couldn't it be heart failure?" I asked.

"You sound as if you want it to be."

This man read my mind well. Anything but heart failure was too horrible to contemplate.

"You think he may have been poisoned, don't you?" I managed to say.

"Not intentionally. He may have eaten something by accident."

"But he couldn't! I prepare most of his food—or Dora does."

"Perhaps some berries when he was outdoors."

I hoped he was right. The idea that someone had deliberately killed poor little Ruffles was too horrible to think about. And why should anyone want to—except to distress me? And the only person I could think of who might want to do that was Miranda, who had never really wanted me at Knight's Keep, but I couldn't credit her with wanting to hurt me that much.

"Tell me what he ate today," Daniel said.

"His normal diet. I went down to the kitchen myself to prepare his breakfast. Dora or I do that in turns."

"Anything at midday?"

"He had some soup. Consommé that was intended for me, so it must have been all right. I gave it to him because I wasn't hungry. Miranda had brought it up to me. I was resting in my room and Ruffles was with me."

"Resting? *You?* That seems out of character with an energetic young woman. Why were you resting?"

The question seemed unnecessary, but perhaps natural enough coming from a doctor.

Because I didn't want to tell him of my quarrel with Justin and my distress following it, the only other excuse I could think of was the truth. I said, "I'm having a baby."

His face went strangely still. After a moment he said, "I see."

"You might congratulate me."

"I thought it was the father who was congratulated in these matters."

"The happiness is mine too."

He smiled. When Daniel smiled his face was quite different —not stern, but surprisingly kind.

"Of course it is," he said. "I'm glad for you, and I'm sure the baby will be beautiful."

"Thank you."

In some ways, I thought in surprise, this man was quite human. His concern for me and for my puppy seemed to be quite genuine.

"Will you leave him with me, Jane?"

It was the first time he had called me by my name, and the pleasure I felt was illogical.

"Yes—I'll leave him with you. But you won't find anything abnormal, I'm sure."

"I hope not—but a healthy young animal doesn't usually drop dead. Come—I'll drive you home."

He used the green carriage again.

"Do you ever take this to London?" I asked.

"Never. Why?"

"I just wondered."

"I can't be troubled with a carriage in London. Hansoms are good enough for me, and handier. I keep this one down here to drive myself, and that old black one for my man to use."

I said unexpectedly, "It was a green carriage that killed Uncle Silas."

"You surely don't imagine it was mine? There must be hundreds of green carriages in London. You might as well suspect all of them! I can assure you that mine has never been used in town."

He made me ashamed of my doubts and I said, anxious now to get away from him, "Will you drop me here? I'll walk back across the park—"

Perhaps he knew that I didn't want him to drive me to the house and possibly meet Justin again, or very likely he was only too glad to be spared the rest of the journey, for he set me down at once. Before we parted he said, "As a doctor, I'd advise an early night. You've had a shock today."

More than one, I thought, remembering the sable cloak. I was glad this man didn't know that my husband had been running up debts, and I couldn't help wondering how many more there might be, for a man who could order costly sables knowing full well that he could not pay for them was just as capable of ordering other things without compunction. My dear, foolish Justin, I thought with the compassion of a mother for her child. Would I often have to cope with situations like that one?

I walked slowly across the park, deep in thought. Perhaps it would be better if I settled my inheritance on him now. That way he would be able to meet any pressing needs, and I firmly believed that a married couple should share their possessions. Besides, it was frustrating to have to communicate with Mr. Claythorne every time I wanted to make any big expenditure, so it would be better all around if my husband had control.

But other questions nagged at me. Why had Mr. Claythorne tied everything up so securely, and why had Justin pretended all along that he had no need of extra money? Obviously he had, but had been too proud to tell me the truth, and equally obviously my solicitor could not have known about the state of Justin's affairs. My husband had definitely not married me for gain, knowing that under the new Act he would get nothing. His love for me was indisputable and he demonstrated it in many ways. I was letting my imagination run riot and perhaps pregnancy was making me doubly sensitive. I decided to tell Justin about the baby as soon as I saw him. An heir to Knight's Keep would make him the happiest man on earth and provide a steadying influence. There would be no more extravagance when he was faced with the responsibility of fatherhood.

But when we met I found it quite impossible to break the news, for my husband's mood was unapproachable.

"Where have you been?" he demanded distantly.

"Walking."

"You must come from a long line of gypsies. You seem to have their love of the highways and byways."

There was acidity in his voice, but I refused to be goaded. "I enjoy the exercise," I answered equably.

Miranda joined us at that moment. She looked at me in concern. "You look pale, my dear. Has something upset you?"

I told them about Ruffles, and watched Miranda carefully as I did so. It was she who had brought the soup, but she didn't know that Ruffles had had it. Was she looking for signs of some physical reaction in me—a reaction which would be longer delayed in an adult human being than in a puppy? The thought was so appalling that I was ashamed.

She seemed genuinely sorry. She put her hand on my shoulder and said gently, "Poor Jane—you loved your pet, I know."

I nodded, unable to speak. My throat ached with unshed tears. She stooped and kissed my cheek, a rare demonstration of affection from Miranda, and said, "I'm sure Justin will buy you another."

"If I do, it will have to be a thoroughbred. I'll have no more mongrels in the house."

I burst out, "I don't want any other! I loved Ruffles. He was sweet and affectionate, even though he hadn't got a pedigree—like many people who don't come from a long line of blue-blooded ancestors!"

"My dear Jane, you're not yourself. Perhaps you should take a rest."

"I've done that once today—and what happened? Ruffles died."

They both looked puzzled.

"*Now* what are you talking about, my love? How could the death of that wretched animal have anything to do with your resting? You're not making sense."

I'd removed my bonnet and now I ran a tired hand through my hair. "I know I'm not. It's just that he drank the consommé meant for me."

"But it couldn't possibly have upset him!" Miranda said. "We had the same at lunch, Justin and I."

My husband put in impatiently, "My dear Jane, I don't know what fancies you're conjuring up now, but it is obvious why that damned puppy died. He was half-dead when you found him. You nursed him back to a brief life, but he simply wasn't strong enough to survive. And since you've done nothing but take the creature for strenuous walks, no one can be blamed for its death but you. You overstrained its heart."

I turned on my heel and went towards the stairs. Halfway there I remembered something.

"Miranda!"

She was on her way to the drawing room. Justin had disappeared into his study. Miranda looked back at me inquiringly.

"Yes, Jane?"

"I'm sorry I disturbed you last night."

"Disturbed me? I don't understand. I went to bed early and fell asleep at once. No one disturbed me."

"I meant in the locked room."

She walked across to me slowly.

"What about the locked room?"

"I know my late father-in-law's things are stored there. Justin told me today that you sometimes sit with them. Last night Ruffles was scratching at the door—he must have seen the light and known someone was inside. I tried the knob, but it wouldn't yield. Then I called. Had I known the truth, I wouldn't have troubled you."

"I wasn't in there. I've already told you. I was in bed and asleep."

"I see."

"You don't see at all. I don't think you even believe me. The room is stacked with trophies from all over the world, and if you want to see them, you can. Come."

Instinctively, I followed her. She took a key from a chain wrist-bag and unlocked the door. The room was exactly as she said, stacked with trophies. Skins of lions and leopards and tigers; tusks and horns and antlers; a stuffed bear rearing on its hind legs; native drums and head-dresses; bows and arrows, primitive weapons, necklaces and amulets—and a cabinet containing a macabre display of shrunken heads, fossilized lizards and snakes, a collection of bones, and the jaws and teeth of nameless creatures.

I shuddered and looked away, glad to find something that didn't send shivers down my spine—a laden bookcase containing endless volumes. I glanced at their titles. Most of them sounded heavy and uninteresting, but on one shelf I saw a selection on witchcraft, ancient beliefs, and primitive rites.

"Do you really think I'd enjoy sitting alone in here, Jane?"

"Frankly, no. But Justin believes you do."

She laughed. "I'll soon enlighten him! You must have been mistaken about a light here last night."

"But I saw it."

"But I am the only person who has a key."

"Then someone must have borrowed it."

"But why?"

"A curious servant?" I suggested.

"I should think the contents of this room would be enough

to frighten any servant away! Besides, none would dare to venture into this part of the house when not on duty. And how could they possibly borrow my key?"

I shook my head, as baffled as she. We left the room and she locked the door behind her.

"If you want the truth, Jane, I'd be more than willing to get rid of those things. They remind me too much of Africa. Only loyalty to my husband makes me keep them."

"But Africa is your country!"

"It *was*," she said.

Dinner that night was a strain. I had no appetite, and Justin's mood had not improved. Conversation was spasmodic, and lapsed altogether when the servants departed. After the meal was over, I made tiredness the excuse to go to bed. I was about to leave when Justin suddenly asked, "What did you do with the dog?"

The question was so unexpected that I echoed stupidly, "What did I do with him?"

"After it died," he said impatiently. "How did you dispose of it?"

"I didn't. I left him with Daniel Firth."

"Why with him?"

"It happened near his house. I took Ruffles there, thinking he was ill and Daniel could help—"

"But the man is in London during the week."

"Not now. Dora tells me he is home more and more."

"*That* woman! And how does she know about the doctor's affairs?"

I shrugged. "I've no idea. He looked after her on the journey from London and in consequence she thinks the world of him. I suppose that makes her take a particular interest in him."

Miranda said pacifically, "All the servants take an interest in the affairs of their betters, Justin, and you know it. It was sensible of Jane to take the dog to Daniel. I expect I would have done the same, in the circumstances."

Justin shrugged, then turned to me.

"Well, it was a good idea to leave it to be disposed of. You could hardly have carried a dead animal all the way home."

I didn't tell him that I had left Ruffles with Daniel Firth so that he could check on the cause of death. In any case, I wasn't sure now that it would serve any useful purpose to know. Ruffles was gone, and nothing could bring him back.

Justin didn't come to my room that night. I lay for a long time, waiting for him, determined to tell him about the baby. I was convinced that the news would delight him and that his difficult mood would disappear at once. The prospect of an heir couldn't fail to please a man so proud of his name.

I don't know when I accepted the fact that he wasn't coming to me at all. I just knew, suddenly, as if some inner voice had told me. Once or twice he had slept in his dressing room, but I knew he wasn't there. The room adjoined our own, and I would have heard him come up.

I felt oppressed. The feeling had increased all day and now, in desperate need for someone to talk to, I thought of Dora. She hadn't heard about the death of Ruffles and although common sense told me that it would be best to tell her tomorrow, something compelled me to go to her now.

Her room was two floors up. I lit a candle and walked along the dark corridor to the stairs. As I climbed them the candle sent leaping shadows up the walls, like mocking ghosts. The house was still as death. I hurried, shivering a little in the empty silence.

I reached the next floor. Miranda's room was near the stairhead, and as I approached I stopped dead, for sounds were coming from that room. Sounds which were unmistakable.

I clung to the banisters for support. Her voice was crying Justin's name over and over again, and I knew that he was with her. I had suffered the same violence on my wedding night, but unlike me, Miranda was enjoying it.

Shock ran through me in an active, physical pain. The dark corridor spun giddily, and through the whirlpool I saw a face watching me.

It was Sarah's.

She stood in the shadows, and I knew why. She was listening to the sounds from within that room, and she knew as well as I what was taking place.

I tried to move. My hand slid down the banisters and my shaking legs took a backward step, but I was mesmerized by the servant's face.

It was smiling. She came towards me, still smiling. She stood at the head of the stairs as I retreated and then she said in a harsh whisper, *"So now you know—my lady."*

CHAPTER TWENTY-FIVE

The candlestick fell from my hand. The flame spluttered into darkness, and I ran—blindly, stumblingly, groping my way down the stairs and along the corridors until I reached my room and threw myself on the bed.

I couldn't cry. Sobs racked me, but they were dry and terrifying. I tried to clutch at reason, and failed. Waves of nausea ran through me, and there was still the pain that had stabbed like a knife in that first moment of shock. It would go, my tormented mind insisted. I had to pull myself together somehow.

But the pain grew worse, dragging at my body. It ebbed and flowed in ever-increasing tides until my whole being was awash with it and I could scarcely tell the difference between consciousness and unconsciousness. Once or twice I heard my voice crying for help, but it was weak and ineffective. No one could possibly hear.

Vaguely, I realized that Dora was beside me. What brought her to me, or how she knew that I needed her, I had no idea, but without her I might have died that night when I lost my baby.

Justin was standing at the foot of the bed.

"Why didn't you tell me?" he demanded. "I had a right to know."

I turned my face into the pillow, refusing to look at him.

He came around beside me and said gently, "Jane—dear Jane—look at me."

"No."

"Why not?"

"I don't want to."

"My love, I want to be patient, but you're being very trying. You've lain here for days, refusing to have anyone but Dora with you. I'm your husband, remember."

I wished with all my heart that I could forget.

"Jane—did you hear me?"

I nodded mutely.

"Why didn't you tell me about the baby?"

"You weren't in an approachable mood."

"But you must have known before that day. You were three months pregnant, Dr. Mayfield tells me."

"I know—he confirmed it that morning."

Justin sat down on the bed and covered my hand with his. I felt nothing. No love, no hatred, nothing. It might have been a stranger who touched me.

"My poor sweet—we quarreled that morning, and all over a sable cloak! And I went on being angry, which was unforgivable, and as a result, this happened. If only you had told me!"

For the first time I looked at him.

"I'm glad I didn't." My voice was expressionless, but it alarmed him.

"You don't mean that."

"I do. If I had told you, you would have been here with me that night and I wouldn't have found out."

"I—don't know what you are talking about, my love."

"Ask Sarah."

"*Sarah?*"

"Yes. She knows what shocked me. She even went along to Dora's room and told her to come to me. It's the only thing I've ever had cause to thank Sarah for. I'm surprised she did it—but people are full of surprises, aren't they? We can never really know what a person is like under the surface."

"You are talking in riddles, my love."

"Riddles have answers. Try to work that one out."

"You must rest again. You need it."

I dragged myself up and, leaning on one arm, I said, "If you can't answer the riddle, my dear husband, I'll give you a clue—I know now why Miranda keeps Sarah supplied with clothes."

"My poor Jane, I don't know what you are talking about, and I'm sure you don't either." He pressed me gently back against the pillows and drew the cover over me. "Sleep now."

"If I do, things will be no different when I wake."

He answered cheerfully, "Yes, they will. Mayfield is working hard to build up your strength and I'm sure he'll succeed if you let him. Losing a baby at three months isn't dangerous. Now be a good girl and cooperate with him, and you'll soon be well enough to have another child."

I clenched my hands beneath the bedcovers, digging my fingernails into my palms to prevent myself from speaking. Throughout the days that I had lain here instinct had urged me to be silent. To hurl the truth at him would only create a scene, worse than we had ever had, and I wasn't strong enough to do battle yet. There were too many things I wanted to know, too many niggling fears that I couldn't understand. Finding out the truth about Miranda and Justin should have explained everything, but it didn't. I felt that it was only part of the truth.

When he had gone, Dora came to me.

"How are you, lovey? C'm on now—eat a little of this for Dora. It's chicken broth and it'll put the roses back in your cheeks."

I took it to please her, and she sat beside me while I did so. She never left me now, sleeping in the boudoir at nights with the door ajar because I refused to have anyone else near. Justin had humored me, but I doubt if he was pleased.

"Dora—has there been any message from Dr. Firth?"

"Not that I know of, dearie. Were you expecting one?"

"Hoping."

"Maybe 'e's tried to see you, but not being your doctor and seeing as 'ow 'is lordship don't like 'im, it ain't likely that 'e'd be able to, now is it?"

I finished all the broth, which pleased Dora, and as she took the tray I said urgently, "I've got to get up!"

"Time enough when Dr. Mayfield says you can."

"No—I'm getting up today. This afternoon, when no one is about. Don't ask me to explain, but it's important that everyone should think I'm still too weak to leave my bed."

The truth was that I didn't want to see Miranda, or to let Justin think that life was back on its normal course. I wanted time and solitude in which to decide what to do.

"And there's another thing, Dora—I want you to go to Dr. Firth and find out why Ruffles died. But don't tell anyone, not *anyone*, understand?"

Her homely face looked at me in concern. "What's up?" she asked. "What's going on?"

"I don't know. Perhaps nothing."

"Don't give me that talk, dearie. You're not the one to lose a baby through shock, unless that shock was a stiff 'un. You've never told me wot 'appened that night—and nor 'as she."

"She?"

"That Sarah. Can't stand the likes of 'er, but she did come'n fetch me that night."

"Tell me exactly what she said."

"Well now, let me think—'You'd best get to your mistress,' she said. I was 'alf asleep but the moment she sez that I'm wide awake, see? 'You'd best get to your mistress—she's 'ad a shock and she'll be needin' you.' And then she walks out of me room in that swaggering way of 'ers. That one's no better 'n she should be, if you arsks me, but I've gotta say this —but for 'er I wouldn't't've known you'd been taken ill and 'is lordship not around an' all."

I looked away. I had known that Justin's absence from my room that night couldn't have passed unnoticed, but until now Dora had made no comment.

"Will you go to Dr. Firth?" I repeated.

"Going right away, dearie. And you be a good girl while I'm gorn. 'Ave a nice nap, and if you want to get up, it's to be no further than this bedside chair. Remember?"

"I'll remember."

But I didn't obey. I didn't sleep, either. I lay there thinking of the horrible moment outside Miranda's room, and the hateful truth of her relationship with my husband. No wonder she had never really made me welcome!

But other things troubled me, questions that forced themselves into my mind no matter how hard I tried to resist them. Justin said he had invited me here to ease Miranda's loneliness, to be a friend and companion to her, but why had it been necessary if they were in love at that time, and if the present relationship had existed between them then, why hadn't they married? Two answers were conceivable: that having fallen in love with me he had turned away from her, which was enough to make her hate me, or—which seemed more likely—recent dissension between us had made him turn to her now. It might be no more than a passing affair, a seeking after comfort on his part. I tried to cling to that thought, but could not really believe it. *"So now you know— my lady!"* The secret relish in Sarah's voice echoed in my ears, taunting and mocking, suggesting that she had known about the liaison for a long time and relished the thought of my having been fooled.

This, then, was the reason for the wardrobe full of clothes from Miranda—bribery, to keep a servant's mouth shut. The situation was so ugly that I felt sick at the thought of it. It was stupid to delude myself that it was a recent affair. My husband had walked into Miranda's room with a familiarity born of custom.

What puzzled me was why Miranda had urged me to tell Justin about the baby. Would a woman normally want her lover to know that his wife was expecting his child? Nothing was more likely to make a man reject his mistress.

When the hush of afternoon descended on the house, I rose. My legs were weak, and I sank gratefully into the bedside chair, but after a while I felt strong enough to slip into a wrap and take a few steps to the window. It was open, for the day was warm. The air was soft and sweet, and the hum of bees came clearly from the vine on the wall. I leaned out, sniffing the scent of summer, and as I did so I saw Miranda standing in the garden below. She was with a man and I recognized him at once. It was the man who had leaped from the shadows of the cedar tree and grabbed my arm, the man I had seen lurking there on the night of my arrival and, later, keeping a clandestine meeting with a woman. So I was right—the woman had indeed been Miranda. Was she just naturally promiscuous, I wondered? Was one man not enough in her life?

She wore riding kit and looked as poised as ever. This was the first time I had seen her since that dreadful night and I found myself studying her with critical detachment, realizing that beneath her veneer she was a primitive woman with primitive passions, and passions of that kind had nothing to do with love.

I was about to turn away, when the breeze suddenly carried her voice up to me.

"It's no use your coming here asking for more money. I've told you before and I tell you again—keep away from this place!"

The words pulled me up short. What *was* the man—a blackmailer, or simply another creditor? Had both Miranda and Justin been running up debts between them and was that the reason—dear God, was *that* the reason for my being invited to Knight's Keep, and wooed, and won? It was a hideous thought, but I had to face it. I was becoming adept at facing ugliness now—too adept, perhaps, imagining wrongs that did not exist. The man demanding money from Miranda could be some unscrupulous rogue she had had an affair with and then discarded, and now he was blackmailing her in return for silence.

But what of Justin? There had been signs of lavish spending before my arrival, and no one would have thought he was anything but rich. By other people's standards he was, but now I knew that these standards were not high enough for him. He yearned too much for the Elam Valley, which his extravagant father had sold piecemeal, and he, Justin, would never rest until he owned it again. He could not be content with being merely Lord of the Manor.

I closed the window quietly, sat down, and thought hard. I was still Justin's wife, however ugly the situation in this house, and if I wanted to make a success of my marriage I could do one of two things—turn a blind eye, which I was incapable of doing, or insist that Miranda should leave at once. To achieve that end I would have to offer inducement, and the inducement would have to be money. Not for Miranda —she was the last person I would bargain with—but for the estate: to buy the land my husband so longed to own and to turn Knight's Keep into the fine kingdom he dreamed of. But in return I would demand Miranda's immediate departure and his fidelity henceforth, and what would that amount to but a financial bid for his devotion? To buy a man's love was not for me.

Perhaps it was sheer physical weakness that made me want to cry—or else disillusion. I had woven idealistic notions about this man, idolizing him as a hero, but now I had to face the fact that he was made as other men, susceptible as most and weaker than many. I also had to decide whether I wanted to stick by him for any reason other than wifely duty. Somehow, the decision seemed too big to face right now, but one thing was certain—the thought of staying in this strange house, part of its unnatural ménage, frightened me.

I walked shakily across the room, opened the door and stepped out into the corridor. At that hour the place was deserted, the domestic staff down in the kitchen quarters and Justin out on the estate with Gavin.

I knew that I had to get strong so that I could cope with things, and that it was impossible for me to continue hiding in my room much longer. I decided to exercise secretly every afternoon, concealing the fact from Justin because the longer he thought me unwell, the longer he would stay away from me, and I needed a breathing space in which to think, and plan, and think, and plan. . . .

I walked the full length of the corridor, slowly at first but with gathering strength. I wondered if I could manage the short one at the end. I turned the corner, took a couple of paces, and stood still. A man was kneeling on the floor outside the door of the locked room, doing something to the keyhole.

It was Gavin Rudge.

CHAPTER TWENTY-SIX

I don't know why I stood there watching. Gavin's duties didn't bring him to this part of the house and he would need a very good excuse for being here. I walked quietly towards him, and as I reached his side the rustle of my gown startled him. He looked up swiftly, his fingers still pressing something on the keyhole. It was a piece of soft wax.

"You're taking an impression of the lock!" I exclaimed. "Why?"

He was neither perturbed nor embarrassed. He finished pressing the wax against the keyhole, removed it carefully, and examined it.

"Excellent," he said. "I'm taking an impression for an obvious reason—another key is needed." He smiled and finished politely, "I'm glad to see you up and about again, ma'am, but shouldn't you return to your room?"

He put his hand beneath my elbow and gently led me back. I felt too weak to protest. All I could say was, "Who needs another key?"

"Lord Ashford. The only key belongs to his stepmother, and he finds this frustrating. He plans to turn that room into an office, and thought the most tactful way to get another key was to have one made."

"Lady Ashford might object to having her husband's trophies turned out."

"They'll be housed elsewhere, ma'am. I'm sure she will yield to Lord Ashford's wishes."

I'm quite sure she will, I thought bitterly, as I went back into my room and shut the door.

Dora returned an hour later.

"Well?" I demanded eagerly. "How did Ruffles die?"

"Straightforward heart failure, dearie—nothing more than that. What did you expect?"

"I—I don't know."

What *had* I expected? That Ruffles had been poisoned,

killed by a dose meant for me? That was wild and nonsensical, and only proved that I was growing morbid and imaginative.

"What did Dr. Firth say?"

"Only to tell you that there wasn't any sign of anything else. I s'pose that meant no illness of any kind. And I was to tell you that he hopes you're coming along well—progressing, 'e said, but it means the same thing don't it?" Dora cocked a knowing eye at me. "But that wasn't all 'e was thinking, not by a long chalk. Never saw a man more anxious about anyone, that I didn't. Folks can't 'ide things from Dora Smee, that they can't, and if ever a man was worried about a woman, that man was Dr. Firth and the woman was you. Anyone would've thought 'e was afraid you were going to die!"

Like Dulcie? Like his sister, who had been Justin's wife before me? Had she experienced what I had experienced, and been shocked as I was shocked? She had been married to Justin for two years before his father returned with his beautiful young wife, a man so old that he couldn't possibly have satisfied Miranda's lustful appetites. How soon after her arrival had her affair with Justin started, and had poor Dulcie found out, perhaps in the same horrible way as I, and turned to Gavin for comfort or help? Had fear grown in her as insidiously as it had grown in me, without any tangible cause?

I now felt an affinity with Daniel's sister. I no longer thought of her as frivolous or neurotic or worthless. Her picture had revealed a sensitive and intelligent girl, a girl I would have liked.

I heard Dora saying, " 'E'd like to see you, that I know. I'd say 'e was desperate to see you, dear, and I can give a good guess why."

I'd been so lost in thought that I came back to the moment with a jerk.

"Who would like to see me?"

"The doctor, o'course. That's who I'm talking about, love."

To my surprise, I heard myself saying fervently, "And I would like to see him!" And I meant it. Just how deeply I meant it came as a shock to me. I could not understand it and attributed the reason solely to a need to lean on someone. For the first time I felt that I could not only lean on Daniel Firth, but be glad to.

CHAPTER TWENTY-SEVEN

I knew that I would have to face Justin sooner or later, and the moment wasn't long in coming. In a few days it was impossible to pretend that I was still ailing and Dr. Mayfield announced my complete recovery.

"So there's no need for Dora to bring your meals up here. You can join Miranda and me for dinner tonight."

"I don't want to."

The doctor had gone. We were alone. I was sitting in an armchair by the bedroom window and Justin stood above me, pretending to be solicitous—but I knew now that he could hide his real feelings expertly.

"You're angry because I lost the baby," I said bluntly. "You're not really concerned about me."

"I have been, my love, but not now. You are perfectly fit again."

"If anything, I'd say I was stronger than before, in every way."

"That's splendid. Perhaps next time you won't cheat me out of an heir."

"Heir to what?" I hazarded. "An estate burdened with debts?"

"They'll be cleared eventually. If you were a loyal wife, you would help me now."

"By clearing the lot? I can see Mr. Claythorne agreeing to that!"

"Damn Claythorne. I'll get the better of him yet."

"How? By demanding that Uncle Silas's money should be made over to you? It can't be, unless I say so. And you refused a generous offer once—he won't forget that." I added bitterly, "Perhaps you're sorry I didn't die in childbirth, then all I possess would have come to you."

"Don't talk like that. What's happened to you? You're not the loving wife I once had. I've made allowances for your being ill—I can't continue to."

"Nor can I make allowances for you—for your lies and your pretenses! You say that I cheated you out of an heir, but *you* were responsible—by cheating me. With Miranda."

His face went absolutely still. Then he shrugged.

"So you know. How did you find out?"

"In the worst possible way. Ask Sarah. She was lurking near Miranda's room when I came upstairs that night. She saw you go in, as I did, but it wasn't a shock to her. How long has she known? How long has Miranda been giving her gifts to keep her silent? And you—have *you* bribed her too?"

I thought for one moment he was going to strike me, but at my glance he checked. I'd spoken the truth when I'd said that I was now stronger than before. I wasn't an inexperienced girl any longer. I was a woman, and confidence had come to me. I held these two in the palm of my hand and no longer would they be able to patronize or condescend.

"You came upstairs spying?" he said. "So you had your suspicions."

"If I'd been suspicious, I would have been prepared, not shocked. I was more than shocked—I was disgusted. Your own stepmother!"

"That doesn't make her a blood relation."

"Then it's a pity the Church forbids you to marry her! That seems to me the only reason for your not doing so."

He answered coolly, "Apart from the legality, there are other reasons why I prefer to have you as my wife."

"The only one I can think of is money."

"You are becoming perceptive, my love, but that is *not* the only reason." He switched on the smile again—coaxing, indulgent, fond. "Miranda is the kind of woman to enjoy, not to marry. My father was in his dotage, besotted with a girl he couldn't get any other way. Marriage was her price, and he paid it. Now you, dear Jane, are different. You're the kind a man does marry, and if you'd be more generous and understanding, you would make the perfect wife."

His self-confidence was almost an audacity. I laughed aloud, and the charm fell away from him.

"Poor Prince Charming," I said, "how thin the veneer is— scratch it, and the shoddiness shows through. You think you can still have me as your wife, to provide respectability, money, and children to carry on your name, and still maintain a mistress beneath our roof. But you are mistaken. I have decided that I shall be your wife no longer."

His eyes narrowed. "You mean that you intend to shut me out of your room? I should advise you not to try it."

"I mean that I intend to divorce you."

I got the reaction I expected.

"That shocks you, doesn't it?" I taunted. "It horrifies you! The scandal, the disgrace to your good name, the ostracism in Society! You'd never be allowed in the Royal Enclosure at Ascot again and every notable door would be shut on you! You can lie and cheat and be as immoral as you like in private, but to be found out, to be publicly exposed, that's the ultimate disgrace in your noble world! Well—I want none of it. I'll be rid of it—and of you."

With characteristic confidence, he rallied.

"Try it, my love. You won't find things easy to prove. Miranda and I will deny everything, and without proof you are lost."

"You forget that Sarah was a witness."

"Hardly a witness, my sweet—nor were you."

"Ring for her. Bring her here. She knew you were going into Miranda's room and I could tell from the look on her face and the tone of her voice that she had known of things for a long time."

"As you please."

He strolled to the bell rope and pulled it. Four times—that was the ring for Sarah. One for the butler, two for the second butler, three the housekeeper, and four for the first housemaid. The first housemaid was Sarah, and she obeyed promptly, closing the door quietly behind her and presenting a polite and incrutable face.

"Sarah—your mistress wants to ask you something."

The inscrutable face turned to me. "Yes—m'lady?"

Questioning a servant about my husband's behavior wasn't easy and it wasn't pleasant, but I did it.

"On the night I was taken ill you saw me upstairs. You know what shocked me. I want you to tell his lordship exactly what you saw."

"Well, m'lady, all I remember was seeing you at the top of the stairs. I'd just taken a warming pan to Lady Ashford —she'd rung for one because the bed was cold, she said. I don't know what shocked you, ma'am—all I know is that you were taken queer all of a sudden, and ran downstairs, and knowing you wouldn't want *me* around, I went to that Dora Smee and sent her to look after you. As for seeing things —what things, m'lady?"

"His lordship—"

"His lordship wasn't around, m'lady. Leastways, not to *my* knowledge."

I gasped, "You're lying!"

Sarah looked offended. She turned to my husband in protest. "Have you ever known me to lie, your lordship?"

"Never, Sarah. You must excuse your mistress. She has been unwell."

"I tell you—she's *lying!*" I insisted.

Justin put an arm about my shoulders. "Calm yourself, my love. You are overwrought and hysterical. That will be all, Sarah—you can go."

The door closed behind her. Justin's arm fell away.

Nothing. Absolutely nothing. I was too distressed to speak. Even worse, I felt trapped, and the feeling was intensified when Justin walked to the door and removed the key from the lock. So he was going to lock me in.

I was wrong. He tossed it on to the bed contemptuously. "You won't need this," he said. "You needn't even trouble to lock your door."

CHAPTER TWENTY-EIGHT

There was a curious lull in the days that followed. I continued to have my meals upstairs and took care to avoid Miranda when I left my room. I scarcely saw Justin, and when I did he was polite, pleasant, and completely cold. I went for walks in the park alone, and Dora watched me anxiously. I wondered if she knew how trapped I felt, and how my desire for escape was increasing daily.

What would Justin do if I left him? I could afford to. I could pack my bags and leave this house. It had suddenly become a gigantic and frightening cage, but in a curious way I hadn't the will to go. I felt tired and listless, unequal to making decisions or taking decisive action. The newly acquired strength seemed to be draining away from me. I was periodically drowsy, and once or twice I was sick. This always seemed to happen on Dora's day off, when I was forced to eat downstairs. Pride forbade me to ring for Sarah to bring me a tray. I couldn't face that young woman again.

On these days, Miranda never appeared in the dining room. I didn't ask where she was, nor could I bring myself to ask

Justin whether he had arranged for her departure. To do so would be tacit consent to becoming his wife again once she was out of the house.

We always ate in comparative silence. I had little appetite, and on one particular day Justin watched me in concern, urging me to eat. "You'll be ill again if you don't, my love." I had a little soup, and a small portion of chicken that he carved for me. He had dismissed the servants and the food was left on the side table. He attended to me like an anxious husband, but there was now a barrier between us that nothing could break down.

I left half my food and went upstairs. I was putting on my bonnet and cloak before setting out for my afternoon walk when I felt a sudden wave of nausea and was violently sick. It left me feeling so weak and exhausted that I was prostrate on my bed when Dora returned.

My pallor shocked her. She cradled me like a child, no longer able to hide her anxiety. "There's something wrong, dear—something 'orribly wrong. You're not the same girl I useter know—not since you came to this 'ouse. It's all the fault of this place, I'll swear—fair gives me the creeps it does, and wot it's doing to you, I dread to think. Told Doctor Firth this afternoon, I did. 'She's fair wasting away,' I told 'im."

I laughed weakly. "I'm doing nothing of the sort. I've slipped back a bit, but I'll pull up again."

"A bit! You've gone right down, lovey. You've got to see Dr. Firth."

"I can't. Mayfield is the family physician."

"But *he* can't do for you what Dr. Firth can, and if you don't know why, it's not for me to tell you. Anyway, you're going to see 'im, 'cos I've fixed it."

"Dora, you can't bring him here! My husband would—"

"I know wot your 'usband would do, dear—d'you think I can't see through 'im?" She sniffed eloquently. "I know 'is type—I've met 'em before. Nice and smooth on top and cruel underneath. But don't worry—Dora won't lead you into any trouble. All I've done is fix it so's you can meet the doctor tomorrow morning—and a nasty shock 'e'll get when 'e sees wot you look like now. Ten o'clock at the south entrance to the park—and if you won't go, I'll drag you there."

My spirits lifted in a surprising way.

"You won't have to drag me," I said. "I'll go. Indeed, I'll go."

She kissed me soundly. "That's more like it! And you're not to worry about a thing. After I've brought your breakfast I'll tell everyone you're off color and are staying in bed. Lunch time, I'll do the same—and I'll eat a bit of the food before taking the tray down again, so's it'll seem as if you're too ill to look at much, and it mightn't be a bad idea if I locked the door to make sure no one disturbs you." She looked at me thoughtfully. "Must've been a poor sort of lunch you ate today, making you sick like that. . . ."

CHAPTER TWENTY-NINE

My relief at seeing Daniel caught me unawares. We stood for a moment, just looking at each other, and I saw shock and concern in his face. Then he put his hands on my shoulders and drew me to him.

I made no resistance. For the first time for weeks, I felt safe and at peace. His shoulder was broad and solid and my head rested there as if it was the most natural place to be. I felt his arms go around me, and that seemed the most natural thing, too, so I closed my eyes and stayed just where I was, and all the doubts and suspicions about him that had once subtly taken seed in my mind no longer seemed to be there.

That brief, revealing moment was soon over. He held me at arm's length and said, "Dora told me I would see a difference in you, but I didn't expect so much. Someone must protect you, and it's going to be me."

"There's nothing to protect me from!"

"Oh yes, there is—but it will be over soon, I promise."

"I've been ill, but I'm getting better. Otherwise, nothing is wrong."

"Don't lie to me, Jane. You can't do it, And don't try to cover things up. My sister was married to Ashford. I knew of things that broke her spirit. He's not going to do it to you."

Daniel's carriage was nearby. He picked me up like a child and put me into it, then sprang to the driver's seat and took the reins. I had slipped out of the house without being seen and the south entrance to the park was so rarely used that no one saw us depart.

"It is kind of you to take me for a drive," I said, relishing the air and the sun.

"It will be a long drive. I hope you'll feel up to it."

I assured him that I would, for I was already feeling better. The shadows and fears and uncertainties of Knight's Keep were behind me.

"Where are we going?" I asked curiously.

"To Rye."

"Rye! But that's over the county border!"

"In Sussex, yes, but these are fast horses and we'll have time to stop for lunch. We'll go to the Mermaid—you'll like that."

We reached Rye shortly after noon and for the first time in weeks I was really hungry. The swift drive across the Romney Marshes and the sharp sea air had whipped color into my cheeks and, catching sight of myself in one of the quaint shop windows, I knew that my appearance had already improved.

I shall never forget that day, nor that lovely little town perched upon its hill, nor the fairy-tale cottages with their lattice panes and heavy oak beams, nor the cobblestoned streets climbing towards the church, nor Dolphin Street itself, steeply rising from the harbor, with the Mermaid Inn halfway up. But most of all I will never forget Daniel's kindness, and the happiness I felt now that I had dropped my guard against this man.

But I ought to have known that there was a purpose behind the visit, Daniel being the man he was. He could have driven me to the old town of Romney, or inland to Appledore and Tenterden, had he merely wanted to give me a pleasant outing, but he had chosen Rye for a definite reason.

After lunch we left the carriage in the inn yard and walked slowly up the street. Near the top was an apothecary's shop and the name above the door leapt out at me—Leo Van der Heul.

"I know that name," I said. "I've heard it, or seen it somewhere. . . ."

"When? Try to remember—" Daniel said urgently.

I stared across at the little shop and suddenly a shutter clicked in my mind. I saw the name written in a feminine hand on a letter I had taken out of the mailbag long ago.

"It was the morning I searched for a letter to Dora—my first letter, which was lost. I went downstairs and emptied the mailbag, looking for it. I wanted to add a postscript to tell her about my marriage, but the letter wasn't there. Nor did it ever turn up." I finished thoughtfully.

"But the apothecary—who was writing to him?"

"It could only be Miranda. The handwriting was a woman's and she was the only woman apart from myself who would use the family mailbag. It wasn't Justin's writing, I do know that. But what does it matter? It's not important."

"More important than you think, perhaps. We're going to call on Mr. Van der Heul now. That is why I've brought you. You won't like what emerges, but later you'll be glad."

We entered the little shop. It was a gloomy place, with a tall mahogany counter and wall shelves laden with apothecary jars. Through a door leading to an inner room I could see a man stooping over a table. I recognized him at once. It was the man who had lurked beneath the cedar tree, the man who had pounced upon me in the dusk, the man I had seen talking to Miranda.

The jangling of the bell brought him into the shop. At close quarters and without his features obscured he was handsome and vaguely familiar. He reminded me of someone.

At the sight of Daniel's well-dressed figure the man bowed and smiled in an unctuous sort of way. His eyes slid to me and away again, but in that brief glance I knew that he had taken in a lot, particularly the quality of my clothes and the air of wealth which now sat naturally upon me, but his otherwise inscrutable face gave no sign of recognition.

Daniel didn't bother to return the man's effusive greeting, but took out his pocket book and extracted a piece of paper.

"Can you prepare this for me?" he asked.

The man glanced at the paper and his shifty eyes were immediately still. The fingers holding the prescription trembled a little, then at last he looked up and said, "I'm afraid not, sir. This drug is unknown to me."

"Are you sure? Strophanthin came originally from Africa, as you did."

"I repeat—I have never heard of it."

The man was handing the prescription back, but Daniel ignored it. He continued conversationally. "It was found originally in the Kombé country. If you haven't heard of it, perhaps your sister has."

"My sister! You know her?"

"Of course. We are near neighbors, and this young lady is her stepdaughter-in-law."

So *that* was why the man looked vaguely familiar! He was Miranda's brother—a brother she never invited to the house and obviously did not want to have around. (*"I've told you before and I tell you again, keep away from this place!"*)

"You probably thought Lord Ashford's wife was dying," Daniel continued, "but as you can see, she is not."

Through my shock I heard the man protest, "Dying! I've heard no such thing, sir!"

"Then why have you supplied your sister with regular doses of strophanthin? You know what it does and how it was first used—on poisoned arrow heads belonging to natives near the Shiré river. An arrow head like this."

I held onto the counter for support, for suddenly I knew that the suspicion I had refused to believe was actually true —Miranda was trying to kill me. She had tried to kill me the day she brought the consommé to my room. . . .

I saw Daniel take a package from his pocket, unwrap it, and reveal a deadly-looking dart.

"This was brought back from Africa as a curio by your sister's husband. It would be simple enough for a skilled apothecary to make a solution from the paste scraped from the head. The Kombé natives used to pound the seed of strophanthus in water and mix it with red clay, then it was smeared over the weapon. Strophanthin is a deadly poison, killing quickly and leaving absolutely no trace."

The man passed his tongue over his dry lips and said, "Why are you telling me this? And why should I supply it to my sister? How could I?"

"By making a solution from the compound which covered the arrow."

The man blustered, "This is nonsense! The paste on some ancient curio would have dried up and lost its potency years ago!"

"On the contrary, an arrow that has been unused remains deadly for many, many years. The poison stays fresh, and any man with a knowledge of chemistry could analyze and copy it. If you examine this arrow, you'll see that the shaft and the head have been scraped, but some of the paste remains. Only a sample has been taken from it."

The man refused to look at it, and again pushed the prescription across the counter.

"Take it! I want none of it. I don't deal in poisons."

"Or dangerous drugs? You know the penalty in this country for that, don't you? Deportation. And with your record they wouldn't have you back in Africa." Daniel leaned across the counter and said deliberately, "I know the truth, so stop lying."

"*If* you knew the truth, you wouldn't accuse Miranda!"

"Ah—then you admit it? If not she, then who? Lord Ashford? And for how long—for weeks before my unhappy sister died? It began in a small way at first—minor ailments, lethargy, sickness, until she was diagnosed as a hypochondriac, always imagining herself ill. But she *was* ill. Slowly and surely she was being poisoned—small doses every now and then to establish a pattern of ailing, not one strong dose to kill within a quarter of an hour. A sudden death in so young a woman would have aroused comment and curiosity, but a slowly-established pattern of ill health culminating in death, with no symptoms to suggest anything but heart failure, made sure of a medical certificate testifying to normal death. And even a post-mortem could reveal no trace of poison." Daniel's hand shot across the counter and grabbed the man's wrist. "I'll force the truth out of you—or give you away to the authorities. They'll search this place and find your notes. You must have made notes. You couldn't memorize the chemical formula for something so complicated."

"I could destroy everything!"

"I'll give you no chance. Lady Ashford will fetch the police the moment I ask her, and I shall remain here until they come. With the evidence they'll be bound to find *and* this arrow head, they'll soon have a confession out of you. You're the kind of man who'll squeal easily enough. You've squealed already."

I spoke for the first time.

"I heard him demanding money from Miranda the first day I was up! They were standing below my window and she was telling him to keep away—"

"But not for that reason!" Van der Heul protested. "She never wanted me around, but she knew nothing of what was going on."

"Well, *someone* took this arrow head, scraped some of the compound from it, and replaced the weapon, and that someone could only be your sister—or Lord Ashford," Daniel declared furiously.

"But Justin didn't have a key!" I said promptly. "Not until recently. I saw Gavin Rudge taking an impression so that one could be made for him."

"That was for himself. He had been helping me from the beginning. He remained at Knight's Keep after Dulcie's death solely for that reason—waiting and watching while I did endless research into obscure poisons, then widening the field to a tropical one. I even gave up my hospital job to take an appointment which would give me greater scope for research. It took a long time, and meanwhile I had to stand aside and watch you fall in love with Ashford and marry him. I could do nothing to stop you. My sister's fortune wasn't very great, and if it hadn't been tied up in a trust she might be alive now. The trust had to be handed on to her descendants, or should she be childless, the beneficiary would be her husband. Much of the land belonging to Knight's Keep had been sold to keep its head above water—my sister's money came in useful. It wasn't enough to buy back the lands, but it restored barns and outbuildings and cottages, and even the carriages were done up, though not all of them needed it. Then you came along, and rumor had it that you were rich—"

"*Rumor?*" the apothecary said sharply, but Daniel ignored the interruption.

"I knew then that my search had to be intensified, but it wasn't until a few months after your marriage that I came across a treatise on African poisons by a doctor in Johannesburg. It had never been published here, and immediately involved me in endless correspondence, but it convinced me that I was on the right track."

"That track couldn't lead to me!" Van der Heul blustered.

"But it did, and I'll tell you how. Somehow, Gavin Rudge had to get into that room and look for evidence—hence the necessity for a key. He found this arrow among a collection of weapons *and* a book on native medicines with heavily-underlined passages about strophanthin—the poison mentioned in the doctor's treatise. It was logical to think of you as the accomplice. It was even possible that you knew of strophanthin when you came to England."

"That's not true! I'd never heard of if before!"

"But you have since. Gavin Rudge watched Ashford's comings and goings. Once he followed him to Rye and saw him come to this shop."

Van der Heul protested ineffectively, "He could have come for anything! A headache powder—"

"All the way to Rye for a headache powder that could be obtained locally? It would have to be something more than that to bring the lord of Knight's Keep all the way to Rye on a personal visit to an apothecary. I followed him on two occasions myself. He paid you well, didn't he?"

"At first," the man muttered.

"And then only with promises? Rich promises, once he married again. He told you his new wife had far more money than his first, didn't he? But he was lying. She has nothing. The story of her wealth *was* only rumor." Daniel turned to me and said, "Tell him it isn't true."

"I haven't a penny," I lied. "My father was an impoverished curate in London. My parents left me nothing."

Van der Heul's eyes blazed. "But he told me you had inherited a fortune—a fortune that should rightfully be his!"

"His uncle was a poor old man who wandered into my father's church, almost destitute. My parents looked after him because he was homeless. Would a man with a fortune live like that?"

"Only if he were mad," the man muttered.

Daniel's hand closed over mine as he turned to me and said, "Silas wasn't, but his family had a history of insanity. His brother died insane in New Zealand, and his sister, Justin Ashford's mother, finished her unhappy life in the same way. Her final breakdown occurred in the small sunken garden at Knight's Keep. Silas was with her at the time. I was a boy then and heard my parents discussing the tragedy. Shortly afterwards Silas sold his home and went away for mental care. My parents told me later that he did so voluntarily, fearing that the strain might be in him. Perhaps that was the reason he never married. It was certainly the reason why I opposed my sister's marriage to Ashford, but she was passionately in love with him and since our parents were dead and she was of age, I could do nothing."

I clung to Daniel's hand, remembering the words Silas had penned at the end of his letter—the words engraved in the little arbor where he had seen his sister go mad. *Repelle, Domine, virtutem diaboli.* . . . They had remained engraved on his memory too. Had he written them in fear, or in prayer?

Daniel said urgently to Van der Heul, "If you don't do as I ask, you will suffer for it and I will see that you do. Ashford won't save you. He will deny all association with you to save incriminating himself. Don't you want to strike back at him for taking you in? He has involved you in a serious crime and you've been involved often enough in the past. You don't want to go to prison again, do you? *He* is the one who should be convicted. Help me to do it."

"And what about me?" the man demanded truculently. "If I do that, I'll convict myself!"

"You haven't any choice—either way, the truth will come out, but my way will be easier for you. If you turn Queen's evidence it will act in your favor—so whether you like it or not you're coming back to Knight's Keep with us *now*."

CHAPTER THIRTY

I went into the great house alone. Daniel had instructed me carefully and I wasn't afraid—not even when I saw the anger in Justin's face.

He met me in the hall.

"I know where you've been," he said. "You're carrying on with another man behind my back—my enemy, too! Don't trouble to lie to me—I got the truth out of that cockney woman, Dora Smee. I have my methods of extracting the truth from lying servants."

"*What have you done to her?*"

"Punished her—and sent her packing. She's out of this house, bag and baggage."

"Where has she gone?" I demanded furiously.

"How should I know? I never wanted the woman here and it was by trickery that you got her."

"Trickery! I wrote to her openly—"

"Only the first time."

"Then it was *you* who took my letter from the mailbag!"

"Of course. I wouldn't allow a future wife of mine to communicate with low-born friends from her past. When I read it, I was even more determined. The familiarity between you and that woman was highly undesirable, so I naturally destroyed the letter. Then you wrote to her secretly. I warn you, Jane—don't ever try to cheat me again, and don't even try to communicate with Dora Smee."

"I shall find out where she has gone and I'll keep in touch with her as long as I live!"

He walked towards me and there was something menacing in his step. My instinct was to retreat, but I knew that Daniel was near, so remained where I was. But I was afraid, and when Justin finally stopped before me I saw that his eyes were cold, fanatical and vicious. Then he struck me. The blow was so hard that I screamed and staggered backwards.

The sound brought Miranda out of the frilly salon. She looked at me and then at my husband, then said sharply, "*Justin—stop it!*"

He turned and looked at her. He moved his head slowly, in the peculiar way of a man whose senses were not fully co-ordinated.

"Do you know where she has been?" he said. "With her lover. With Daniel Firth."

"He is not my lover!"

"But you've been with him, haven't you, my sweet?" His voice was soft now. "You met him at the south gate this morning, and spent the day with him. Being a devoted and loving husband I was concerned to hear that you were unwell again. I went upstairs to see you. The door was locked. Dora Smee wasn't very bright, was she? She forgot that access can be gained through my dressing-room as well as through your boudoir. She forgot to lock the third door—and there she was, sitting in my wife's room, with a lunch my wife wasn't there to eat! She had even connived with you to make it appear that you had eaten some—just a little, as befits an invalid." He dropped the honeyed tone and shouted, "*What have you been up to with that man?*"

"Proving your guilt," I said quietly. "Proving that you have been planning to murder me as you murdered poor Dulcie. Was it strophanthin that made me sick the other day? Small and regular doses produce lethargy and increasing ail-ment—but you have only just started on me, so it hasn't had time to accumulate as it did with Dulcie. Poor Dulcie! How much money did she leave you, Justin? Not nearly so much as you would inherit from me, but enough to deal with urgent repairs and have the carriages repainted—*all* of them, because one in particular might be recognized, and to have only one disguised might arouse comment."

He laughed. "Disguised? What are you talking about?"

"The green carriage you followed Uncle Silas around in.

You had traced him, hadn't you, and followed him for some time, waiting for an opportunity to kill him? A man so old and frail wouldn't stand much chance of survival if he were run down one foggy night—and there was his money, lying just beyond your reach, and you his only remaining relative. But I got in the way, didn't I? You didn't dream that he would have willed his fortune to anyone else. You pretended to be pleased when Mr. Claythorne informed you. You made a noble and sacrificial gesture by refusing to accept a penny, but only to avert suspicion from bigger plans. If you couldn't get rid of me, you would marry me before the year was out and the new law came into force."

"Get rid of you?" he scoffed. "And how do you imagine I planned to do that? Run *you* down as well with a team of galloping horses?"

"No—by hiring a thug of a driver to do it somehow, anyhow. Did the man watch the house in Long Acre day after day, waiting for an opportunity and seizing it when I obligingly hired a cab to take me to the solicitor's office? And when that plan failed did he, or you, or some other hired assassin, try to catch up with me on my way home through Covent Garden?"

Daniel came in unexpectedly, "I was that man, Jane. I was walking back to my lodgings and saw you distributing sovereigns to the flower sellers. That was asking for trouble and I hurried to catch up with you—to see you home safely."

"You see?" Justin said triumphantly. "The girl has taken leave of her senses, imagining a lot of nonsense. She's insane."

I retorted, "No—you are. And that reminds me—driving home just now I saw Sarah's child again."

"I know nothing about Sarah's child."

"The poor mite has the Ashford features. *That* is why Sarah lied the other day. She couldn't do anything else, relying on you for the child's maintenance, and on Miranda's bounty to keep her mouth shut about other things." I turned to his stepmother, who had been silent all this time. "Yes, Miranda, I know about you and Justin. I know about your brother too, and how my husband has been using him."

There was a moment's deadly silence, and then Miranda's face crumpled tragically.

"Dear God, it isn't true!" she sobbed. "Not Leo—not poor Leo!"

"He is here," I said, and went to the door and opened it.

At the sight of her brother, Miranda's pride finally cracked. She went to him and put her arms about him, weeping distractedly, and I saw pity in Daniel's eyes, a pity which I found myself sharing.

Leo Van der Heul said bitterly, "Why weep for me now, Miranda? You haven't wanted me around—not since you became the great lady with a title. You didn't want me to follow you to England—"

"I wanted to be accepted!" she cried. "Don't you understand? I've told you that many times. I've given you money to stay away, until I could give you no more. Do you think I wanted it known that I had a brother with a criminal record? I left Africa to escape the shame and ostracism it brought on the family. I even married that vile old man as a means of escape. I thought if I could get to England with a new name, and one that was respected I could start a new life. But you had to turn up and threaten to ruin everything! Even so, I didn't want to hurt you. Believe me, if you had stayed quietly in Rye, running your shop, going straight, and staying out of my life, I could have put up with it so long as no one associated me with you—but then you started coming here, demanding money not only from me, but from Justin. I heard you in his study one day, so he can't deny it, but I didn't know what was going on. I thought you must have revealed your identity to <u>him</u> and were making <u>him</u> buy your silence, as you made me. What is strophanthin, anyway?" she finished.

"The doctor can tell you," her brother said. "It's no use trying to lie your way out of it, Ashford. I've admitted everything."

"Everything about what?" Justin scoffed.

"Everything about this," Daniel answered, and produced the arrow.

Miranda looked at it curiously.

"Don't touch it!" Daniel said quickly. "There's still enough poison on it to kill."

"But that belongs in the trophy room! It's kept in the cabinet with Matthew's other horrible souvenirs. God, how I hate that room!"

"Hate it?" Justin echoed in surprise. "I've always found it fascinating. I've spent hours in there, poring over my father's things and reading his books. . . ."

The fanatical light was back in his eyes again, and I knew

then that in the dark corridors of his mind was a blackness no sanity could penetrate.

"Yes, Miranda, the arrow was in the cabinet," Daniel agreed. "It was left there to avoid suspicion. Had it been removed, you might have missed it. You thought you had the only key to that room, but Ashford has just confirmed that he had one, too. He could come and go at will."

"Then there *was* a light beneath the door that night!"

"I've told you," I said. "I saw it. But Justin told me it must have been you."

She smiled half contemptuously, half sadly.

"Justin always was a liar. He told me he loved me, but even so he married you, although I could give him everything he wanted."

"Except money, my dear. And I certainly wouldn't have married a woman with a criminal for a brother, whether the church or the law permitted it or not."

Miranda's lovely mouth curled. "What a cold and calculating devil you are, Justin!"

"You don't understand. I have a name to live up to, an estate to maintain. I *had* to have money, and if that damned lawyer of Jane's hadn't dilly-dallied, the fortune would have been hers long before the year was out and I could then have laid hands on it. Believe me, Jane, it would have been better so. I could have lived with you very happily then."

Daniel put in, "Claythorne dilly-dallied because I asked him to. I went to see him, told him of my suspicions, and urged him to delay completion until it would be too late for you to take everything. He was more than willing. When he heard about Jane's marriage he was as anxious as I, because he too knew about your mother's family."

"My mother's family didn't matter. My father's was a fine and noble one!" Justin declared proudly.

"Once upon a time it was, but you've brought it to an end. You can't lie your way out of things now. Van der Heul is willing to turn Queen's evidence and even if he tried to change his mind, he can't. I have all the evidence I need to have you both arrested. I swore when my sister died that I'd bring you to trial for her murder, Ashford, and by God, I will!"

"Never!" Justin cried, and snatched the arrow, plunging it into his wrist. Not even Daniel was swift enough to stop him.

Everything was over very quickly after that, and it was Miranda who wept for him.

CHAPTER THIRTY-ONE

All that happened long ago. Beechwood Close is now my home, and Dora is with us. She was there that night, waiting for Daniel's return, sitting on the doorstep with her shabby grip. Daniel told me about it later. "Blimey," she said when he at last arrived, "I was beginning to think you'd never come! I've been sitting 'ere for hours and perishing cold I am, so you'd better take me in, sir 'cos it's all your fault I was kicked outa that 'ouse, but I ain't going far from it so long as my Jane lives there. The day'll come that she needs me, *that* I know!"

Her heart is as warm as ever, and always will be. We love her as our children love her, even though she bosses them unmercifully. My marriage with Daniel is a good one, a real one, and our children are fine and healthy, all four of them. They make a din romping on the lawn, and the youngest, two-year-old Paul, protests forcibly when called in to bed, and yells even more forcibly when his father swings him shoulder-high and carries him indoors, but this is a house of noise and life and always will be, and young Paul's nose will be slightly out of joint when his younger brother or sister arrives. Our family is large and I hope will be larger. It has completed our happiness and our world.

Miranda has her world too, alone at Knight's Keep. I was glad to let her have it and, being the strange woman she is, it holds no shadows for her. She sold the Home Farm, the hundred-acre park, and all the surrounding lands and buildings, keeping only the house and a portion of the gardens for herself, and after Justin's debts were settled there was enough left for her to live in reasonable comfort, although Justin would have called it penury.

She alone holds the Ashford title now. That is her pride, and she carries it with dignity. Sometimes I see her driving in the one stately carriage she possesses, visiting local families who have become her friends, opening bazaars, and in general playing the country lady of title to perfection. She is a leading rider with the local Hunt and always looks magnificent at Hunt balls.

Sometimes she comes to see us. I can feel no ill-will because of the past, and although I suppose the memory of it will always be there between us, there is liking too. Once she even admitted that she had liked me all along, against her will.

"I wanted to hate you as I hated Dulcie. When I first arrived in England and met my husband's daughter-in-law, I still had the feeling of inferiority I had at home. Dulcie was so very much at ease in her surroundings that she made me even more conscious of the fact that I was not. I had a lot to learn, and I used to watch her and copy her, and hate her because I had to take my example from a girl younger than myself. Also she was Justin's wife, and I had become infatuated with him. If you had ever met my late husband, you'd understand why."

"And Justin could do nothing wrong in your eyes?"

"Nothing at all! I was ready to give him anything he wanted, in any way he wanted, and I was jealous because Dulcie was his wife and I was not. When she became ill and died, I was glad, but I never suspected that it wasn't a natural death. I didn't even know that Justin was in touch with my brother until I heard Leo's voice in the study that day." Her lip curled. "I despised Leo. He was weak, and above all things I despise weakness. I hated him too—hated him for the disgrace he had brought on my family, and even more for following me to England, but in the end I felt sorry for him."

"Did you ever find out how he and Justin met?"

"Yes—but not for a long time. One day, after you had lost your baby, Leo arrived at the Keep, demanding money again. This time he insisted that Justin owed it to him, but I didn't believe him and ordered him off the premises. I thought it was one of Leo's lies, but then he told me that shortly after his arrival in England, long before Dulcie died, Justin had walked into his shop. Apparently he had been in Rye on business, and had seen the newly-opened apothecary shop and the name above the door. Only one person he knew had ever had that name—Miranda Van der Heul, who married his father. I suppose it was curiosity that made Justin go inside. Anyway, he met Leo, and later made good use of him. All Leo told me was that Justin owed him money for cattle medicine he had supplied!"

I asked a question I had long wanted to ask.

"Why did you urge me to tell Justin about the baby?"

"I don't know—some instinct to protect you, perhaps, although I've never been interested in protecting anyone but myself. As I said, against my will I liked you, and I could tell that Justin's attitude to you had changed, and you were unhappy. I ought to have been glad. I had every reason to hate you both—particularly Justin. I had no idea he had invited you to Knight's Keep until the day before you arrived. He then ordered me to welcome you and urge you to stay. I tried to obey, but it was hard. I think it was then that I first began to mistrust Justin. He was devious, and I knew it—but still I was enamored of him."

I shall always find Miranda an enigma, and I know that underneath her poise and assurance her passionate nature still lies dormant. I have heard that she has lovers, and very likely it is true, for no doubt a woman of her nature could not live without them. but I know that she has the thing she wants most of all—a place in the world and one which, in our country society, commands respect.

One day, to my surprise, she brought me a gift. It was a puppy. I don't know if she intentionally chose one as near like Ruffles as it was possible to find, but I suspect so. She has never forgiven herself for carrying that soup up to me, though she was completely innocent in the affair. Justin had asked her to bring it. "Try to coax her to eat, the poor darling," he had said as, with his back to the table, he ladled the soup from the tureen on the sideboard.

As for Leo, he disappeared on the night of Justin's death. Daniel and I suspect that Miranda helped him—one has only to travel into nearby Folkestone to take a packet steamer across the twenty-six miles of the English Channel that divide this coast from France, and a fast carriage from the Keep could have got him there in time for the night boat. Perhaps it was also Miranda who burned the papers that were found charred to ashes in his shop. Whatever happened, he has never been seen or heard of again.

Gavin Rudge is a close friend. With his savings and a loan from his parents he bought the Home Farm, and it is more successful now than it ever was. Eventually he married, but not for a long time. His wife is a nice girl, affectionate and with a sense of humor. Dulcie would have liked her, I'm sure.

Before his marriage I asked him to give me Dulcie's picture. I have it now, and it is better so. It is on my desk in the morning room—the busiest room in our noisy house, where the children have their meals and life hums daily—and in some strange way I feel that she shares it all, and is part of our family. I don't think it is in my imagination that our eldest girl, called after her, also has her dark good looks and sweetness of expression. Sometimes I think that Gavin notices it too, and I know that my husband does.

Occasionally I visit Miranda at Knight's Keep, but only because she begs me to. When I do, I feel none of the awe that I experienced at first sight of it. I feel nothing at all, for the place means nothing to me, and the life I lived there means nothing, either. The one I have now is rich and full, and I would not exchange it for any other.